Sheena Joughin has twice been a winner of the London Short Story Competition, and is a regular contributor to *The Times Literary Supplement*. She lives in west London with her son.

Acclaim for *Things to do Indoors*:

'Joughin's intriguing first novel, set in west London in the 1980s, vividly conveys the textures and rhythms of life on the shabby, crowded streets . . . coolly perceptive'
Sunday Times

'Very funny, very edgy, very acute. I love this book'
Julie Burchill

'Bookshops' shelves groan under the strain of coming-of-age novels, but Joughin's début is an addition not to be overlooked'
Glamour

'Wryly funny . . . wholly true'
The List

'Joughin's beautifully sparse writing balances the drama perfectly'
Big Issue

'A quirky and delightfully witty novel'
Tablet

'What elevates the book far above the level of soap opera is the richness of the descriptive writing. Every vignette within the teeming human panorama . . . has the ring of truth'
Sunday Telegraph

'Sheena Joughin handles her material with elegance and wit . . . recommended'
Irish Post

'Joughin has a merciless eye for unflattering detail and for the insecurities of both sexes . . . extremely funny'
Daily Telegraph

'Joughin writes an early 80s London of complex personal disloyalties that is vividly and vigorously recognisable . . . sensuously rich'
Time Out

'Joughin conjures up atmosphere brilliantly . . . a stylish writer'
Irish Examiner

'Her wry insights, economical characterisation and idiosyncratic voice mark her out as a talent to watch'
Daily Mail

'She writes like an angel and thinks like the devil. Joughin is a major discovery'
Fay Weldon

'Sheena Joughin has an unusual clarity of voice and a crafty duality, something brooding and light, in her writing. The hurts and nastiness between her characters are paralleled with a casual persistence of good nature and good humour in this funny, piercing book about lostness, childishness and growing up'
Ali Smith, *TLS*

THINGS TO DO INDOORS

Sheena Joughin

BLACK SWAN

THINGS TO DO INDOORS
A BLACK SWAN BOOK: 0 552 77153 8

Originally published in Great Britain by Doubleday,
a division of Transworld Publishers

PRINTING HISTORY
Doubleday edition published 2003
Black Swan edition published 2004

1 3 5 7 9 10 8 6 4 2

The lines from 'Sad Steps' by Philip Larkin, from *High Windows* (Faber & Faber, 1974), are used by permission of Faber & Faber. 'Blythe Road' first appeared as 'A Mackintosh Sky' in *Well Sorted: The London Short Story Collection, 2* (Serpent's Tail, 1995). 'Lunchtime' was first published in *Does the Sun Rise over Dagenham? New Writing from London* (Fourth Estate, 1998).

Set in 11/14pt Ehrhardt by
Falcon Oast Graphic Art Ltd.

Black Swan Books are published by Transworld Publishers,
61–63 Uxbridge Road, London W5 5SA,
a division of The Random House Group Ltd,
in Australia by Random House Australia (Pty) Ltd,
20 Alfred Street, Milsons Point, Sydney, NSW 2061, Australia,
in New Zealand by Random House New Zealand Ltd,
18 Poland Road, Glenfield, Auckland 10, New Zealand
and in South Africa by Random House (Pty) Ltd,
Endulini, 5a Jubilee Road, Parktown 2193, South Africa.

Printed and bound in Great Britain by
Cox & Wyman Ltd, Reading, Berkshire.

Papers used by Transworld Publishers are natural, recyclable products made from wood grown in sustainable forests. The manufacturing processes conform to the environmental regulations of the country of origin.

For Josh

One shivers slightly, looking up there.
The hardness and the brightness and the plain
Far-reaching singleness of that wide stare

Is a reminder of the strength and pain
Of being young; that it can't come again,
But is for others undiminished somewhere.

FROM 'SAD STEPS' BY PHILIP LARKIN

One Blythe Road

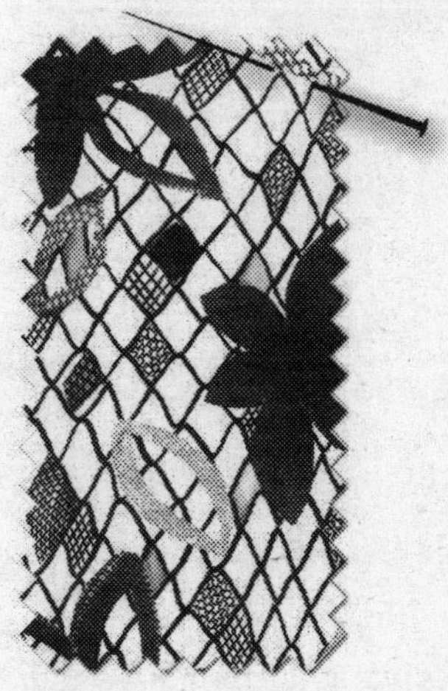

HE WAS KISSING ME, VERY BADLY. HE OBVIOUSLY HAD TO THINK to do it, so while his hands were moving over my trunk, trying to find something to pull up or down or off, his tongue was resting. It rested on mine, thick and filling like a spare lip in my mouth that I could have bitten into. Eventually he found a way through to one of my breasts and moved his mouth to that. We heard my breathing change.

'Take your jumper off,' he said and rolled on top of me.

'I can smell you,' he said for some reason.

I could smell him. The top of his head was a twisted mix of Silk Cut and scent and blue Stilton. Stilton soup had been soup of the day again. I'd scratched it onto the downstairs blackboard myself, and nearly broken my leg when the chair I was stretching from had collapsed. They often did that. Nick used to keep a camping chair behind the bar, and take it out to sit on if he came in for a nightcap. The customers were mostly fat.

'I want you,' said Jake, and moved his legs apart so I was trapped between them. I felt rather sick. The collar of his shirt was poking my nose. I could barely breathe with his wardrobe-weight pressed against me.

'I think I'm going to throw up,' I said.

I opened my eyes to see the tassels of my standard lamp making tiny jerks above my head. I belched some cheesy red wine.

'I feel sick,' I said.

'You're gorgeous. Take your jumper off.'

He explained that he'd been wanting to take my jumper off all night, which seemed unlikely since he'd been flirting with Alison since the place opened. They'd been leaning into each other, drinking Buck's Fizz as I arrived for my seven-thirty start. There were no ashtrays on the table and no Perrier in the fridge. She'd been sheathed in her usual black elastic. He'd only walked me home because I'd said I needed another drink and taken two bottles from behind the bar. We called that pilfering, rather than stealing. We were very badly paid.

I had to drink every night before I went to bed that summer because Nick had left me. Well I'd left him, but he'd been seeing someone else so I had to, everyone said. Every other customer who came in told me about the Spanish girl they'd seen him with in The Dome. I told them he was teaching her English, which was what he'd told me, but in the end I started not sleeping and I left a bitter note one morning and moved back to Blythe Road. I hadn't seen him since, although everyone said he was in a state and she'd gone back to wherever she came from. Perhaps I should see him. I still couldn't sleep. I told Jake the mean details and the measure of my unhappiness as we chain-smoked back at my place.

'Sex,' he'd said. 'You need some good sex to clear your head. He's a mummy's boy. You were wasted on him.'

Then he blew in my ear and we lay on the couch and my feet ached and I realized that I'd drunk too much. Nick always said it was best to be sick if you'd drunk too much.

'Get off,' I said to Jake's stubble, and he did this time. He lay on his back and trailed his right hand around my crotch.

'I'm going to the bathroom,' I told him.

'I'll be waiting for you.' He smiled. He had tiny teeth.

'You're gorgeous,' he called to my back.

'Don't,' I said, and I held the door handle for a swaying moment before I attempted the stairs.

When I got back, after brushing my teeth and swilling out the bath, I felt much better. Jake was snoring on his back with his arms by his side, like a fallen boulder on my couch. I needed a cigarette to clear my mouth, but all the packets were empty or stuffed with wrinkled stubs and crumpled gold paper. I lit the longest butt I could find, which tasted disgusting. I must get to a 7-Eleven before anything else occurred.

'I'm going to find some cigarettes,' I told the lump on my couch, which snored evenly on.

'I'll buy you some, too.'

I unfolded his jacket from the back of a chair and took a fiver from the inside pocket, then I spread it on top of him to keep his body heat stable and hoped he didn't mind about the money. I'd get Silk Cut, I decided, because those were what he smoked. I pulled my bra straps right and tucked everything in and looked at myself in the mirror. I was very flushed and looked about twenty-six, I thought, which was good, because that's how old I was. I smoothed my hair down and put on some lipstick. I laced my shoes, found my bag and left the room. The 7-Eleven was about a twenty-minute trip, one way. Jake might wake up and go home in the meantime. I left the light on, and checked that I had my key before I pulled the front door behind me and moved into the warm wet outside air. I noticed that I couldn't walk in a very straight line and that the street lamps were blue. A cyclist passed, spinning light rain from his glossy tyres.

'Hi,' I said to him.

'Hi,' he said.

Outside Au Temps Perdu, the black bin liners of empties that I'd dragged up to the dustbins a couple of hours before were waterlogged and leaning. I kicked one to hear the bottles ring, but it sagged into itself, so I tried again and it worked. I locked my hands over my head to block the steady rain as I loped on through pooled leaves and puddles of litter and my own voice singing 'Every Time We Say Goodbye'. We'd had it on that night a lot. Alison liked Ella Fitzgerald.

Across Brook Green I slowly sang and down the Shepherd's Bush Road. There was too much movement there – people with beer cans and bare limbs and lorries and unstuck posters; cars with headlamp rain and steam-train smoke. Too wide and noisy with sirens – so I wavered back into a sidestreet with festoon blinds, coloured doors and narrow pavements. Low houses with families and dustbins and gates. Occasional scaffolding cut into the skyline and many skips half-blocked my way. There were floorboards and a narrow mattress to negotiate and a car alarm to ignore. And then there was a pair of legs with cowboy boots on the end of them, sticking out of a blanket like odd props on a stage set. A snoring man on his back at three thirty in the morning, halfway down Luxemburg Gardens, where in Paris, of course, there are always men asleep. They sleep on their backs there too. Flat-out and unafraid of what might fall from the sky, or of passers-by, trying to kill them. I couldn't sleep like that if you paid me, but men don't seem to mind. This one was clearly very drunk. He didn't stir when I patted him with my foot, so I bent down to check he was not hurt and realized that it was Jasper, Suzanne's man, who was one of our most regular punters. And it wasn't a blanket on top of him, but a coat. Suzanne's blue cotton coat, which I'd helped her to find on the coat rack as she'd left the bar all those hours ago. She and Jasper had left together, after-hours as usual, banging into collapsing chairs and holding one another through the door. Jasper had kissed me tenderly goodbye and said see you very soon, and what a nice skirt I was wearing and, 'Enjoy it, you're a long time dead,' which was what he often said when he'd had a few drinks. I was fond of him. He helped with the rubbish and had a high forehead I liked, like Nick. His head was lolling back now onto a tumbled wall, so I felt it to check the temperature. It was cool and solid. He seemed at rest. I was tempted to lie down beside him, but could see that would be irresponsible. I tucked his coat covering firmly round him and pulled the collar up over his chin, and then I felt the cold of the brooch there, which Suzanne wore on most of her clothes. Her art nouveau tulip head, upturned for the taking. I mustn't leave it there. Someone would steal it because it was silver. I must take it to her before I did anything else, and then I could ask why Jasper was asleep in the street and perhaps she would come to collect him. She lived nearby, off the Fulham Palace Road. It would be nice to see her. She'd have lots of cigarettes, and anyway, she liked me. She'd held my hand as I'd served her banana meringue thing that night and asked if I'd been in touch with Nick. She always knew all about everything because everyone always asked her opinion. She wore strappy sandals, like glamorous mothers in old photographs, and red lipstick and laughed a lot, and held court on emotional matters.

'See what Suzanne says when she comes in,' we'd say to each other.

It was the best advice to give. But I think we thought she lived with Jasper. Maybe they'd had a row. She'd know what to do about Jake on my couch either way, and this humming inside the top of my head that was making the world so twitchy. She might let me stay on her couch if she had one. I unpinned the brooch from her coat, fastened it onto my jumper and set off. At the bend in the road I turned to shout goodbye to Jasper. Perhaps he would wake up and go home, wherever that turned out to be.

*

Something thudded against the basement window from the inside where the light was as I negotiated the steps down to Suzanne's front door.

'Stuff Jasper's farm in France,' a male voice shouted. 'Stuff the marinated peaches.'

A woman made a noise and then I rang the doorbell, pleased that its green square button that shone seemed to be staying quite still. I noticed that I was now humming 'Every Time We Say Goodbye', which sounded nice. I ran my hand over the tulip brooch. I was a useful guest with a valuable thing and they would be glad to see me.

I rang the bell again until a man was standing in front of me with a long scarlet hallway behind him. He was wearing a Fair Isle jumper, which confused me because it was like one Nick had which I often wore myself. The man stared at me so I stared back.

'Suzanne's in bed,' he said.

'I am not in bed,' Suzanne shouted, and walked out of a door frame with no door, which she then leaned back onto. She had a glass in her hand and no shoes on.

'Chrissie, darling.' She smiled out, so I walked in past the jumper and she slid towards me to hold my arm through the shapes of the paintings on the wall.

'I found your brooch on your coat,' I explained. 'It was on Jasper in Luxemburg Gardens. He was asleep.'

'Passed out, more like,' said the man.

'Did he seem OK?' Suzanne asked, frowning into my face. 'I've never seen him so wrecked before. He lost his keys. He's hopeless. Did he seem OK?'

'I'd say he's very comfortable.' I nodded as she pulled me into a kitchen by my fingers, like a child.

'This is Oliver,' she told me. 'We're divorced. His cigarette lighter has just broken.'

'I've got one,' I said, 'but nothing to light.'

'Perfect.'

She smiled and lifted a soft pack from a half-finished crossword puzzle lying across the table. We smoked. I didn't sit down but Suzanne did and crossed her long legs up onto the chair next to hers.

'This is Chrissie, Ol.' She exhaled as she tapped ash into a saucer that had a geranium on it. 'She works at Temps Perdu.'

Then she said, 'My mother's dying.'

Oliver took a peach from a box of them on the floor and a knife from the cluttered table. He started finely slicing the fruit and said Suzanne was being hysterical.

'Ring the hospital, stupid,' he partly shouted.

I was surprised that Suzanne let someone call her stupid, and surprised, too, that she still had a mother to die. She'd never mentioned her to me. Not even when I'd gone on about my own being so sick and had to stop working to be with her for weeks.

'You're probably better off when they're dead,' she'd once decided, I remember. 'You can't expect any more from them then.'

But I didn't want mine to die and I'd told her so. It's bad enough not being able to see people who are still alive.

I sat down and wondered if I should phone my mother right now and check that she was all right, but then she'd suspect that there was something wrong with me and start phoning every day, which would put a great strain on my life. I'd write. That would be best. I'd send a card in the morning. It would be silly to ring her in the middle of the night. She hates interruptions to her sleep.

'Just ring them up, for Christ's sake.' Oliver was not sitting down. 'No one said anything about death to me. They just said she's had a mild stroke, that's all.'

'Are you sure? They didn't say she might die?'

Suzanne seemed to be still holding my fingers.

'Of course not. Why should she die? She's tucked up in a

nice white bed, being taken care of by nice clean nurses. And even if she was dead, they wouldn't tell me. They don't say things like that on the phone. I'm just a man taking a message as far as they're concerned. A message my wife is ignoring.' Oliver glared at me. 'Although I've been waiting for Suzanne to come back for three hours. I don't even like her mother.'

'Oh that's nice.' Suzanne turned to stare at me too. 'My mother knitted the jumper he's wearing. She gave us her car.'

'The car that you wrote off six weeks later.'

Oliver poured himself a drink from one of three half-bottles of our house red open on the table top. I wondered how they'd got there as Oliver ate a peach and juice trickled onto his jumper front. Suzanne watched him carefully, then picked up a peach of her own and said how come Oliver was in her house in the first place? I picked up a teaspoon and studied the sugar stuck to it in case anyone started talking to me.

'How did you get in here anyway?' she said to her fruit. 'How come you were here when they rang? This house isn't a wine bar, you know, that you just call into when you've nothing better to do. And stop drinking my wine.'

Oliver put his glass down.

'I got in by using my door key. My key to my house where my son lives, remember? The one you asked me to call in and say hello to, remember?'

'The one who always stays with my sister on Fridays, remember?'

'Look, ring the hospital. Have a drink. Or don't have a drink, in fact. You're drunk. Just make the phone call, then we can all go to bed. It's four o'clock in the morning.'

We all looked at the fake station clock above the door. It was four eighteen. Suzanne poured herself another drink.

'Stop bossing me about. I'll ring when I'm ready.'

She stood up, then sat down again.

'When did they call anyway? Was it ages ago? How long does it take when they have a stroke?'

'How long does what take?'

Suzanne put her head on her arms. I rolled a peach out of the table area that she might slip further into and spun it for a while, watching the pale parts move. I asked where her mother was, but no one answered, and then she started to cry noisily, with lots of gulping in of air. It sounded quite like my own crying in the mornings, when I would wake up and feel the dark space of the day. It was tiring to cry like that.

'Don't cry, Suzanne,' said her husband, like men always do. Then he walked around the table to her and stroked her hair, which was red and had been tied up but was now straggling down. He lifted odd strands from around her face to tuck them into something. He was surprisingly good at it. It looked quite neat when she lifted her head.

'I can't.' She sniffed, rubbing her nose with her hand. She bit into a finger. 'I can't ring them. What if she's dead already?'

She pushed her face into the zigzags of his jumper and squeezed the folds of his corduroy legs. Her nails were nicely shaped and painted.

'You do it, Ollie,' she whimpered. 'You ring them for me. Please. Just this once. Please.'

She took his hand and kissed it.

'Please,' she said.

Then she was looking at me, and I felt I should do it if he refused, but he said he would, after a while of silence, so I started spinning my peach again and remembered my sister running into the wine bar the night we were told about our own mother and how I had asked Nick to please come with us to be with her, too. He said he couldn't, of course, but he did three days later. Isa and I had to take it in turns to go to the hospital, which we hated because of the noise and the heat and the nurses who stared. Nick stayed in my mother's house and made soup, which my sister and I never ate, because of anxiety we said, but actually it was not very nice. I wouldn't have minded a bowl of soup now though.

Oliver was still collecting Suzanne's hair up onto the top of her head. I thought I should leave, but didn't want to disturb them.

'Have a cigarette,' I said to the room and felt foolish.

'I'll ring,' Oliver decided. 'I'll do it now. Have a cigarette.'

He went into the hall to the phone and we heard him saying 'My wife' and 'I see' and 'Fine' and 'Thankyou' as we smoked in the yellowing air.

'Your hair looks lovely,' I said, 'like that.'

Then Oliver was in the room again saying it was all OK but Suzanne should go up there, and looking in his pockets for a wallet that he found and telling her to take something to read. He'd wait here for word, he said. He explained that I would walk her down to the tube, so I stood up and went to the door while they kissed, I supposed, and then Suzanne and I were out in the rain under a mackintosh sky, saying nothing to each other at all. I hummed 'Every Time We Say Goodbye' for a few yards, then stopped but carried it on in my head.

At the tube station Suzanne remembered Jasper. I said I'd ring Oliver for her and ask him to go and check up on him if she liked. Or we could ring the police and tell them he was there.

'What would you do?' she asked, very pale in her black plastic, and I said I wouldn't do anything if I was her, with everything else to do.

'He'll manage,' I said. 'Have you got change for a ticket?'

She hadn't and neither had I. I only had Jake's £5 note. She had a twenty from Oliver. We walked through the swimming-pool light of the ticket hall, with the opening flower stall and the mirror on the photo booth, and the fluorescent-strip clock that said 5:05, and we stared at the neat buttons of the wall of machines. Apparently they took notes. I smoothed the twenty into a slot.

'Press King's Cross,' Suzanne told me. 'We can walk from there. She's in UCH. Will you come, too?'

She watched the flower-stall man's shiny dog.

'Please come with me, Chrissie.'

I bought two adult singles to King's Cross and hoped the chocolate machine on the platform was working.

The tube was pleasingly empty with more suitcases on it than people. Great heaps of cases plastered with airline labels sprawled around a dozing man with a moustache and no lips. Not a good kisser, I decided, and wondered what had happened to Jake. I supposed he'd be fine. He seemed like a man who might be used to waking up somewhere he didn't normally sleep, wherever he normally slept might be.

Two girls talked and yawned to each other with their legs side by side and their open-toed feet up on the faded plaid seats. They had bags with bright labels tied to them, like miniature postcards or over-sized stamps. They were all from Heathrow, of course, at this time in the morning.

'Must be nice to be getting home from a holiday on Saturday morning, all salty and sunburnt,' I thought out loud to Suzanne at Barons Court, where she had her head on my shoulder and her hair slipping down onto her face. She didn't answer. She was falling woozily asleep in the fluid movement of the train. Her hand was limp on my leg. I moved it onto her bag and watched the strip lights rush past the windows as we rocked in and out of more or less empty stations.

Earls Court.

A woman with a pleated skirt and a newspaper got on and sat as far away from us as she could have. I hoped we didn't smell of our long and trailing night. Somehow my fingernails felt much dirtier than they looked.

Gloucester Road.

'Sting a burglar today,' I read above the No Smoking sign, next to a poem by Elizabeth Bishop about losing a watch and houses and a person. I stared at a picture of a giant wasp and ate my last piece of fruit & nut. Strange that Jasper had lost his keys. He had a large Filofax and a Porsche. He had a child, he'd told me once, drinking sweet strong white wine one snowy late night. Suzanne had fallen asleep on that night, too. She must be one of those people who sleeps when there's nothing to be done. I don't do that. I can't sleep until I've done everything I can.

South Kensington.

Knightsbridge.

The man with no lips struggled his luggage out just in time. He'd be staying in some soft-lit plush-walled hotel. I worked in one around there once and got a £50 tip from a drunk and handsome man.

Then it was Hyde Park Corner, with its brown and cream tiles like a Jersey cow and its arrows and scratched Way Out signs.

Suzanne started to snore softly and re-crossed her legs. It would be Green Park next. Green Park with its deckchairs opposite the Rolls-Royce shops, where Nick and I spent our summer holiday once and had a picnic on my twenty-first birthday. There'd been no buses by the time we left, so we walked back through the park to the Palace gates where I was too tired to walk any more so we got into a taxi. It cost £4.80, I remember, so we had to use all our change and had no money left for the old gas meter back at his house. Back at our house, because we lived there together then.

Suzanne's head lolled onto my breasts. I rolled it to rest on her own seatback and hoped she would wake up before King's Cross. I'd never met her mother and I wouldn't expect her to meet mine.

When Green Park arrived I stood up and I minded the gap and gulped the dust. I liked the slam of the doors and the train lurching away and I smiled into a poster of a beach in Greece, because I knew by then that I was going to Nick's. I would hail the pale light of a taxi against the sweep of Piccadilly and the milky pool of the park, and I would pay with Jake's £5 note. Suzanne couldn't blame me. She'd see that. I'd known Nick since I was seventeen. I had the key to his house and he still had one to mine. I didn't want to go to a hospital. I wanted to see a man I knew, in his own bed, on his back.

Two Lisbon

MOST CONVERSATIONS I HAD WITH NICK AFTER HE LEFT ME took place in my head as I was falling asleep, when it was hard to make them stop. The best thing to do was to talk to someone else on the telephone, and a few nights after my tube ride with Suzanne, I rang Geraldine in Lisbon because she was someone who answered the phone whatever time it was.

'Come here,' she said, 'I've got a car now. Come to Lisbon and cry on my shoulder.' It seemed straightforward advice, so I took it, and booked a flight from Gatwick for the following weekend.

When I arrived I found that the car was still half owned by Danby, who was still half owned by Geraldine, but since he was never in it with us, I thought of it as ours. It was our hottest and happiest place, with its sun-softened seats that we had to peel ourselves off, and its tin floor rolling with pebbles and warm bottles of water and small change and swimsuits. Cigarettes tasted better there and biscuits more complex. Conversations were more careful, reassurance less casual. The car and I were introduced when Geraldine met me at the airport just after midnight.

'There's our car,' she said, as she pulled me along through the tingling sound of wide-awake crickets and the throb of planes taking off.

'You thought I was lying about the car, didn't you?' She

whooped and dropped my bag to squeeze me tightly with my arms against my sides so I couldn't hug her back, which unnerved me slightly.

On the drive back to her place Geraldine explained that Danby didn't use the car any more. He had a motorbike now, and anyway, he owed her some small comfort since she'd been the one to move out of their flat.

'I mean, if Nick and you shared a car, you'd have taken it by now, wouldn't you?'

I was too confused by the notion to respond in the short gap she allowed for my answer.

'Well, anyway, he's got a bike. He's got everything. I deserve the car.'

Danby did indeed have a beautiful bike. He'd always be standing beside it or sitting astride it, smoking, if we arranged to meet him anywhere, as we often did. He had two motor-bikes in fact, but they looked the same to me, except when I saw the one that was borrowed in pieces outside his flat when we went there to collect some maps one day. He was taking care of the second bike for a friend who'd gone home for the summer he told me. One of Danby's cats had gone missing that afternoon and I found it in the motorbike's back box having sex with one of its sisters. I said I didn't know cats did that with their siblings, but Danby said yes, of course they did. He seemed cross that I knew nothing about cats, but I had the feeling he mightn't have liked it if I'd known anything either. He was hard to please that week, and I might not have bothered if I hadn't seen that he liked to please me sometimes, and that when he did it made Geraldine jealous. That made him interesting, naturally. So I watched with measured surprise and interest as his cat bounded away, scattering dust and cigarette butts. That one was called Brando, I was told. The white one was Boss, and she stayed put in her post-coital softness to roll into Danby's spread palms and writhe luxuriously there, with her back legs loose and a sliver of a tongue stretched out to smooth her tousled fur. Danby closed one of his hands loosely around her head and wriggled his fine guitar-playing nails around in her neck, which made Boss purr very loudly.

'Sounds not unlike a motorbike,' I hazarded, but Danby didn't respond. He was absorbed in Boss, who was his favourite now that Garbo was dead, Geraldine explained to me later.

Geraldine hated all Danby's cats, she told me after a long run in the car, which had overheated and purred enormously itself as boiling water gurgled through its insides. Geraldine doesn't usually drink, but the drive in the erratic vehicle had made her tense, along with a phone call from Danby as we arrived back at her flat, so she was on her third beer when she started about the cats.

'Would you believe that Danby brought them to bed when we lived together?' she asked me, clearly certain that no one could believe any such thing.

She flicked her cigarette lighter and held its flame a few inches from her roll-up for a moment, to add drama to this outrageous fact. She lit up then exhaled slowly, shaking her head. Smoke drifted into the wrought-iron fence of her balcony, which our bare feet were resting on side by side.

Danby brought the cats into their bed, she continued, and fondled them to sleep, as far as she could make out, while refusing to touch an inch of her.

'I mean, he knew I wanted a baby,' she said, flicking her lighter on and off, watching the flame come and go.

'He was always too tired to have sex, of course, after sunbathing all day, but not too tired to keep me awake half the night whispering with those creatures.'

She poured the last of a beer bottle into my glass and pulled her bare knees up to her chin, then stretched her legs out to the railings again. She took my hand, as she sometimes did, and stared into my eyes, blinking hard.

'It was like they were lovers, you know?'

Geraldine would often say 'You know' at the end of a statement. It went with touching the back of my hand, my shoulder, my cheek perhaps.

'You know, Chrissie?' she'd say with a soft lift to her voice and a raising of her hairline. I would generally nod rather than making a verbal assent. I did know, of course. Of course I knew. We shared these things that hurt her, just as she shared my misery about losing Nick, although in fact she'd never liked him. But this time I forgot to nod knowingly (empathetically? thoughtfully?), because I really was intrigued by the idea of cats in her bed. My sister had a black kitten once, and I loved the feel of its feet against my skin, but since it was winter when it arrived I was always wrapped up in clothing, and never felt that timidity anywhere tender. I thought it might be nice to have a kitten in bed. Nick wouldn't let us get one because they gave him asthma, but I could have one now if I wanted.

I was wondering whether the pet shop in Shepherd's Bush Market sold kittens, and was beginning to think it did when Geraldine's fingers touched my arm. Her hand was cool by now.

'I felt so lonely, you know?'

I remembered sliding my legs into the cold sheets of my large bed lately, and did indeed know what lonely felt like. Although being lonely with someone else beside you in bed is worse than being alone there, of course.

'It was as if I didn't exist, you know?'

I squeezed Geraldine's small cold hand and nodded pensively. I thought of Danby's firm body, which I'd seen drying on hot sand the day before. I must concentrate on Geraldine.

'Did you try saying anything about it? Or did you pretend not to notice?'

'Not notice?'

She emptied her glass. I took it and poured her some of my beer so she wouldn't get up for more from the fridge. I wanted her to keep talking.

'You couldn't not notice, Chrissie. He was all over them. Rubbing noses, chewing their ears, pulling their legs about. It was disgusting, in fact.'

'Did he have an erection?'

I wasn't concentrating properly or I wouldn't have said that word to Geraldine. She ignored it.

'And if I did say anything he'd go mad with me and say how could I be jealous of a kitten, and why didn't I see an analyst?'

'But I thought you did?'

'I stopped when I moved in with Danby. And I can't go back because I can't afford it now I'm paying for this place. The rent's about double here, you know.'

'Why didn't he move out? That place was so cheap. I mean, you found it, you said? And he earns millions now, he says.'

'He says lots of things.'

She stood up and folded her arms around herself, looking skinny.

'I think I'll make some camomile tea,' she told the wall to my right.

Then, kneeling in front of me, with her face as white as the full moon behind her, 'Stop frowning. You need a jumper.'

Our conversations would often end with my needing something, I noticed, as the hot, white-cobbled-street week eked away.

Most of my days in Lisbon with Geraldine began with a phone call from her to Danby, which seemed to be mostly about the car. Then, when we were in it and away from her flat, skidding around a cathedral or a cluster of lost tourists or a building sided with shiny tiling, Geraldine would start to 'talk the car thing through'.

The 'car thing' was a simpler issue than that of the cats, at first, and seemed wholly unrelated. A straightforward example of how tough life was now and of Danby's desire to hurt her. He said he needed it back for a while because his mother was coming to stay, but Geraldine needed it more. The car was her main pleasure these days and there was no reason why Danby should have it even for only two weeks. Of course he had paid for the insurance since they split up, but he'd wanted to do that, and actually she'd asked him not to, knowing that this would happen, and now of course it had and what could she do? Couldn't he see how it was for her? Did he have to spoil her holidays? He'd made her unhappy enough as it was. He could rent a car, couldn't he, when his mother arrived?

'Of course he could. He's loaded. The car is obviously symbolic of something.'

I was watching a sail boat curl into a harbour where a string of pale lights had just burst on. The sea to our right, through my dust-streaked window, had faded into pale powder on the violet horizon, but was still rolling in Day-Glo breakers for the straggling paddlers to run with, close-up. I lifted my feet onto a collapsing shelf, which was probably meant to hold maps but was crammed with tapes and beer cans and a battered English–Portuguese dictionary, which I browsed through whenever we stopped for petrol.

Geraldine put her hand on my knee.

'Let's stop for a swim. You need a wash.'

'Let's not. I need a drink.'

So we veered onto some split tarmac by a bar with a corrugated roof with a pink neon sign and a turquoise tarpaulin, and I thought of the word 'delightful', as I often did when

Geraldine stopped the car and we found ourselves upright, in a blast of lavender air, with our limbs bare and brown, our shadows side by side and a similar size.

'Inebriate of air,' I said, quoting Emily Dickinson, which made Geraldine raise her eyes, but she was beyond whimsicality now, and looking an uneasy mix of defiant and beaten as she moved towards the bar with her back very straight. I sat down at a tin-topped table.

'You couldn't be without the car. It's ridiculous,' I insisted, to relax the atmosphere when she came back with the beers. I squinted at the heat-pleated air above our car bonnet through the smoke of a cigarette, which made little firework noises as it burned, like Greek cigarettes do.

'I mean, we couldn't be here together if Danby had the car now, could we?'

I thought what a sweet taste the beer had, and enjoyed the weight of my glass as I watched her fingering sand out of her fine straw-coloured hair. She wriggled matted strands through her fingers and thumb and frowned at the salty texture of it, or maybe at what she was thinking.

'I can't stand Danby's mother,' she said, which didn't surprise me.

Then she said, 'And his daughter's coming as well this time,' which did, because I didn't know Danby had one.

By our second beer and final bowl of some salty hybrid of peanuts and baked beans, I thought I knew everything Geraldine knew about Danby's daughter. The girl's name was Lily. She'd lived in Sydney all her life. She'd been born when Danby was only nineteen and he'd hardly seen her since. Lily's mother was a woman called Crystal, who Danby had met when he was on his way to find himself somewhere in Turkey. They'd fallen in love and read *The Whole Earth Catalogue* together and got stoned on someone's verandah one afternoon and decided to set off for the west coast of Ireland. They were going to breed goats and live in a bus and all that crap, Geraldine said, although they'd actually had a perfectly good cottage all to themselves, which of course they decided to leave as soon as Crystal got pregnant.

'She wanted to start a commune in Cork. Can you imagine? What a joke.'

I tried to look as horrified at the muddle-headedness of Danby's past as Geraldine clearly felt. I didn't mention that Nick and I once moved to Scotland for a week with the same sort of plan, but discovered we liked hot water. Anyway, we were in the wrong place: everyone else had moved to Wales or Devon or Yorkshire.

'Why did they choose Cork?' I wondered, but Geraldine didn't want details snagging her broad-sweep canvas of Danby's wilderness years.

'Because it was there.'

She lit a cigarette and went on to explain that things in Cork had gone badly for Danby. Crystal had met someone else, who she followed to Dublin. From there the happy couple had gone to Australia, where this new love of her life came from, and it was there that Lily was born. Danby was heartbroken and went back to London.

'So he never saw his baby?'

I wished he was there suddenly to ask him all about it. I wished he'd lived with his baby. I could see Danby with a baby in his arms. The only baby I knew at that time was a nephew of Nick's and I loved to see them together.

'Well, he saw her eventually. Couldn't stay away, could he? But by the time he got to Sydney, Crystal was expecting another one and it was all sewn up. Danby went out a few times, though, I think after that. They've always been in touch, although he pretends he's not that interested when I ask. He won't discuss his family with me. He's afraid I'll start complaining that he won't let me have a baby. Which I wouldn't, of course, if he'd be reasonable about the whole thing.' She bit a fingernail loudly.

'But Lily must know Danby's mother, then? I mean, they must be quite close if they're coming to Lisbon together?'

'Danby's mother isn't close to anyone, as far as I know.'

Geraldine lifted a small insect from the skim of her beer.

'No, but . . . well, they must have met?'

The whole thing was beginning to intrigue me. I wished again that Danby was with us. I thought he'd tell me more than Geraldine would.

'So how does Danby's mother know Lily?'

Geraldine wrinkled her nose. 'God. You're full of questions, aren't you? Well, they've met in London. There was a big family do there last Easter, when Lily was over, applying to art schools. She's seventeen now. The image of her beautiful mother, apparently. So friendly, so bright and so nice.' Geraldine warped the word into a sneer, stretching her face away from itself.

And now that the 'amazing Lily' was coming to Lisbon with his amazing mother, she went on, of course Danby must have the car back.

'Because, I mean, Daddy would have a car, wouldn't he? But not a girlfriend, of course. And not a baby, either, would he?'

I watched an American motorbike pull in beside the contentious Renault 4.

'I can't believe she calls him Daddy?'

'She calls him Daniel, in fact. Unlike everyone else in the world.'

'Have you met her?'

'We've talked on the phone. I wasn't invited to her coming-out dinner, naturally. Didn't even know it was happening till afterwards, although I was in London at the time.'

'That's terrible for you,' I said as she rolled herself one of her tiny roll-ups. 'You must feel horrible about the whole thing. Why doesn't Danby include you?'

She gave a little sniff, looking away into the haze with a slight bitter smile, then looked back at me with narrowed eyes.

'He wants her to have him all to herself, I suppose. I'm glad you can see that I ought to be involved, though. It makes me sad, you know?'

At first the 'car question' seemed to have little to do with me, but as the burning tarmac of the next few days glossed by I could see that I had to share it. Sometimes I felt as if I was the 'car question'. On the sardine night, for instance, Geraldine and I got back late from the beach, and as I went out to the balcony to dangle our costumes to dry, I heard Geraldine on the telephone. I moved nearer to the doorway to listen.

'Well I can't ruin Chrissie's holiday because you want to empty the car ashtrays I'm afraid, Daniel.'

Her best insulted tone at full pitch. The clock tower ballooned out nine firm strokes. There was more excited conversation with my name in it, which I couldn't quite get the drift of.

I moved to stand inside the flat, waiting for Geraldine to say goodbye. I was hungry.

'Well I'll ask her. But there are only seven sardines.' Pause. 'Do you, Danby?' Her low tone, reassuring but slightly reproving too. 'Do you? Well I feel like that some days too, you know?'

I watched the back of her stone-smooth shoulders as she scratched her neck through her hair, then I went to stand beside her and she took my hand, smiling into the phone.

'OK, we'll be there in half an hour. Get something to drink.' She winked at me. 'You know how Chrissie is.'

Eyes down again for a new intimacy with the phone and a tenderness in her 'goodbye' that threw me. She made its privacy seem complete. I stood to watch her while she took sardines from the fridge, then I sat and watched her wrap them, after which she changed her sandals. Did those look better? They did, so she wore them out, down the narrow stairs and across the clattering courtyard to stop outside her door of the car. She smiled at me over its bird-stained roof. We were going to eat with Danby.

The drive was splashy through a freak shower and very dark along a minor motorway with traffic lights, pointlessly placed, it seemed, since there was never anything crossing our path. As she fingered the fragile gearstick into neutral for our third or fourth wait at an oval of red, Geraldine said she'd like a cigarette and would I roll one for her? I often did that and liked the conspiracy of lighting it myself, then passing it over, and the way she sometimes passed it back if she needed her hand free for a moment. It was like a silent conversation. It was seductive to feel so at home with someone after being at home by myself for too long.

'I was thinking, Chrissie,' she started, as a lorry swayed past us much too close. She held her cigarette in her mouth to blast the horn and we raised eyebrows at one another.

'I was thinking it might be best if you could tell Danby that you're not going back till Monday night. He thinks you're only here for a week.'

That was because it was true, I thought. I was flying back to Gatwick early on Saturday morning.

'You see, he wants the car on Saturday to collect his mother and Lily from the airport.'

We swung off the well-lit road onto a smaller one with industrial buildings massed black all around.

'And I don't want him to have it then, you know?'

She stubbed her cigarette and put a hand on my knee.

'Do you see what I mean? He always wants everything exactly his own way.'

'Most people I know do.'

It was the wrong response, clearly. She put her hand back on the wheel. She turned the windscreen wipers off.

'But what reason shall I give for changing my flight, then?'

'You don't have to say you've changed your flight. He got it wrong, that's all. He misunderstood me, I've told him. You always planned to stay ten days. A week isn't enough, is it?'

We ground into second and up a tiny dirt track with a low modern building against the sailing sky.

'I mean, a week to see someone you haven't seen for two years who you used to see practically every day? You should have come for two weeks really. A week couldn't possibly be nearly enough.'

She turned the engine off and reached for her bag on the floor by my feet, which meant I had to pull my knees up into my chin. When she had her bag safely on her midriff, she leaned back in her seat, sighed deeply, then rolled her head heavily onto my shoulder. I smoothed her hair away from her forehead, with its scar that intrigued me, and I said, 'We'll say I'm staying ten days then, if that's the deal.'

'That's the deal, if he buys it. Can you reach the sardines from there?'

They were on the floor behind my seat, so I groped them into my hands and eased myself out of the car. She locked my door behind me as I straightened out into the smell of rainy pine and candle wax and decomposing cardboard and something else that I don't know the word for, which you only smell in Lisbon.

The cats smelt our sardines as soon as we arrived and swarmed to our ankles like a soft installation on the kitchen's checked floor. Much soothing and stroking from Danby, which prevented him finding a corkscrew. Geraldine had gone straight out to construct a barbecue on his corridor of a balcony, which he'd adorned with candles that kept blowing out. They distracted him from the corkscrew question, too, and he went outside to do something with the windbreak, so I started looking through drawers myself. There was no corkscrew, but I found a photograph of Danby's mother and a black-haired girl with a nose like his. Must be Lily, I thought, and wished I could look at it longer, but slid it back as he came through and started pulling at something that had stuck to the back of my shorts.

'Where's the corkscrew, Gerry?' he called out to make her turn and see us so close, I assumed. I was pleased, but tried not to seem so.

'How should I know where your corkscrew is? Mine is in my kitchen.'

Sardonic smile at me from him and then a stretch to a wall cupboard and the problem was solved.

'None for me, thanks,' she called. 'I'll stick to beer if there is any.'

There was plenty. I washed the sardines and tried to kick the cats away discreetly. They were making a lot of noise.

Everything seemed to take much longer than it should have, there being only seven sardines and a lettuce. We didn't finish eating until nearly twelve, by which time a bottle of almond liqueur was on the table and two small cats were on Danby and Geraldine was asking if the washing machine worked yet, and if Matthew Arnold's 'Dover Beach' would be a suitable poem for her students to translate.

I felt rather homesick with Danby saying, 'Ah, love, let us be true / To one another!' especially when I went to his bathroom and saw the Christmas card Nick and I had made the year before. It had two fat people embracing in glittery clothes. I'd put the glitter on myself. Glitter was my job on the night we assembled the cards, as well as filling our glasses with assorted wines left over from his birthday two days before. I gave him a typewriter that year – it's the one I still use now.

*

When I got back from the bathroom, where I brushed my hair, the mood on the balcony had changed. Geraldine was now half sitting on Danby's muscular legs, holding a white kitten, which he was feeding with dangling fish skin. I had to squeeze through their intimacy to get back to my chair, which was filled with a different cat. I was grateful to have something to lift onto my knee, and something to talk about in the molten silence.

'Where do they all sleep?' I heard myself say, which was silly because Geraldine had told me, but Danby ignored the question to say why didn't we all sleep there at his flat tonight? Lots of room, he said, pulling bits of bone apart for a stripey kitten called Pocket, because it liked to be inside anything at all, they told me.

I said I'd like to be in a pocket myself. It was getting cool in the now cloudless midnight. The candles were mostly out.

'You can enclose yourself in the back bedroom,' Danby said, leaning across at me, making it sound like our secret. 'I've just cleaned it up so my mother doesn't realize I'm a slob. The whole place will be transformed by Saturday.'

'You know we need the car till Monday, don't you?' Geraldine stood up and stretched with emphatic pleasure. 'Chrissie's flight is at midnight on Sunday.'

Danby took Pocket's tail and brushed the cat's nose with it until Geraldine lifted the animal from him and dropped it onto me. I stood up, feeling suddenly cross and tired and bored with them and their cats and their car and mothers and sardines and candles and the wrong sort of drink, that gave you a headache instead of cheering you up.

'If we're staying, can I go to bed? I'm shattered.'

Finding myself asking their permission to do what I wanted annoyed me more.

'I mean, I think I'll go and lie down.'

Geraldine stared at me sharply.

'I'm just tired, you know?'

She couldn't argue with that. Silence, except for the crickets and feline teeth on sardine. Geraldine moved her chair nearer to Danby's.

'I've run out of beer.'

She kicked him playfully, as they say.

'Are you staying?'

Danby ran his hand down her side, from her waist to the floor, and I watched his backbone stretch through his T-shirt. It looked good from where I was standing.

'Go on. I'll get you a nice cold beer.'

She ruffled his head, which was at her breast-level.

'I think I should take Chrissie home and tuck her up. She needs her sleep. She likes my bed.'

'I don't mind where I sleep, Gerry. I couldn't care less.'

My voice was almost shrill.

'I'll sleep out here if you bring me a blanket.'

'Have a drink. You're on holiday. Relax.'

Danby refilled my glass and I sipped some more sickly thick liquid. I was bound to feel disgusting in the morning. Yet another cat appeared on the balcony wall and he lifted it to him and Geraldine said all right we'd stay, if nobody cared and yes, she'd have another drink, why not? In fact, she thought she'd have some of the almond stuff, now that she wasn't driving.

'I wouldn't if I were you,' said Danby, passing her the bottle. 'You know how ratty you get.'

Some time later somebody offered to show me my bedroom, but I went by myself and fell asleep in most of my clothes and dreamt that Lily and Nick were lovers and that she wrote to me and said he had my photograph on their kitchen wall, and they had a baby called Gerald who looked like me. Then I woke up and there was shouting somewhere and I didn't know where I was or where the light would be, and I had a headache and a taste in my mouth.

'You're the one who's sick.' It was Geraldine, screaming.

'You're completely screwed up, you know that, don't you? Why did you ask me to stay?'

A slower voice now, but still hers and still louder. 'Why do you do this to me? Give me that.' Banging noises. 'Just give me that thing now. I won't have it, do you understand? I will not have this happening to me any more, you fuck-up.'

More fumbled banging, during which I wondered vaguely if I could climb out of my window. Then my door was open and Geraldine was coming towards me in a T-shirt, carrying her skirt, then her hand was around my wrist pulling me up.

'We're leaving. Get up. We're leaving right now.'

So I got up and found my shoes and we left right then, and Danby's door stayed shut. As the headlights hit the gravel outside, a white cat stopped and stared still into us and Geraldine got out and caught it. She threw it inside the car over my head, and drove off down the dirt track onto the motorway and said nothing until the car made a strange grinding noise, then a burning smell, then smoked, then stopped completely.

'Shit. We'll have to walk it.'

'How far away are we?'

'About two miles. We could try hitching. We'll have to push the car into the side, though.'

We got out of the car. The cat mewed loudly and tried to squeeze out past Geraldine's window, which she had her right hand pushed through to hold the steering wheel. She told me to stop pushing and get back in and steer, and keep all the windows shut. I was amazed at how she moved us forward all by herself then, up a slight hill, into a lay-by. I thought of some woman I'd met at someone's house telling me she once threw a chest of drawers down a staircase as her husband was leaving. Rage makes you strong, she'd explained.

So there we were, walking home side by side, with the cat and the car keys and the tent – which we thought might get stolen – and the sea breeze and my goose-pimpled arms and white lines on the wet road and a slight snuffle as Geraldine wept.

Geraldine's flat was one enormous room with a cupboard for a bedroom, where I slept. She'd been using the sofa bed, where she woke up long before I did to smoke and read John Updike stories, continuing them out loud to me when I got up, while I dressed or made my tea. I never saw her asleep. But after Danby's, at ten to three, as we collapsed into the familiarity of her pale grey walls, she said we'd have to sleep together in her bed because of the cat. We must shut Boss in the main room and hope she behaved. We watched the animal rubbing against the table leg. We stared at it like you might look at a pan of something that's just exploded all over the stove.

'I threw it out of his bedroom window back there,' Geraldine told me, holding my arm now as if to protect me.

'I think we'll give it away in the morning. I want Danby not to have that cat any more. I want him to think it's left him.'

She held my arm tighter so that it began to hurt.

'He's got to understand that you can't reject a person who loves you without paying for it somehow. He owes me that cat.'

She moved away from me to sit on the floor. She hugged up her knees and talked to a flowering cactus at her side. I thought for the first time how like her mother she looked. Her mother was a maths teacher.

'I wouldn't mind poisoning it actually. Then we could take it back and leave it on his motorbike. See if that teaches him.'

'Teaches him what?'

'To like me more.'

‘Why would he like someone who’d murdered his cat?’

‘Stupid. You’re completely missing the point. Anyway, he couldn’t possibly connect it with us. I mean, why would we bother ourselves with his cat when our car’s broken down and we’ve been abducted, most likely?’

I didn’t like all this ‘us’ business. I thought of my bedspread at home with sudden affection.

‘Yes. A dead cat. That should put him off them for a bit. Unless dead animals turn him on.’

She twisted her mouth and groaned, like children do when they’re given something unattractive but wholesome to eat. She looked at me, grinning. I said nothing, but watched her thoughtful face and wriggled my toes discreetly to circulate the blood. My fingers were cold, too. I would have tucked them into the cat, but thought Geraldine might attack me.

‘What will you do about the car?’

‘Leave it. Someone’ll take it. It’s insured anyway. In his name, as luck would have it.’

She pulled a fallen flower head from the base of the cactus and threw it towards me.

‘In fact, I’ll ring the police myself and tell them where the car is now. But not that I left it there, naturally.’

She stretched out on her back and then rolled over a few times so that she was lying beside me.

‘Yes, indeed. He’ll be a worried man when he hears about the car left on the road and goes there and realizes we’ve probably been murdered.’

‘Less worried when he gets round here and finds us safe and well, however.’

‘Shut up. We won’t answer the door.’

‘Who murdered us?’

‘A psychopath. There are loads of them.’

‘There’s you.’

'I'll ring the police and tell them. They'll ring Danby when they identify the registration.'

She stood up and talked on in a cheerful way, looking down at the blue rug she'd bought in Morocco with Danby the summer before.

'I'll say I've seen an abandoned car and they'll see it's his and ring him and he'll ring here and won't know where we are. It's illegal to leave vehicles on the motorway, you know.'

'It's in a lay-by. It broke down. What else could we do?'

I was tired.

'They'll be on the case right away. We could easily have been murdered walking home, you know.'

She picked up the phone and winked at me. She had a very particular wink. She must have practised as a teenager.

'Now you're being stupid,' I said, surprising myself. 'If he hears about it now, he'll get on his bike and come straight here. He'll wake the landlady up, and she'll bring him here to find us safe and sound with his favourite cat and he'll never speak to you again.'

She put the phone down and came to sit beside me, sweet-smelling in an afterglow of almond brandy.

'How clever. You know about men, don't you?' A hand on my head. 'I'll make us some herb tea then we'll go to bed. We'll have a lovely sleep and I'll ring the police in the morning, then we'll go straight out. We'll go camping. We won't be here when he comes. We can go to that place you liked on the ferry. I adore you, Chrissie, sometimes, you know. But now I need a pee.'

As she splashed in the bathroom with its stencilled walls, I unfolded the sofa bed and called through that I'd sleep there so we could both get some rest. She came out with a towel bunched around her, scowling.

'But I thought we were sleeping together. That cat will attack you.'

'I'm not scared of cats.'

'Are you scared I'll snore?'

'I'm not scared of snoring.'

'What are you scared of?'

I'm scared of small women who want to kill cats and can push cars up hills single handed, but I didn't tell her that. I told her she needed some sleep.

One of the first things we realized the next day was that we couldn't go camping because the tent poles and pegs were still in the car. Geraldine said we'd take a tram to the ferry then walk to a beach and think of what to do next later on.

'We'll get some cat food first to keep it quiet. Do you want to go to the shops or shall I?'

I didn't. I could never work out how much anything cost or how to please the onion-skinned shopkeeper, who was forever grabbing my hand and pressing it into the folds of her apron. I'd make coffee, I said, and read my guide book.

'Have a shower,' she said. 'I'm going to.'

She took off her T-shirt and looked down at her breasts for a moment, before turning her back to me and shutting the door of the bedroom behind her. When she reappeared she was wearing a flowery wraparound thing and carrying a pair of my espadrilles that she wanted to borrow.

'You don't mind, do you?'

'Not really.'

'You do. I can tell. I won't then.'

'I don't.' I minded something, though. My heart was beating too hard.

'I'm sorry, Chrissie. I had a deprived childhood, you know?'

Half laughing, slipping into their faded grey fronts. Boss rubbed up to her calves, butting and weaving her perfect tail.

'A hungry cat.' She smiled up to me.

'Deprived,' I agreed. 'And I need some cigarettes while you're out.'

'Yes, Mummy.' She kissed my cheek.

'Don't be long.'

'I'll run all the way.'

I drank a pot of coffee and smoked my last cigarette and emptied ashtrays and picked things up then put them down, and still Geraldine stayed at the shops. The church tower struck another half hour, the sky clouded over, a ball was bounced and the landlady sang and I started looking through Geraldine's books, then some wallets of photographs jammed into the end of a shelf. They were pictures of holidays mostly, in rolling heatscapes in Geraldine's happier days as a half of a couple. Danby in trunks, leaning into his bike with an ice-cream, against an emerald sky. The car on beaches or slumbering next to a tent. Soft smiles at the camera over plates of scarlet fish and tables crowded with maps and beer. Cafés with coloured lights and people in big-printed clothing. 'The party I've been going to all my life,' as we'd read in Updike that morning. Everyone's holiday photographs. I had dozens like them myself.

And then there was a set developed by Boots on Kensington High Street the April before, which made me sit down on the unfolded sofa bed, to spread them out and stare. Boss clawed up beside me and the photos slithered underneath cushions, so I shut the cat in the bedroom and went back to examine these unexpected pictures of Lily. The photographs in this set were nothing but Lily. She was not unlike Danby but more Celtic and much slighter. Not that unlike Geraldine either, in fact. The same wide, startled soft eyes. Dressed in black in most of them. In Holland Park, smiling at squirrels or eating cake or holding hands with Danby's mother. Then in a restaurant with clouded walls where Geraldine seemed to be sitting beside her. Certainly it was Geraldine. I knew the dress. And a tense Danby there, too, with various other flash-red-eyed family members, presumably. The family gathering that Geraldine had not been invited to was all here to see, with Geraldine very much at it. Geraldine, very drunk in some of the pictures, by the look of her, and Lily, too pale in one, staring aghast at something. At Geraldine herself, it seemed. Danby then, in front of Lily, and Geraldine leaning into both of them. Or was she pushing Lily out from behind her father? It was hard to tell, but it looked chaotic.

The telephone rang as I was trying to piece together a picture that had been torn up, so I scrambled the photos together, then dropped them all somehow as I took the phone in my left hand and heard Danby saying Hi. I didn't answer at first, so he said it again.

'She's not here,' I said, pushing the slidy squares back into their wallet. 'This is Chrissie.'

I had to get the photographs back on the shelf.

'Is she OK?'

They didn't seem to want to go back in their packet. I wondered if it mattered what order they were in.

'Geraldine's at the shops.'

I hoped there was still a long queue, or that she'd met someone she knew, or forgotten how to get home, perhaps. Boss mewed loudly from the bedroom. I jammed everything back more or less where I'd found it. Danby wasn't saying anything, so I said, 'How are you?'

'Tired.'

'Me, too. It was a late night.' I was blushing, I could tell.

'Yes. Chrissie?'

I looked over to the door and saw Geraldine's camera hanging on a hook with the coats there on the back of it. I thought of all the photos she'd taken of me that week as Danby said my name again, like someone in a horror film who thinks the person is dead at the other end of the line. I must say something back.

'She's at the shops,' I said.

'Yes, you said that. Look, Chrissie, can you tell Gerry something for me when she gets back from the shops? Tell her I'm going home for a while, can you? I'm flying out this afternoon.'

'Don't you want your camera back?'

'What camera?'

'Your cat, I mean. Do you want the cat?'

'Look, Chrissie, I've got a plane to catch.'

'We've got Boss here. By accident.'

'Well, someone's feeding the cats here, so Gerry can drop her back if she feels like it. She's got keys to this place. I don't really care.'

He sounded as if he didn't.

'The car broke down.'

I started chewing on one of my fingers, which isn't something I do.

'I know. They told me. Are you OK?'

'I don't know why Geraldine's taking so long. Shall I get her to ring you back?'

'No, just tell her I've gone to London for a while, can you? The car's at Graham's, tell her. She can ring him tonight to see how it's going.'

'Will it be OK?'

'Hope so.'

I concentrated on the telephone being awkward to hold. Its wire was too short, so I had to stoop down to speak.

'Are you going to London to see Lily?'

He said he didn't know I knew about Lily.

'I don't. I mean I didn't, but Geraldine told me. She's met her, hasn't she?'

'She certainly has. I'm surprised she told you about that

little nightmare, I must say. It's not something I'd be proud of.'

'No.'

'No. Well anyway, I'm not going to see Lily, although I'm hoping I will see her. But she's changed her plans. In fact, Chrissie . . .' His voice changed as he said my name, as if we were lovers and he'd met someone else. 'In fact, I don't know where Lily is. She's disappeared. She was last seen in Sydney boarding a plane to Heathrow, but her grandmother couldn't find her when the plane arrived. She'd disappeared from the airport. She's disappeared, full stop. They just phoned me. I mean, everyone's been on the phone. No one knows where she is. So I'm going to London, though it's probably pointless. I'm just tired. I'm just upset.'

He was saying he was just something else, too, which wasn't quite said when Geraldine's key slid into the lock and she saw me on the phone.

'It's Danby,' I told her. She stayed by the door.

'She's back,' I told the telephone. 'I'll put her on. Goodbye then. Take care,' I said, although it's not something I say, and I pulled at the tangled flex to get it nearer to Geraldine, but Danby hung up in the time she took to come over and say hello.

My last hour in Lisbon was far from delightful, although the sun was burning hard as my taxi slid over cobbles and followed the steel-grey tramlines' curve to sweep me out of the centre, through dazzled traffic lights and into the airport. Geraldine was mad that Danby was going to London. He should have asked her to go with him, she said. He needed her now. She could calm him down. She could help him find Lily, who had obviously only pulled this stunt to get some attention.

'She'll do anything to get him away from me.'

I watched as she stood on a chair to slide a suitcase from the top of a cupboard. She started folding things into it from her bedroom chair. She threw her camera on top of the pile.

'Can I wear your shoes for now?' she said, and also that I could collect the car for her and would I feed Boss for the next few days and there was a bus that went to the airport that I could get on Saturday morning and maybe we could all meet up in London on Sunday?

'If he's looking for Lily, I want to be there,' she said. 'I know the places a girl like that goes.'

'But you've never met her.'

'She's a cow,' Geraldine said. She glared at me. 'But Danby won't let me say so.'

I watched her drag dresses from her louvre-doored wardrobe and told her I would not be seeing her in London. She'd got the car now and the cats and both of their flats and Danby needed her in Lisbon to take care of things while he went to look for his daughter. And that's what she would do, if she loved him, I said. If she cared, she'd leave him alone to sort things out. But I didn't care what she did, I said, almost shouting, like she had the night before. I didn't care what she did any more, but I wouldn't be doing it with her. Or for her, either, I went on as she stared, and I was pleased to be making a noise for a change.

She got off her chair then and came towards me and I thought she might slap me. Her right hand was up and her face was tight.

'What do you know about what I'd do if I loved him? How could you possibly know? You're the one who's come on a holiday, remember? Getting over your boyfriend who left you, remember? You're the one who got the plane.'

Now she was taking my shoes off her feet and slapping them into my rucksack. Gathering all my things together. Packing for me now, I noticed, instead of herself.

'What could you know about doing things you know you

shouldn't do? D'you think it's all a question of being nice enough to make everyone think you're the nicest? Do you really think that's how it works? Does everyone just do what they ought to do, stupid?'

Then she sat down and stopped screaming, and said I was simple. She wasn't surprised Nick had left me, she said, seeing as how I'd just left him to it. That wasn't the way love worked, she explained. You had to fight to get what you wanted, but I was too simple for that.

'You're simple, Chrissie,' she told me. 'You really are, you know?'

Three Moscow Road

I HADN'T BEEN BACK FROM LISBON FOR MORE THAN A FEW days when I learned what my sister had been up to all summer. And since Isa is not a simple person I can only assume that she wanted me to discover that for myself, or she wouldn't have got me up to Moscow Road. It was an uphill bike ride from my flat to Isa's, through the crammed, silky cars of Holland Park Avenue, which were annoying if your legs were already tired from being a waitress, so my sister usually cycled down to see me, but she refused to that afternoon. She couldn't, she explained.

'I can't.' My sister always shouts when she's on the phone.

'I can't move. I spent the night in a luggage compartment.'

'Oh really? What was it? An installation or something?'

Isa was still an art student at the time.

'Stupid. I was on the boat train from Paris.'

I was surprised she was home. The last I'd heard she'd been in Greece and planning to stay there indefinitely.

'Can you do my evenings at Temps Perdu for a while?' her loopy scrawl had asked two weeks before, on the back of a picture of an off-printed squid, intertwined with a complex postmark. I could and I did and was glad of the money. Her shifts had provided the air fare to Lisbon.

'I thought you were on Corfu with Charlie?'

'Charlie got off the train in Venice. We're not talking to each other.'

I heeled my left pump off with the toe of my right one.

'So when can you get here? I need to see you.'

I've never liked my family needing to see me. I said I was undressed.

'Why? It's two o'clock. Are you in bed with somebody?'

I explained that I'd just finished doing a lunchtime and was planning a nice cool bath.

'Was it busy? How much did you make?'

'Nothing. We've been empty all month. Everyone's away, except the estate agents.'

'And me. Have you heard from Nick?'

'No. Has Charlie?'

'How should I know? So when can you get here?'

'Why don't you come here? We can lie on the roof.'

'I can't,' she said. 'I can't move. I spent the night in a luggage compartment.'

Moscow Road when I got there was blocked and hot. I already blamed Isa for my first-gear journey through noise and exhaust fumes and taxis' black close-ups, and now I couldn't cross her street. Jammed surfaces of plate-glass cars were queuing behind the zebra crossing, where a woman was collecting tumbled doughnuts. I watched with everyone else for a while, then squeezed my bicycle basket through car fenders to collide with a man with a ponytail who often lunched in the wine bar. He was carrying a child and a briefcase and loaves of long bread, and was sweating impressively. I said sorry and hello and he said, 'Hi, Isa,' and strode on before I could draw his attention to the fact that I was not my sister. We don't really look like each other, but people used to think we did. Nick said it was the way we held our heads, although I couldn't see how else to do it if you want to see where you're going.

In the alley opposite the Greek shop I uncoiled my warm chain from my waist and locked my bike to Isa's green one, which had a missing mudguard and a flat back tyre. She should have told me that, it would have been a good excuse. I watched our customer's well-fed back with his child's hands against it as he turned left into Queensway, then I followed him into our favourite bakery. He stopped and read an Italian newspaper headline while I bought myself a roll which I ate on the pavement, gazing through the window of Oddbins. 'Confused?' a yellow poster questioned; 'Bewildered? Perplexed? Uncertain? Ask for help.' I must tell Isa that; she'd love it. She was nuts about the American with white Levi's who worked there. He once asked me out for a drink, but Isa said I couldn't accept because Nick would find out. When she said that, she meant she would tell him, although I don't think she ever really did.

I was still hungry when I'd eaten my roll, so went back into the bakery and bought more to share with Isa, then I squashed myself through jangled languages and sunglasses and suitcases on wheels to the olive-oil afternoon of Moscow Road.

Inverness Mansions has a pale stained front door that looks randomly damp, but which was warm and dry to shoulder open. It's always locked, but I had a key, though I hadn't lived there for years. Sometimes Isa used to ask for the key back, but I had to have it because she was often out when she said she'd be in, and there's no doorstep to sit on until you're inside the building. The stairwell then had marbled lino that smelled of old wood and brown-pink concrete walls that held decades of Decembers, so you froze in winter in spite of the antique radiators on every other landing. The stairs are pleasingly scooped, with trills of wrought iron in the banister struts and an echo, like railway arches. I was pleased to be there again. Pleased to be in familiar territory, and pleased at the idea of seeing Isa so soon, and telling her all about Geraldine and Danby and the cats and the car and comparing our tans and hearing about her disaffection with Charlie. Being her elder sister, I would be bound to be asked for advice. I could smoke my Portuguese cigarettes and hold forth.

The flat Isa lived in is on the top floor of the building. She shared it with Charlie, as Nick and I had once done, before Isa got involved with Charlie and moved in herself. Charlie's father is an art dealer and he owns the flat, but never bothers himself with whether it stays in one piece or not. Since no one has ever paid rent as far as I know, I suppose that's fair enough. When Nick and I lived through our winter there in the icy French-window room, there was a piano in the hall which a German musician gave lessons on from time to time. Charlie liked the arrangement because he had meandering affairs with the German's students, and I liked it because he'd ask my advice on what to do next, or how to undo what he'd done when these affairs went wrong, which gave rise to a lot of pleasant late-night conversations. I didn't think he'd fall for Isa, however, so maybe my emotional counselling wasn't as perceptive as I liked to imagine. Nick said I didn't want Charlie to be truly contented anyway, and that was probably true because I liked him in the kitchen, playing gloomy tunes on his saxophone between swigs of warm Czech beer. Nick said Isa didn't really want Charlie to be happy, either. She just wanted to share his flat, he said. I denied that, of course, because she is my sister, but it may have been somewhat true. She wasn't slow to move in anyway, and to see that the attic would be perfect for her paintings, which were garage-door sized at the time. She filled the attic with them slowly, bedding them down in our remaindered old clothing and the duvets we left in case we ever came back.

I hadn't been to visit my little sister since before her birthday in June. She'd been mostly out in July. I knew this because

I'd often ring her, and find that Charlie thought she was with me at my house. I'd have to say that I wasn't at home myself – whether I was or was not – and that Isa may well be there with Nick. I had a suspicion she was being naughty, but I never asked her directly. If it was important, I thought she'd have told me. She used to call having affairs 'being naughty', which I tried to point out was babyish. She was a grown-up, I used to say, and what about Charlie? She'd say Charlie was grown-up too and she wasn't his mother, and anyway, it was none of my business. I got the wine-bar shifts she should have been working through that July when she escaped on her mysterious dates, so as business goes it wasn't bad. But I wished she wasn't my sister. I could have given Charlie advice.

The bakery clock had chimed three as I tinkled its glass door on my first bun-buying trip. Now, outside Isa's, it was three fifteen. I had a glamorous plastic watch that I'd found in the wine bar and been told I could keep, so long as no one asked for it back. Jasper said it would be a collector's item in time. It told the right time at least, which was more than the one Nick had given me did since Isa wore it to go swimming. She probably broke it on purpose. She never liked me to have things I didn't really need, she told me once in a pub at last orders. She was referring to alcohol at the time, but I think it was a fairly general observation. Charlie was there and said he thought so too. He also told me that I seemed to need to have things that Isa wanted.

'Your boyfriend hates me,' I said, hungover, on the phone the next morning.

'Well of course he does, sometimes,' she shouted. 'It's only natural. You're my sister.'

Three thirty now and three rolls to go. I was sitting on the stone-cold mosaic floor outside Isa and Charlie's front door.

It was the sort of surface that gave you piles, I thought; I'd blame Isa if I got them. She'd promised to be home by three. At three thirty-seven the front door closed itself with a crash and someone with something bulky bumped up towards me. I leaned over the banisters to see the back of a head with grey hair pinned raggedly up, and then the white collar of a neckline, then a stoop-shouldered body jerking itself into view. A woman was pulling a pushchair up, with carrier bags hanging from everywhere on it. She stopped on the landing below ours to breathe heavily and mutter to herself, then turned to look at the final flight of stairs and noticed me at the top. She smiled. I decided to help her.

The pushchair rocked unevenly as she went up backwards, holding the handles, and I followed behind lifting the foot-rest part.

'Thanks everso,' she whispered, as we touched down on Isa's landing. 'I'm not used to this mountaineering.'

Her voice was Scottish. She pointed to an upholstered bundle sleeping deeply inside the pushchair, and winked at me, nodding and pleased for some reason.

'Thanks everso.' A knowing, nodding whisper. 'And you'll be Chrissie, won't you?'

I nodded too. It seemed not unnatural that she should know my name.

'There you go then, hen.'

She handed me a feeding bottle with a murky teat and something vinegar-coloured swilling inside it. We both looked at the baby with its tiny flared nostrils that glowed, as if there were a small torch inside them, and its bare feet, like a talcum-powder advert.

'She'll no wake now, hen. Not till Isa's back. And if she does, just give her a wee suck o' the bottle.'

She seemed to be preparing to go back down the stairs

alone, unwrapping a jumper from her Stonehenge hips and firming down her hair.

'Where is Isa?'

I found myself holding her arm.

'In Boots, poor wee thing. Crushed almost to death.'

She scoured my face for some shared concern, and indeed I was worried by this information. Isa can spend days in Boots. I may not see her at all this afternoon.

'Well, Chrissie.' The woman was lifting my hand from her blouse. 'I'm late. Have fun with wee Jane.'

She twinkled me a last slow wink and set off, on theatrical tiptoe, down the stairs.

At three fifty-five I was crouching beside my borrowed baby, growing rather fond of the side of her face, when I heard the downstairs door slam itself shut. It was Isa, I could tell. Her espadrilles were flapping, like wet fish on summer-holiday concrete. I leaned over the banister to see the top of her sun-bleached head appearing, with uneven plaits straggling from a tangle of ribbon.

She was bent to read a letter, which seemed to perturb her because she stopped on the first step of the last flight of stairs and twisted the hem of her short skirt round her fingers, like we used to in school if we had to stand up at the front of the class. I thought of my grandmother, saying, 'Nice straight legs,' as I watched her for a moment. Our granny used to say that phrase whenever she saw either of us with our legs exposed, as if most teenagers she'd seen had knock knees or rickets. It used to make us laugh.

'Nice straight legs,' I called down to Isa, and when she looked up I said she was bad.

'You're incredibly late. And why have we got this baby?'

'Chrissie.'

She ran up and sort of lunged towards me.

'Chrissie, thank God. Something terrible's happened.'

There was no choice but to hug her and keep on doing it. She does that to me sometimes. Used to, anyway.

'What's wrong? Calm down. What's happened?'

There was obviously something very wrong, from the way she was breathing and mauling my shoulders.

'What is it? Isa, tell me what's happened.'

I began to feel scared as no answer came and the baby started to make a small noise, not unlike the one my sister had started.

'Who is that letter from? Give me the letter.'

But she pulled it away from me and said it was only from Charlie and he was fine and coming home sometime. It wasn't Charlie, she said. It was that she'd had a test, she'd had the results, just now in Boots, and the test was positive. She was pregnant.

'I'm pregnant,' she shouted, as well as you can when you're crying. The baby started to cry as well. I thought we should all go inside and see how it seemed in the kitchen. I took the key from her pocket and opened the door.

By four o'clock the three of us were sitting comfortably at the big round table in the kitchen of Charlie's father's flat. I'd discovered that wee Jane stopped crying if I put sugar on my thumb and let her suck it off. It was a pleasant sensation, but it meant that I couldn't drink the tea which I'd persuaded Isa to make, to calm herself and stop her weeping everywhere.

I tried to interest her in discussing the Scottish woman and why we seemed to be looking after her baby just now, but all Isa would say was that she lived across the hall and the baby didn't belong to her really. It was her daughter's.

'She's very nice. She's got a washing machine,' Isa said.

The idea seemed to start her crying again. I explained that

the woman and her washing machine would be extremely useful if she decided to have the baby.

'Not everyone has a babysitter and a washing machine just across their hallway. That's a good start,' I explained.

I began to think, in a chaotic moment, that we should phone our own mother. I knew better than to suggest such a thing to Isa, but I did feel that we needed a seasoned mother to call on somehow. Someone who knew what a baby is and does and means in the long run.

'But it can't live across the hallway, can it? I mean, we haven't got a room or anything.'

'Do they need a room?' I thought it unlikely. Babies were tiny and had no possessions.

'Anyway, you've got the attic. It's huge.'

She said her paintings were up there and I said so what, she could move them if necessary, and that seemed to work because she stopped weeping to watch our baby's face. She wondered aloud what it felt like breastfeeding. She said her breasts ached, and asked if mine had when I got pregnant. I pretended I couldn't remember. She said she didn't know anyone who had a child.

'Do you?' she asked. 'Do you wish you'd had yours?' And then, moving towards me, 'Let me have a hold.'

She lifted my little bundle of baby suddenly up high above her head, which it seemed to like, then she arranged wee Jane on her lap, like a pile of paperbacks, or something electrical, broken. Baby cried, so Isa licked her finger and dipped it in sugar and wrinkled her nose, laughing, as the sucking began.

'How weird,' she said. 'Does it suit me?'

I said it didn't not suit her at least, which was good since we might have to keep it for ever.

'You can have it,' she said. 'Then we'll have one each if I have mine.'

'I don't want one,' I said, 'or I would have had my own.'

'But that was Nick who didn't want it, wasn't it? I thought he told you not to have a baby.'

She suddenly stared at me hard.

'He didn't want it, did he? He doesn't want to be a father, you said.'

I said it wasn't that simple. I stood up and got a drink of water from the sink, which looks over the roofs of the whole of Bayswater, and drank the glass down in one, keeping my back to the room.

'Do I look like you?' she said then, louder. 'Did I look like you when we were babies, do you think? Would my baby look like yours?'

I looked round at her then and said how should I know, and that they usually look like their fathers as well.

'You look like Mum,' I told her, 'with that on your lap.'

She told me not to be offensive, but she did look like our mother, in a photograph there is on the kitchen wall at home, where our family is having one of their catastrophic picnics. I told her that too and she made a face.

'So why didn't you have your baby then, if Nick wanted one?'

'I didn't say he wanted one. I said he didn't not want one.'

'So you could have had it if you'd wanted to?'

'Of course I could. Yes, I could have, of course.'

Trying not to get cross with her now, or with Nick, or with myself either. Trying not to shout about it.

'Do you think I'd just let Nick decide the whole thing? I mean, it wasn't like that, Isa.'

'What was it like then?'

'We weren't getting on. I was about to move out. The whole thing was a mess. I didn't want a baby to arrive into that.'

'But you and Nick never got on in that way.'

'What do you mean, "that way"? Like you and Charlie, you mean, who leave each other on trains halfway across Europe.

You don't know anything about me and Nick, so shut up.'

Silence. She gave the baby more sugar. I was surprised she hadn't started crying again and wished I'd shut up myself.

'Look, let's not argue about me and Nick. Let's talk about you, shall we? I mean, I'm not the one who's pregnant right now.'

'All right.'

Her sullen look. We watched the baby's hopeful face for a while as it sucked on sugar from Isa's tanned fingers.

'Well, would you have mine if you were me?'

I'd wondered when she'd say that.

'How should I know. I'm not you and Charlie's not Nick. I think if I were you I'd tell Charlie, for a start. Where is he anyway? You'd better get him back.'

Isa stroked the little head on her breasts, which I noticed had grown. They were much bigger than mine now, instead of just slightly so, which is normally the case. I watched her hand as she stroked, followed the slow back-and-forth of a turquoise ring I hadn't seen before and was about to ask where she'd got it from when I heard her say her baby might not in fact be Charlie's.

'It could be his or it might be somebody else's. That's the thing. I don't know whose it is.'

I felt her not looking at me and slowly felt I wanted not to see her with that baby and her sun-smoothed hand and those skinny plaits and my mother's mouth that was moist and full and almost smiling.

'I've been seeing someone else, Chrissie,' she said, still not looking up, and then I didn't want to know any more.

'That's stupid,' I said, although it wasn't what I meant.

I might have meant unfair, but who could I have meant she was being unfair to just then?

I threw the glass I had in my hand into the sink, then I left the room and went to the bathroom.

*

The bathroom at Isa and Charlie's is too big. You can't have baths there in winter because of the draught from the cracked sash window above the airing cupboard. It faces North, so it's good to paint in until your limbs go numb. Nick used to wear an old fur coat to work there when we were staying. I'd take him cups of tea from time to time, and roll him cigarettes, which he couldn't manage because of the colours smudged into his fingertips. We'd had some of our nicest times in that bathroom, before his final show, thinking up titles for his watery canvasses. *Chrissie's Wet Hat* was one of my favourites, because I was in it, of course, in theory. He said the swooping blues of it could be mine to keep, but the painting was still there in the bathroom, standing on the dribbled pink floor, supported by a carved towel rail that belongs to me too. The swirling rug by the bath is mine as well. You couldn't see much of it that August afternoon because the contents of Isa's rucksack were spilled all over the floor. There was a red swimsuit I hadn't seen before, and a copy of *The Golden Notebook*. There were faded T-shirts and my Japanese blouse, frayed towels and tubs of sunscreen creams, and Greek toothpaste in a flat red tube, with 'PEPP-UP-PASTEY' across it in green.

I chose a toothbrush with a woman's leg for a handle from a brace of them in a coronation mug by the wide Victorian sink. I liked to use the sink in Inverness Mansions. I liked the oval mirror and the taps, which are long and brass and narrow and look as if they belong on a bedhead. I often brushed my teeth at Isa's, for old times' sake, I'd tell myself. So that was how I came to see the postcard from Nick, stuck into the frame of the mirror at just about eye level above a Ken Kiff print, as I was watching the PEPP-UP-PASTEY lather on my teeth and remembering that I'd forgotten to go to the dentist the day before. The card was large and gaudy. It had a wrinkled peasant woman in black standing next to a threadbare donkey on it, and the woman's head had a huge bunch of flowers coming out of it, which had been drawn on in smudging felt-tip pens. There was an arrow pointing into the scribbled flowers, and the writing above it said, 'Wish you were just here.' It was obviously from Nick. It's the sort of thing he'd been sending me ever since I'd known him. I used to think they were sweet. I pulled it out from the mirror frame and turned it over. It was a lurch to look at his writing again, and I thought I couldn't read it, but of course I did.

Isa, Dear Isa,
This lady is dying to see you. She'll be in Corfu in the bar next to the station from seven till ten, on the 5th and 6th of August. You'd better arrive or the flowers will die. I am keeping her company.
Kisses. Nick.

Something bulky and porous slid into my stomach, and my hand holding the card began to judder like the old man's I'd served spinach soup to at lunchtime, so I held it by the wrist with my other one and bit hard into the flesh of my thumb.

Kisses from Nick to Isa. Kisses, it said. Dear Isa. Dying to see you. Kisses from Nick, and I was with him myself then in that same bathroom, feeling the point of his nose on my face, and the fur of his coat in my fingers. Kisses from Nick. Dying to. Kissing the smell of his neck. Kissing his skin with no clothes on and the shape of his shoulder, and the press of his head and the noise he makes just before he comes. It's her noise now. She's heard it too. Kisses from Nick to Isa.

'She's got great legs, your sister,' I heard him say and watched her walk across a beach towards us in Cornwall with her dress clutched up last April.

'She's got lovely legs,' he said.

*

When Isa called me I was sitting on the side of the bath tearing the postcard into pieces, trying to make them all the exact same size, and piling them up on a stain on the fabric of my trouser leg. It was a perfectly circular stain and I hadn't seen it before. Isa was calling me and the doorbell had rung and the Scottish lady's voice was out there saying thanks and thanks everso and Isa saying no problem and Chrissie loves babies and banging and goodbye and laughing, and calling me now again from a long way away.

'Chrissie.' She's calling, that's what she's doing. 'Chrissie, come out.' She sounds pleased, and she's calling her sister from her kitchen down the corridor of where I used to live with my boyfriend, who she has been kissing in Corfu.

She says she needs a pee now and she's just outside the door.

'Go away,' I say. 'Get right away. Go back to the kitchen. I'm leaving and I don't want to see you.'

'I need a pee,' she says. 'I'm pregnant, remember?'

'Get into the kitchen.' I sound like I'm howling. 'Go back into the kitchen.'

She stops turning the handle. The kitchen door slams.

In the corridor, dragging *Chrissie's Wet Hat* and with my Japanese blouse around my neck, I banged a plant over and there was earth on the carpet, then a rope of low-hanging ivy trailing along beside me. Isa came out of the kitchen to watch and asked where I was going and why I was taking her painting. I told her it was mine and had always been mine and she couldn't have my things any more. I kicked over a three-legged stool that once was in my mother's house and she picked it up and held it against her front and backed into the kitchen doorway.

I opened the front door and pushed my picture out ahead of me onto the landing, where I'd been with the pushchair when

I'd seen her arrive. Where I'd waited for her and looked after her neighbour's baby and rubbed her back.

'You can't have my boyfriend's baby,' I said, quietly now, as I left. Then louder, with the canvas slithering at an angle down the stairwell, banging into the walls, 'You cannot, do you understand that? I won't let you.'

I don't know how long it took me to walk all the way home, but I do remember knocking into people down Holland Park Avenue, and the stares I got. I remember stopping on a corner in the gooey air of Pizza Pronto and bursting into tears, and some man on a bicycle asking if I was OK and saying no, what does it look like, then being silent as he locked his bike to a railing and took one end of the painting and walked me down to Shepherd's Bush.

'I live just here,' I told him when we got to the green. It wasn't true, but I didn't want him to be there any more. I didn't want to be any more grateful.

At my corner shop I put the canvas down and bought a bar of chocolate with peppermint cream inside and a bottle of Peroni that made my bag awkward, too heavy, banging into my hip.

I thought I might as well leave Nick's painting on the pavement now that it was out of Isa's bathroom. No one had ever liked it except me. Charlie hates all Nick's work. He once threatened to burn a great pile of abstracts when there was ice on the insides of the windows one March, and his father was away and we didn't know how to start up the boiler again. Even Nick didn't like this one I'd taken, so I left it, with its face to the wall, about three streets away from Blythe Road.

At home I went to my own small bathroom and ran a hot bath. I ate my chocolate, which I had to lick off its wrapper. I drank beer from the bottle, watching the bath water cover the links of the plug chain, then I undressed and climbed in, and then the telephone rang. I thought it must be Isa and that I would leave it to ring, but found myself in the bedroom, dripping, listening to Nick, who was saying my name.

'Chrissie, at last. You're there.'

He exhaled. Nick always smokes on the phone.

'I was having a bath.'

Silence. Tell him you've just been to see Isa. Make him go away.

'How are you?' I said. His voice was so warm.

'Tired. I've been in bed all day.'

'How nice.'

I picked up a blouse and rubbed drips off my legs. Nice straight legs. Nick was still smoking.

'What do you want anyway?' I said. 'I thought you were in Greece.'

'Not any more. I just got back. I spent the night in a luggage compartment.' He sort of laughed.

'I see.'

I listened to someone trying to start a lawnmower next door.

'Were you on the boat train from Paris?'

'Close. The ferry from Boulogne.'

A man's voice was swearing in the garden next to mine. The mower was broken, he was shouting to someone.

'Chrissie, I need to see you.'

I looked at my legs. Hers were browner.

'Do you?'

'I really do. Can I come over?'

'I don't think so.'

'Chrissie, it's important. I'm all over the place. I could come in an hour. An hour and a half.'

I listened to a match striking, as another duty-free Camel found his mouth. I watched him watch it burning, like he does. And the way he blows smoke was with me too, and the way he tastes when you're kissing.

'I need to talk to you, Chrissie.'

'Talk to Isa, Nick, like I just did.'

Then I like to think he said he still loved me, but I wasn't listening any more. I didn't have time to put the phone down properly, because I had to run to the bathroom as fast as I could. I was sick before I could get to the sink. A strangely violent sort of vomiting, in a succession of watery bursts. I hadn't retched like that for years. Not since those pregnant mornings in Moscow Road, when I could have been having Nick's baby too.

Four The Gaiety

NICK WAS IN THE GAIETY, HALFWAY DOWN HIS PINT, AND ISA was as usual not there, although she'd said she'd be on time this time. 'I will, I really will. I promise. I'll be there at nine thirty. I will.' She was a hysteric when all was said and done and he was starving, which was her fault, because he'd decided to shave rather than eat because he'd been coming to see her. He had to know what had happened when Chrissie had gone round to see her. He wanted to know what the sisters had said. Not that he'd ever really find out, of course. He opened the box of matches he'd had in his hand for some time to find there were none in it which weren't already burnt.

'He comes too fast, that's the trouble. It's all over in about ten minutes.'

Some women at the next table were discussing someone he probably knew. They were smoking heavily, but he didn't want to risk asking them for a light.

'And then he just sits up. He always sits bolt upright straight away afterwards.'

The satisfying smack of a cigarette lighter flinting, then smoke blowing over Nick's lingering drink.

'God. You poor thing.'

'I know. But what can I do?'

Nick fingered his matchbox and twisted himself round to see that it was almost ten on the dark clock above the glass case where the sandwiches should have been. He should have said nine, not nine thirty, then arrived about now himself. He couldn't understand how a person could get herself to Greece at an appointed time, but not make it to a pub down the road from her flat. She was hopeless.

'You could try him on massage. Aromatic oils and all that. Olive oil works, in fact. Olive oil's good.'

'I'd need a tanker of the stuff.'

A spray of fizz as the other one laughed and swallowed at the same time.

Nick stood up and walked a few steps to lift a transparent lighter from the rock pool of their table.

'May I?' he said and smiled at the blonde one with the larger breasts.

'Cheers,' he said through the cork of his last Camel Light and felt proud of his size as he pushed politely away through suits on shoulders and corduroy elbows and hands on glass to the bar.

If Isa had been anyone else Nick would have rung her up to see if she'd left home yet, and maybe complained if she hadn't, but Isa lived with Charlie, so he couldn't do that, although someone else probably would. He wished it wasn't Charlie. Sometimes Isa scared him by saying that she might have to stop living with Charlie. She'd last said it to him about a week ago now, when they were still on Corfu, renting a room with a caged bird outside that woke them up at six every day. She'd stopped counting her paper money out to say that maybe she ought to tell Charlie she was seeing someone else.

'It's only fair if we're going to go on,' she said, staring at him as if it was a question he would know the answer to. He didn't respond.

'Can't do it straight away, though,' she'd continued, moving to undangle a towel and some knickers from the washing line he'd mended, strung across the balcony. The bird attacked the lacy white bars of its cage.

'We can't risk upsetting everything until it's certain.'

'Till what's certain? Your uncertain affections?'

She'd annoyed him a bit now, so she went over and kissed him. Her waist dipped, smooth and warm underneath the almost nothing she had on.

'Your show, stupid. We don't want to screw that up, do we?'

Putting the flat of her hands against his eyes like she did so that everything was black until she took them away and her face was all he could see instead.

'Charlie's going to get you a show because I've asked him to, remember?'

Charlie's father owned a gallery on the Portobello Road, among other things, and Isa worked there on Saturdays, among other things, and she'd been persuading Charlie to ask his father to give Nick a show there sometime after Christmas.

'You're going to be rich and famous before I leave Charlie.'

'Sure,' he'd said into below her shoulder, and they'd made love instead of him finishing his sketch of the yard.

'Nick. You're still here. Shit.'

A rattle of laugh and a hand on his own, which had been peeling a beer mat apart. And there was Jake beside him, in his brass-buttoned coat and his new beard that nobody liked. Jake didn't drink in The Gaiety.

'Isa said you'd be waiting, but I wouldn't have thought it. Commitment, man, or what?' Unbuttoning his coat now with short grubby fingers.

'You've got faith, Nicky boy, and your faith has now been rewarded, because Isa says to tell you the whole thing's in the bag.'

'Where is Isa?'

Jake had a slow, wide-vowelled way of talking, and always used more words than he needed to, in Nick's opinion. It was irritating if you wanted information.

'She's at home, man. She's sick. But the show's all going ahead. Charlie's old man's OK'd it. You've got the first two weeks of next year.'

Nick wasn't particularly interested in next year. He hadn't done more than touch a paintbrush since June. Jake's fingernails were covered in acrylic paint. That was irritating too. Jake seemed to get on with his work however many girls he was seeing. He didn't seem to need any sleep.

'Yep, fame is coming your way, Nicky boy, you lucky sod. It's in the bag. And now buy me a drink, 'cos I need one badly.'

He ruffled his hair and looked round the bar, as if he'd expected to arrive somewhere else.

'Alison's stopped talking to me and I've got to meet her to talk about it later.'

Nick had had conversations with Alison on plenty of occasions in the wine bar. He couldn't think her not talking would be any great loss.

'But where is Isa? I mean, how come you saw her if she couldn't get here to meet me?'

'Isa's sick, Nick. She can't come out, OK? She's at the flat, like I said. She's sick. But she gave me your slides to hand over and said to come and tell you the dates of the show.'

Nick watched Jake struggle to free himself from his coat, which was covered with badges. He then had to untangle the duty-free bag he was holding from some bangle thing he affected. The yellow bag said something in German across it. Isa hadn't been to Germany as far as Nick knew.

'Is that Isa's bag? Did she give you that?'

Jake said yes she had, and what was the problem, and what about 'thanks for bringing my slides to me, Jake'? He'd only come as a favour, he said, seeing as how Isa was so wound up and Nick needed his slides back for Friday.

Nick didn't know what slides of his Isa had, or why he could possibly need them back before Friday.

'And she says sorry she couldn't make it to be here and you should give her a call.'

Nick groped the folds of his lining for change that wasn't there, then waved his last note at the Irish woman at the till while asking Jake if he had a twenty pence piece on him. Jake had and he handed it over, but held Nick's arm as he ordered a pint and said he shouldn't phone Isa now.

'Call in the morning. Don't phone tonight, she said.'

Paying for his drink with Nick's money. Nick didn't want a drink. He wanted to see Isa. Jake had seen her. There must be something up, but unless it was Charlie who'd found something out, Nick couldn't imagine why she hadn't come out to meet him.

'Well, I think I'll go round there, then. I mean, she is capable of being visited, I assume? I mean, she managed to talk to you all right.'

Then Nick looked away across the pub and asked if Charlie was in tonight.

A low cackle from Jake and long gulping and shaking his too-big head. No, Charlie wouldn't be there tonight, he reckoned. Not for a good long while, anyway. Charlie'd be out getting wrecked at The Star, he suspected. That's where Jake'd be, he said, in Charlie's shoes. Nick decided he would have another pint after all. He needed more liquid. His mouth was sticky and thick. When it arrived he drank half of it down in one, and then turned and asked Jake to tell him again.

'Tell what? What is this? Look you've got the show, man. Calm down.'

Jake looked at his watch. He blew his nose on a rag that was brittle with paint. He said he thought he'd be making a move, but Nick said he wanted to know more about Isa, and Jake'd better tell him the truth now or he'd go round there himself. He didn't think Charlie was out at all, he said, so Jake'd better dream up something else if he wanted to see Alison later tonight. No one was going anywhere, he said, until Jake had told him the truth. He drank the second half of his pint down. He felt feverish now he thought about it. A ringing in his ears and his neck swollen and weak. It was too hot in here. Some bug most likely, picked up on the journey home. He should have come home with Isa, instead of spending three days balled up with backpacks and students with weird diseases. He should have brought Isa back. She shouldn't have set off without him.

'I need to see her,' he said.

Then, because Jake was staring, he tried to slow down and told Jake to tell him all about Isa again, and Jake spoke more slowly than ever and said that she was sick. She was lying on the couch watching *Twin Peaks* when he'd got there, he said, and she stayed on the couch the whole time. Charlie was out. Charlie had left the flat before he'd arrived. There'd been a row. A hell of a row, Isa said. He looked sideways at Nick, then up at the spirits, mirrored on glass, like a chemistry set. A scene had just happened, Isa had told him, and Charlie had gone off to get pissed.

'How could they have a row if she was sick? What could a sick person argue about?'

Nick said he was going round there. None of this made any sense and Isa should be here to explain herself.

'For Christ's sake, man.'

Jake didn't shout often, but he almost shouted that, then he shut up and tilted his beer back and forth and said all right then, well, the fact was, Nick. The fact was, he said then, you see, Nick, the thing is that Isa's got pregnant.

'See? There. So now you know. What's your show got to do with Isa and Charlie anyway? You think he's jealous or what? You think they'd argue about that? Charlie doesn't want a show. He's a musician, man, and a fine one too.'

Nick's underarms were wet and his knees suddenly jutting the front of the bar.

'Jesus, Jake. What did she say? I mean, what else did she tell you? I mean, about being pregnant. How does she know?'

The beer wet now in his stomach, like dirty surf at Dover.

'How should I know how she knows? Did a test, I guess. I mean, she didn't go into details, man. Said she feels crap. That queasy thing they get. I mean, I didn't ask.'

'Shit. And she's told Charlie, right?'

'Yep. That's old Charlie stitched up all right.'

'So she told Charlie and it's his then, is it?'

Jake looked into his glass, then at Nick. He looked like he might be about to shout again.

'Of course it's Charlie's. What are you saying, Nicky boy? Hold on there. How much have you had to drink?'

Silence as Jake drank a while, then a low laugh from his ambled direction, then more silence, then he said not to tell anyone about it. Isa didn't want people to know, he said, but shit, enough was enough, and he'd had it with this crap and accusations and he'd be off now, unless Nick wanted to buy him another pint to make amends.

'Amends for what? You're full of shit.'

'Look, don't shoot the messenger, that's all,' Jake said, and was pleased with the phrase so he said it again and that he thought he had time for one more. Alison was bound to be late.

'They're always late, or pregnant, I guess. What do you think, Nicky? How's Chrissie by the way? Is she over you yet? Good-looking girl, old Chrissie. Wasted on you, some would say. What do you think, Nicky boy? Think a reconciliation's on the cards there or what?'

Nick thought he might hit Jake if he didn't shut up. He was like a television set stuck on the wrong channel with the volume too loud. Nick moved away, found he was in the Gents then, where his face was white but red at the top and his hands shaky stone cold as he splashed trickled tap water over and onto his hairline and some on the back of his neck. Now his sleeves were wet and he couldn't roll them up right. The hairs on his arms seemed different. He sat down on some shiny wet tiles by a wall, but stood up when someone with a mobile phone came in and started pressing buttons.

Halfway down the next pint, Jake was thinking he'd better get to Alison, and Nick was on the phone to Isa for the fourth time, but hadn't spoken to her yet. Jake thought he should stop pestering Isa about his show and come on with him to the Temps Perdu gig and celebrate the facts.

'Chrissie'll be there. She might be halfway pleased to see you now you're nearly famous, you shit,' he said as he came over to Nick on the phone to borrow more money.

'Leave Isa alone. She's sick. She won't want to talk to you, man.'

Then he was back with another pint of sloping foam beside the grey top of the pay phone, then off to talk to the barmaid. One of the olive-oil women from hours ago was waiting for the phone as Nick waited for Isa to answer. She was smoking something menthol, staring at the side of his face. She smelt like a hospital ward. He decided Isa's phone must be unplugged.

'Sorry to make you wait,' he told the smoker as he handed her the ringing tone, curdling on and on.

'Sorry to take so long, but someone's just got pregnant.'

'Oh God,' she said. 'How awful.'

*

At eleven forty someone held the brass handle of the glass door of The Gaiety against their chest so the last of the drinkers could leave. Nick and Jake moved side by side up to Kensington Church Street, then Nick thought he'd cross over the road, although he had nowhere to go, and Jake wheeled his bike off to the left to look at Holland Park and explained that the trees would do Nick good too. Nick walked away before Jake stopped talking. He supposed he might as well go home to the jasmine bush in his own backyard. There should still be a bus and the stop was close. Maybe he should ring Chrissie. Maybe she'd know what he should do. He stood still for a while on the swirling pavement, which was a supermarket of clutter to move through by now. He couldn't ring Chrissie. That was a stupid idea. A mass of drink-filled bodies swept him along, struggling into jackets, holding onto each other. Holding plastic bags with cans angling through them, disagreeing about what to do next in the eerie white light of the record-and-tape-exchange window. A couple squeezing out of the takeaway giggled, bent closely over chips. Nick wondered if he might as well walk round to Isa's, but found himself at a bus stop, where a man had a dog on a lead. The lead was tangled up in some girl's ankles. She was arguing loudly about her right to some floor space and animals messing up London. Her friend joined in, and a couple in leather, so the man lifted his dog and walked away. Nick watched him and shared his lonely stroll, and realized there was no point going to Isa's. Charlie would probably be there. He folded himself down onto the lumps of a low wall and wished he'd stayed with Jake. Jake was all right in a way. Familiar, at least. Familiarity counted for a lot at a time like this. He wondered if Isa had told Chrissie. They told each other everything. Neither of them told him anything really. A bus came and went, banging its violent doors, and more people shouted and the world was bleak. In times gone by Nick might have walked to his studio now and painted through until two or three. There would have been something to work on, like a person to talk to. Lately he'd mostly talked to Isa. He should talk to her now. He needed to know what everyone knew, about this thing he wasn't supposed to know. This new thing, that might be his.

He stood up and started off with his hands in his jacket's zip pockets along the Bayswater Road. Fifteen minutes to Moscow Road at the most. Past the top of Kensington Gardens and the red-brick six-storeys that no one ever came out of. Watching one of his laces trailing to the left of his right foot. Stopping to tie it at last, wet and heavy and thinking then that going to Isa's was hopeless. What could he say when he got there? She might be in bed. She was sick. She was pregnant, and Charlie knew, and he wasn't supposed to. He sat down on another narrower wall, watched another lone man with a dog strain towards him and past now and pressing the button to cross the road. Nick had a dog once, though he'd never much liked it. It had epileptic fits and had to be put down. His mother was upset and got a Siamese cat. 'Put down,' Nick said in his head a few times. What a nasty expression.

'Hey, Nick. How's it going?'

He looked up from the thoughts on his knees to see a face he knew burning orange in the light between him and the sky. A hand clasp. A finger down the back of his neck. A fake fur beside him and a straggle of boots and shoes, clustering like pigeons at his own two feet. A boot kicking the wall in an off-hand way. They were all going on to a party, they told him.

'Why?' he said. 'What's the point?'

'What's the point of you sitting on that wall?' some girl said, and he could see she was right, and good looking too, so he allowed her to take his arm in a motherly way, and then they were all walking along towards Myra's, going the long way round, he noticed, as they passed their third man with a mongrel.

'Great news about the show, Nick. You lucky bastard.'

The congratulations came from a man he hardly knew with a flat wide nose.

'How come you know about that? I only just heard myself.'

'Saw Charlie in The Star earlier. His dad told Isa this afternoon.'

'I see. That makes sense then.'

Charlie knew everything first.

By twelve thirty-five they'd arrived. Nick was being squeezed up a narrow staircase towards a reggae of bass and squashed paper cups and bolts of radio-play laughter. Someone in front of him pulled the handrail away from the wall, so Nick's face was filled with suede and a boot heel stung into his calf. He staggered backwards, but managed to steady the falling body and his own against the flaking plaster of the wall slightly lower down. The girl who'd been holding Nick's arm bent to the body he'd saved and shrieked, 'Charlie, darling.' She kissed him, said it was so good to see him again and anyway, where had he been? Charlie kissed her hand and said in The Star with everyone else, and where had she been since April?

'Around,' she said. 'With everyone else.' She laughed and winked and Nick felt awkward. He didn't know Charlie flirted.

'Is Isa here?'

The girl asked the question. Nick sat on the stairs.

'Hope not,' said Charlie. 'I'm here to enjoy myself.'

He decided that Nick had saved his life.

'I owe you some duty-free gin.'

He dropped a bag from Paris airport down into Nick's

knees, but the girl put her hand on his shoulder and hauled it up to herself, like a jam jar full of water from a pond, and said she would find them all something to drink from.

Being drunk did not suit Charlie. There was too much of him to be drunk. He seemed to take up most of the kitchen. His paisley shirt front was askew and Nick was bewildered to see some grey hair on his visible chest.

'So Isa's not with you?' he said, instead of thanking Charlie for the cup of gin he was handed. How crass. Why would he ask about Isa?

'I mean, I heard she's sick. Not well or something.'

Charlie stopped stretching a six-pack apart to stare at him.

'So anyway. How was Amsterdam?'

Charlie said it was Brussels, and fine. They'd been asked to play an extra week. Met some extreme musicians. But who'd told Nick Isa was ill?

'Jake mentioned it. We were in The Gaiety. We met by accident. By chance, I mean.'

Intense staring from Charlie's cliff-face grey squint. Accident, too right, he said. The Gaiety was a mistake by nature. Full of lizard-skin and takeaways, he said, last time he'd gone there by mistake. He looked at Nick's face as if it had a sudden skin complaint. Surprised he could stand it, he said, and drank noisily from his beer can.

'Oh well. Just passing. So is Isa OK or what?'

Stop talking about Isa. She's just Chrissie's sister, and you don't see Chrissie any more.

'I mean, did she have a good time?'

'Isa? When? She's sick. How's your painting anyhow? What did you do with that blue I mixed in the end?'

Charlie's band practised in the same building that Nick's studio was in. He came in for a coffee sometimes. His colour-sense was impressive.

'No, I mean on holiday. She's been away, I thought. So Jake was saying in The Gaiety. Before.'

Babbling. Stop talking to Charlie.

'Oh that. I guess so.'

The girl with striped tights helped herself to more gin. She poured Charlie one too. She buttoned his shirt up.

'So you're still with Isa, Charlie.'

'She seems to think so.'

Charlie must like the girl. He was watching her neck as she tilted her drink. You wouldn't think his girlfriend was at home, being pregnant. Still, it might not be his baby, so why should he care? Although Isa might not have told him it might not be his. But she couldn't have told him about Nick. She wouldn't do that. Or would she? She could do anything now.

'So Nick. Congratulations.'

Charlie's grin was pleased and warm. A warm smile when it sometimes came.

'We just heard this afternoon. When do the private-view invites arrive? I trust I'll get a credit. I could play there, in fact, for the punters. You could have a band on your opening night.'

Great. And Isa in those dungaree things they wear in the Mothercare adverts.

Charlie was holding a bottle of white between lean knees now to uncork it. He shouldn't mix like that. Filling the girl's cup up and touching her face. A hand on her hair. He was out of it. He shouldn't be doing all that.

'Well, the show's not till January. You probably know that already? Jake just told me the gallery dates. I mean, Isa told him to tell me. She fixed it up with your dad, I guess.'

Charlie's eyes swirled again. Fuzzy drunk blue, burning in his Eskimo cheekbones. Charlie didn't get on with his father much. Nick should've kept him out of it.

'Jake, Jake, Jake.'

Charlie spattered the name out and threw a can towards a bin that had its lid jammed open. A man with a beret put his head into the door and backed out into the hallway.

'Who's Jake?'

The girl leaned back against the fridge, then casually closer into Charlie's arm. In the next room the music was turned up and something banged against the kitchen wall with the table against it. Bottles rattled, but nothing fell off.

'Jake's a creep. But Isa likes him. Isa thinks he has a nice bum.'

'Does she? She doesn't.'

She'd never said so to Nick.

'Sure she does. She's mad about Jake. Didn't he tell you?'

'Did she tell you?'

'She doesn't have to, Nick. I live with her, remember.'

Charlie watched the girl's long striped legs scissor into each other as she moved to the table to break up some French bread, which she brought back to offer in chunks, like sugar to horses.

'What sort of paintings do you do?' she asked Nick as Charlie nibbled into her fingers, which she pretended she didn't enjoy.

'Are they abstract?'

She liked abstract, she said. She brushed crumbs from her breasts.

'Not exactly. You'd have to see them.'

'What are they about?'

This was ridiculous. He had to talk to Charlie. He should find a phone and see what Isa had told him. She mustn't tell Charlie anything. It might as well be Charlie's baby. Charlie wasn't a threat. He drank too much. Nick was a painter. He had a show to prepare for.

'So what are your paintings about?'

As if she cared.

'Well, you'd have to see them. About space, I suppose.'

Banal, banal, but he couldn't remember. It was a stupid question.

'About light. The way light makes things. Space. You'd have to see them.'

She moved nearer to him. She liked space, she said. She put a slim patent-leather shoe with a buckle onto one of his boots.

'I'd like to see them sometime.'

She smiled near his chin. Space, she said, and looked thoughtful and pleased. How good space was. Did Charlie like space?

'Love it,' he said, and then that he'd like some now, because there was something he had to say.

'I'd like some space,' he went on too loudly, 'to say that Jake is a creep.'

He nodded, wide-eyed, then said again more slowly that Jake was a creep. The last person eating taramasalata left the room holding half a carrot.

'Nick's not a creep, because Nick's a good painter. Though he could be if he hangs out with Jake enough.'

Charlie drank, then thought on out loud about Nick.

'The trouble with Nick is he's not committed. He's not self-obsessed enough, see? But he's not a creep like Jake. He's too self-obsessed for that.'

He chuckled and took the girl's drink from her fingers so that he could take them in his own to tell her that he was a musician. He liked her hair, he said. He liked that colour, what colour was it, and what would Nick call it? Nick said how would he know, Charlie?, and the girl said mahogany and that she tried to be self-obsessed too. It was a good way of getting people to be obsessed with you, she found. Nick wondered where the telephone was.

'What do you want with a telephone?'

Charlie's voice was hard and slurred.

'One of your girlfriends, I suppose? Checking up on your baby, right? Well, I'll tell you something, Nick Watson. You want to know what I think? I think you'll never be a proper painter. And the reason you'll never be a proper painter is that you're not a serious person, see? You're not involved enough, see? You don't know how to be seriously involved. With anything. 'Cos you're too busy drinking with creeps called Jake and sucking off people you think you can use and hanging round parties no one invited you to.'

Nick leaned in through the edge of Charlie's jaw to put his drink down on the top of the fridge. He didn't know what to say. He wanted both his hands free.

'That's right, put your drink down, Nicky boy.'

Charlie took a long slug of his own.

'You've got a phone to find, right? And who's the lucky girl?'

He held Nick's eyes in his, narrow and knowing and older and slow, as Nick wondered what he knew, exactly, about Isa's holiday in Greece. He wished he knew what Charlie knew, and it was hard to hold his head at the right angle suddenly. But he mustn't turn away from Charlie. He moved his eyes only to address the girl.

'Do you know where there might be a telephone here?'

Like a line from a bad translation. She shook her mahogany locks. She'd come with him, remember?

'But there's a phone at my place. I know where that is. I live just round the corner. Want to come over? We can talk about painting.'

Charlie laughed bitterly, rubbing his hand loosely round his front, his shirt unbuttoned again. He seemed to be expanding.

'Artists don't look for telephones, Nick. You have to understand that.'

His elasticated metal watch strap caught on a button,

so he dragged it out towards Nick and the button ripped off.

'They look for meaning, see? That's what artists do, Nick. That's why you won't be one.'

He slid his back down the fridge front and sat on the lino, like a homeless person in an underpass.

'Meaning,' he muttered and twisted the thread where his sprung-off button had been.

'Buttons,' he said meaningfully.

Nick repossessed his drink. The girl slipped her hand into the crease of his elbow.

'So what meaning do you make then, Charlie?'

'A lot. A great deal.'

Whaling to his feet and caressing the girl's head with the hand that wasn't holding the top of the fridge. She moved back, pulling Nick with her.

'A lot of big meaning. Yes indeed. An enormous amount of meaning, I'm making right now, as it happens. Because Isa is having a baby, see? You didn't know that, did you? And you didn't know that, did you, either?'

Demonstrating his new invention to the department store of the world. Both Nick and the girl stepped further back. Primitives confronted with their first box camera.

'Yes. Isa's having a baby. Not planned exactly, but what the hell? Chance, see? Meaning from chaos. That's where it's at, Nick. That's what art's all about, and that's what my life's about too. That's my music. Creation, see? Babies. Music. That's what we're here for.'

His forehead was bright and there was a lock of wet hair there that he pushed back but only partly removed.

'That's reality, see? Not making deals with other people's fathers about a show you can't be arsed to work at. But you wouldn't understand that because you're not a serious person. You're full of shit.'

He leaned his head back and squinted up at the vast paper

lampshade, smiling at brightness, smiling at smiling, as if it was something he'd just discovered.

'And I'm full of babies.'

Nick looked right, up the wall to a Cézanne print of swelling fruit, then to the fridge door above Charlie's talking head, where there were some magnetic shapes for grown-ups to play with. They were shaped like articles of clothing that you could lift and stick onto a cartoon man who was wearing nothing but boxer shorts. Nick looked at the flat figure's legs, which were bulging with muscle, then down over Charlie's, which were wrinkled in leather, crossed loosely over the black-and-white floor, blocking his way to the door if he wanted to leave. He wanted to leave, he realized.

'It was good to see you, Charlie,' he said, and his voice was steady and purposeful now.

'Nice to meet you too,' he told the girl, and she took his head in her hands and kissed him stickily, slipping her tongue up to the top of his mouth.

'Come and meet my telephone,' she said when it was over.

Nick pinched her nice nose and shook his head slowly. 'Another time, perhaps.'

'Tell your girlfriend I'm jealous,' she shouted as he zig-zagged down the stairs, avoiding the banister rail. Some people moved in as he let himself onto the street.

'Charlie here?' a man with a guitar case asked.

'Charlie who?' Nick said.

Outside it was raining again.

Nick walked for a while towards Notting Hill Gate, then turned back down towards Shepherd's Bush. No lone men with dogs around now, and not many cars. A pizza-delivery bike backfiring into the oily film of slick Holland Park Avenue tarmac. A black cab which stopped to let a pair of American women out. Their luggage blocked the pavement for a while.

The slighter of the two almost fell into Nick, who steadied her, then let his hands drop as she asked who he was.

'Do we know you?'

'Don't think so.'

'Perhaps it's time we did.'

They giggled, collecting their bags as the driver's soft cockney sway told them all to take care. Then the For Hire light was back on again and Nick decided that was just what he needed right now. He'd get a ride up to Isa's before his feet could turn back, and be there without having to think. Go to Isa and tell her he wanted a baby. He wanted her baby, which he could see now had to be his. Charlie couldn't get anyone pregnant.

'Queensway,' he told the glass between himself and the driver and settled back into the width of the space he had hired.

'Moscow Road. A bit down, on the left.'

Queensway, where Queen Isa lived with her baby inside her. He sank deep into the substantial seamed seats, with an advert in French in front of his feet, and opened the window and held its slim silver ledge and leaned his face into the blow of the sky. Green lights all the way and the throb of diesel in fourth gear. Fast clouds that were white on a half-lit moon. A plane with two flashing blue lights. Holiday people asleep on each other. Homing down into Heathrow with their duty-free whisky and their airline food inside them, with sea salt still matting their hair. They'd be sleepy and suntanned and possibly pregnant. Travelling people, like himself and Isa, who'd made love in warm white rooms that morning, like he and Isa had the day she came back. They'd probably all left their swimming things hanging outside their rooms like he had. A plane full of meaningful people, with children beside them, work to get on with and paintings to make. That's what he'd be like this time next year. A portable paintbox and a baby's basket thing and Isa's head on his shoulder. He'd paint portraits of his baby in airports and grass, and in his studio too. He'd have toys for it there, with bottles and blankets and space it would learn to crawl over. A space with a baby, with fat little legs like adverts after the news on breakfast TV. And Isa would be there with those weird biscuits she brought him that the baby would suck on before it got teeth. His baby. Isa's baby. They'd have it together, of course, and call it somebody's mother's name.

'Stop here. This is fine.'

Still Westbourne Grove, but he wanted to run out and on and along now. Past Whiteleys and windows and closed cafés to rattle the door at Moscow Road and tell Isa about his plans for their life.

'Cheers,' he shouted over his shoulder into the slam of the door and his feet were smacking the pavement fast for a while, then smoothing down to a smoker's walk. He passed a man with a cap, who looked like a photo of someone. He'd have liked to tell him about the baby and ask if he had one. He probably did. Everyone had babies. The Tate was full of them on Saturday mornings. And mothers too. His own mother would be glad. Mothers liked babies. He thought they did.

Moscow Road corner now before glowing Bayswater Station. The phone box. The flash-lit Casino. The sign for the Rendezvous Café. And now someone tilting from a mountain bike just outside Inverness Mansions, with one foot on a pedal and one on the road to steady himself as he kissed someone like Isa goodbye. Leaning deep into a female, with an arm round her waist and his face into hers for a kiss.

'Goodbye.' It was Isa. 'Goodbye and thanks.'

Then she laughed her small laugh and they kissed again before the bike sliced off into navy, and she turned slowly back to her front door. The front door she shared with Charlie, where Charlie would be arriving any time now, to tell her all his thoughts on chaos and meaning.

Nick's feet were wet, he noticed, as he wandered back the way he'd come. He stopped to tie his laces outside the window of Oddbins, where he looked at the bottles and read a sign in the window. 'Confused? Bewildered? Ask for help,' it said. He nodded. He'd seen it before.

Five Triangle

I WAS GLAD WHEN DANBY RANG BECAUSE IT PROVED THAT buying an answering machine had been a sensible thing to do. Now I could talk on the phone without having to talk to Isa, who'd been ringing me all the time, despite the fact that I'd told her I would never speak to her again every time we spoke. I wouldn't have to talk to Nick, either, if he ever rang me again, which he'd have to sometime. He couldn't not speak to me for ever.

On the late afternoon that Danby's voice broke into my kitchen I hadn't spoken to anyone all day, except the man in the corner shop, who had sold me some tobacco. I was working on a design with layered newsprint and tissue paper, thinking I must ring the wine bar to cancel more shifts, when the phone rang and it was Danby, saying he was still in London and to give him a call. He was halfway through telling me a telephone number when I decided to pick up.

'Danby. I'm here.'

'Chrissie. Why didn't you answer the phone?'

'I'm sort of trying to work.'

I looked across the room at the blocks of colour I'd assembled so far. They looked all right, but in need of some focus. I asked Danby why he was still in London.

'Oh, sorry. Should I have asked you first? Don't do a Geraldine on me.'

I laughed and said I was simply surprised. He could stay as long as he wanted.

'That's good of you,' he said and went on to explain that he was still here because he still hadn't seen his daughter. He'd been in London almost ten days now, he told me, and no one he knew had seen her. No one her mother knew had either, apparently.

I certainly hadn't, I said, if that was what he wanted.

'I didn't want anything, Chrissie. Does everyone have to want something?'

'Are you being sarcastic?'

'No, just disingenuous. I want some information. About Yorkshire, in fact.'

'It's lovely. Go there. And how's Geraldine?'

'She wants me to go back to Lisbon, unless I want her to come over here, which I don't.'

'How are your cats?'

'Wouldn't know. Look, can I meet you for a coffee or something?'

It might have been nice to say, 'Let's have a drink, right now,' but I thought that might seem as if I wanted something myself, so we arranged to meet for lunch the following day.

We met at one in Holland Park, where Danby looked good against wet wood and mud-trodden leaves and imposing in the low-ceilinged café, where the steam from the coffee soft-focused his features. He had a Lisbon tan and a way with spaghetti that he must have picked up in Europe. He suited being subdued, and there was a certain tension in his presence beyond our two selves and the table between us, because of Lily being lost and his wanting to find her. Her absence haloed his well-made head as he spooned up the last of his cappuccino froth and suggested we take a walk. My own loneliness lifted at the prospect of an afternoon with a handsome man who had a crisis to discuss and no plans for the rest of the day. The trouble with not talking to my sister, mostly, was that she was the only person who could properly discuss our current crisis with me. Being in the world without Isa's advice was odd. Just walking around seemed different now that we were doing it separately.

Danby and I walked in the park together after lunch. We went to look at the duck-pond, which hosted no ducks but was hard-edged and still and consolingly black. We walked down the gravelly slope of the widest path to our left, where I saw Jake cycling towards us. He slowed down, but didn't exactly stop. We said hi to each other, and he looked Danby over, and I was glad to be there in the park with an attractive man no one else really knew.

'Who's he?' Danby asked as he cycled away.

'Oh, nobody. Just someone I know.'

We meandered on towards the echoing shapes of the looming Adventure Playground. A woman in pink was doing t'ai chi, holding onto a pole in a clearing. A mother with a pushchair had a bag of nuts for the squirrels, who ran away from her rustling. Over split conkers and the litter of rain-softened leaves we walked, with Danby increasingly silent as the noise of excited children in the playground ahead grew louder. When we were almost there, he decided he didn't think he wanted to see masses of small children just now. He stopped and almost took my arm.

'I don't really want to see any children either,' I said. 'My sister wants to have a baby with someone who should be living with me.'

'Tough one.'

Danby didn't seem to be taking much in. Certainly my revelation did not intrigue him. He seemed to be talking mostly to himself.

'On the other hand, seeing loads of happy kids might do me

good,' he said, some time after I had stopped talking.

He stood still to stare at a small black rabbit, which stared back at him before plopping away.

'I mean, Lily's eighteen now. I didn't even see her messing about when she was little. I don't look at children. Do you?'

I said not really, although I had been studying mothers lately, and wondering what it must be like to be one. He looked at me, puzzled, then said he might like to go down to watch the children ahead by himself for a while. He wouldn't be long. Could we meet back in the café in twenty minutes or so? I watched him move away with a slight limp I hadn't ever asked him about. His jacket was a good colour. It blended well with the dark-blotted leaves on the September trees.

Back in the café I drank hot chocolate until Danby arrived to eat cake and talk on about Lily and wanting to find her. I told him he ought perhaps to go home to Lisbon and wait until she contacted him. You couldn't find anyone in London unless they wanted you to.

'She does,' he assured me. 'That's why I'm here. She rang me in Lisbon, just as I left. She's in love with someone called Gabriel.'

We decided that that should make things slightly easier for him, since neither of us had ever known anyone of that name.

'He's Dutch. But he lives in Yorkshire now. That's what I wanted to ask you about, Chrissie, since you come from there.'

He lifted crumbs of chocolate cake to his mouth with licked fingers and watched me watch him doing it.

'Have you heard of a place called Planet Ten?'

I never had. It didn't sound very Brontë Country to me.

'It's a bookshop in some Pennine village and this Gabriel person works there. That's what one of Lily's friends told me yesterday, anyway. She said he was there in May, and she hasn't heard of him being anywhere else.'

He turned his plate upside down, then back the right way again, and I almost wiped some chocolate off his face, but he did it himself before I had time.

'I thought I might drive up to see if I can find it. It must be worth a try.'

I said it was probably in the hippie enclave, in Hebden Bridge, which I'd once lived on the fringes of. We talked about some friends of his who lived up there, and I grew wistful, remembering the twilights I'd walked through when everything seemed simple and we all had knitting machines, when Nick and I inhabited a half-converted chapel through one very wet windy springtime.

'You might as well go up there,' I told him, when we parted and he kissed my cheek. 'What have you got to lose?'

By six o'clock I was tearing out newspaper shapes again, and had started to print onto some of them with potato-cut stencils. The designs had to be large, since they were for upholstery fabric, but I had a lot of potatoes, having more or less stopped cooking some time ago. I was considering a green bit I'd stamped with red, when the phone rang and I listened for the voice. It might just be Nick, saying that Isa had gone to Australia, or Mars, perhaps.

It was Danby. I picked up.

'Chrissie. Why don't you answer the phone?'

'I just have.'

'I was about to leave a message.'

'What was it going to say?'

'That you need a change of scene.'

I thought he must mean the local pub, but he explained that he'd borrowed a car and was driving north that night, and wondered if I'd like to go for the ride. I seemed a bit lost, he said. I stayed silent as he went on that he'd like company on the journey, and I'd like the friends he was going to stay with, who were called Kenneth and Sarah and lived on a farm. Sarah was our age, he said, which made me realize he was older than I was.

'But my agent is going to Italy in a fortnight, and she has nothing of mine to take with her.'

'And will that ruin your life?'

He left a long gap as I looked at the assorted pieces of paper I'd been supposed to be filling with colour for days, then I said it would be lovely to get out of London.

'It'll improve my eye.'

'And your mood,' Danby decided.

He said he'd be round to collect me in half an hour.

Bob Dylan was singing as I lifted a soft-pack map from the warm passenger seat of Danby's borrowed red Mini. A stained-glass evening sun cast an oblong across my knees as I strapped myself in and Danby sang along to the tape, smiling at his nasal imitation. He placed an *A–Z* in my hands and told me we'd be on page 58, then 42, though he thought he knew the way out of London well enough. I did anyway, I said, and dropped the map to the floor, where a pile of crisps and boxed juice was stacked, like a tuck shop, with Yeats' *Collected Poems* there too for some reason.

We crawled through the rush-hour red lights of Shepherd's Bush Green, then we were somewhere I hadn't been for years but knew well as the best route onto the M1. We passed straggling hitchers with cereal-packet signs, and a lorry stopping for a girl in a cloak, then we were in the outside lane in fifth gear, with Dylan singing that someone must say hello to his girlfriend, who might be in Tangiers. Nick might be in Tangiers with Isa, or even someone else by now, I supposed. Perhaps that's what she'd been trying to tell me the last time she rang my machine and told it she had something important to say.

The tape ended and Danby left it silent, so we talked in waves through the fading light, with the dashboard's flashes glowing more and more brightly and the motorway darkening into a skimming black line, looped up into long orange strip lamps.

We ate crisps, which I had to pass to Danby, one by one.

We smoked.

We talked about Geraldine, and how he didn't know what she wanted, but I didn't like that conversation much, so we talked about Lily's mother, who'd wanted an Australian man, and got one and kept him, which we both admired.

We didn't talk about Geraldine and Lily, although I might have liked to know more, but I really wanted Danby to talk about me, so I talked about Nick and how he wanted Isa, and how she always got what she wanted.

Then I found myself saying something I hadn't said before, to myself I suppose, that what I wanted as I tried to sleep most nights, was to tell them both violently how cruel they were. But I couldn't do that, because I was punishing them by refusing to speak to them at all.

'That's the best way,' Danby said and accepted some crisps. 'But they probably couldn't care less just now.'

A woman wouldn't have said that, I thought. But it probably was true.

From Leeds to Halifax we discussed Sarah and Kenneth between black, smashed-window mill buildings and long areas of industrial scrubland. Danby explained how he'd met Sarah in London when she was doing her houseman year at UCH. He'd been doing a TEFL course, having dropped out of Oxford and decided to go abroad for the rest of his life. They'd met at a party in Crouch End and had a brief affair – he sneezed before he said that intimate word – then she made friends with his sister, so they'd all carried on knowing each other. Her husband was a surgeon who was older than she was and had a son called Jamie who Sarah used to dislike. But Jamie was grown up now and was at university, so she had Ken all to herself again, as well as a little girl of her own.

'What's the little girl called?'

I was almost falling asleep in the blur of darkness and the heater that whirred like a launderette or an expensive hotel. I liked the notion of both.

'Daisy. I've never met her.'

Danby hadn't seen Sarah and Kenneth since the Christmas before Daisy was born, which was two years ago this year.

We drove on past the needled chimneys of Halifax town centre and the bulbous shapes of its municipal buildings, then on through ribbon village fronts with superstores and bus stops, into hills, like vast animals asleep against the clouded sky. Then a steeper lane up past a sign saying Triangle, which was the nearest village to our destination. We drove on up past far-apart lamp-posts and the smell of wet wood through the glass of the car. The clock behind the steering wheel flickered out ten thirty-five and stray barbed wire made eerie shapes outside. We wound round up into open country, with nothing in it but a square silhouette high ahead. That was the side of the farmhouse. There seemed to be no windows.

'Does Sarah know I'm coming with you to see them?'

'Hope so. I told Kenneth. She wasn't there when I rang.'

His knuckles brushed my hand as he changed down into first for an almost perpendicular bend. I took the last of the soft-pack drinks from between my feet and sucked deeply on the plastic straw. I hoped the child who lived here would be in bed and not cry like the last one I'd met.

We pulled up beside a tall stone boulder. Danby got out to open a gate, then back in to bump us to a stop behind a Land-Rover. There were gorse bushes on either side of us, blowing like Arthur Rackham witches' hair. I stepped out into one of them, scratched my hand and made a shrieking noise that surprised me and startled a sheep somewhere near into violent bleating. It was a hopeful sound, so I made it too, then Danby came round from the open boot with a sleeping bag over his shoulder, and he baa'd quite convincingly. Then someone else made the noise as well, and a man with a tweed hat was beside me, his soft forearms pale in the shine of a spotlight from somewhere.

'Kenneth,' he said before I'd asked him.

He shook my hand firmly. He lifted my bag.

'And so,' he went on, turning away, 'another unhappy couple arrives in the country. Come in. Come in.'

He strode off towards an open door with barrels of plants cluttered around it. We followed into a low-ceilinged kitchen that smelled of animals and banana. There was a black and cream Aga with little socks hung along it, and painted plates on the walls, which were built with slabs of flat stone. There was a dresser with rows of small drawers, like the one in Walt Disney's *Snow White*. There was a tall fridge that throbbed. There was a piano against one wall. And there was Sarah, I assumed, far away and somehow incongruous, like a stick-on figure in a fuzzy-felt set.

I pushed my hair back and smiled across as she stood leaning against a work surface, with one hand in her jeans pocket and the other round the stem of a glass. A dishwasher was whirring behind her legs, which ended in two shapely bare feet. Kenneth was beside her already, but I could only see his sturdy bull-terrier back, because he was doing something with something on the draining board. Scrabbling around for a bottle opener, it transpired, and not finding one but knocking spoons to the floor, then putting two running wet glasses onto the table between us anyway and making much of the fact that we all needed a drink. Expansive head movement and up-and-down corduroy shoulders. A good square face, but a line-drawing mouth, that was stuck in a smile that had nothing to do with his eyes, which flickered nervously on and off Sarah.

'Are you going to say hello properly, Danby?'

Our hostess's smile widened and she stooped her head somewhat as Danby dropped bags and bedding at my feet. He went over to kiss her. She folded her arms around his neck and rocked from side to side.

'So long, so long,' she crooned. 'And now introduce me nicely. Who is this lovely lady?'

She winked at me. I went forward to hold out my hand, which she took like a present. She kissed my cheek. She knew I was Chrissie, she explained, because Kenneth had told her ten minutes ago, when he'd finally decided to speak this evening. We were honoured to find her husband here, she continued, picking a grape from a bedraggled bunch of them. He would normally be down at The Flag at this hour.

Kenneth didn't react. He concentrated on his corkscrew. Sarah smiled wearily at me. I thought I'd better say something about how nice the room was, but a dog arrived, so I looked at that instead. We all watched it nose at a bowl of mush until Sarah bent to take the dish away, saying the dog was fat. She winked at me, or maybe Danby, then swayed over to the refectory table and curled into a wicker-backed chair. She drew her narrow shoulders up into her neck and patted the table top just to her right.

'Chrissie, sit here. Kenneth, give Chrissie a drink.'

She wrinkled her nose in a girlish way.

'And Danby, come too. Tell me everything.'

The dog wanted to join us, but Sarah pushed it away and asked Kenneth why it wasn't in the barn with the others. He put a litre bottle in front of her, filled a glass for himself, then scooped the dog up into the crook of an arm.

'Drink up,' he told us, 'I'll soon sort this one out.'

He left the door ajar behind him. Sarah raised her eyebrows at Danby.

'You couldn't, could you?' she said, so he got up and closed it.

Halfway down our first glass of wine we heard the phone ringing from a few rooms away. Kenneth shouted through that Danby was wanted.

'Lisbon wants to talk to you urgently,' he informed us all, frowning into the room. This was a complexity beyond the dog to be sorted out, clearly. When he'd described exactly where the phone was and Danby had rushed to find it, Kenneth stayed on in the doorway to tell Sarah that he'd been clearing up dog sick. He might have to go down to The Flag and root out the vet. Get him to drop by in the morning.

'Don't want dogs throwing up all week, do we? Might be a symptom of something. We can't be complacent.'

Sarah said the vet would be here in the morning anyway to inject the sheep. She sighed at me, wide-eyed, as Kenneth struggled into a waxed jacket, apologizing for leaving like this, but reassuring me that Sarah would like Danby to herself for a bit.

'A bientôt, Sweetie.'

He touched the top of her head. She poured us both more wine as the door slammed behind him.

'Typical,' she said. 'Just typical.'

He was a monster, she explained. Couldn't wait to get down to that pub. The vet was one of his favourite excuses. He couldn't spend an evening with his wife, of course. She drank in little gulps as I waited for her to let me know they didn't have sex any more.

'He hasn't made love to me for months. Not that I'd want him to, the state he's in most nights.'

I rolled a cigarette and wondered what she wanted me to

say. Some shared disgust was probably called for. I could agree that Kenneth was dreadful, but this was his kitchen after all. She might decide she liked him later on. I could tell her the facts of my own love-life at the moment, but that might be considered a bid for attention. I said that it was very nice to meet her and tried to sound anxious, and warm.

'I'm sorry.' She folded her hand over mine. 'I'm sorry. I'm spoiling it, aren't I? But I have no one to talk to. It's hell. You can't imagine what it's like.'

I probably could because I'd lived there myself, with nothing but space and the weather, but I shook my head and looked sorry that she had to live with a monster, in hell.

'I can't tell you how sick I am of it,' she said, pulling at her bottom lip with perfect teeth before beginning to tell me. She was sick of the dog. Sick of sheep. Sick of Kenneth. Sick of Jamie, his useless son, who rang up all the time. Sick of her pregnant patients, with their pains that came mostly from boredom, and the gaggles of infants they brought along with them to infest the air of her clinic. She didn't know why these people had children. She didn't know why she'd had hers really. Daisy was almost two now, and exhausting.

'I thought a baby would even things out between me and Kenneth. I thought when Daisy was born we could start again. Be a happy family.'

She sipped wine and laughed grimly as she said that had been the stupidest idea she'd had in her life, apart from agreeing to marry Ken.

'Because I forgot that Jamie would always come first, you see? I could have set fire to myself every morning and Ken wouldn't have noticed, as long as Jamie's breakfast was properly cooked.'

She went on to say her marriage had ruined her career, her nerves, her looks. Kenneth and Jamie had ruined her life, if she thought about it. She refilled our glasses as I wondered if Danby would ever come back from the phone.

'Don't ever fall in love with a man with children, Chrissie,' she warned me as she wandered over to the fridge, which she opened. She ate a lump of cold meat, wiped her hands on her thighs, then came back to nestle beside me.

'I mean, look what a state Danby's in about this daughter of his. God, he's changed. He used to be fun. But this is what they get like about their children, you see? Completely obsessed.'

And now Jamie was threatening to come home for a while, which was why Kenneth was being especially shitty. The boy had screwed up his first year at Bristol and expected to come back to do nothing.

'Well this isn't a rehabilitation centre for drop-outs, I'm afraid.' She glared at me. 'This isn't a rest home for losers.'

I thought I must tell her that I had a job and an agent who sold my fabric designs and not mention anything about being unhappy. I should wash up or unpack or help her do something, not sit here drinking someone else's wine.

'And anyway,' she went on in a softer voice, 'there's you to take care of now. Danby's told Kenneth that you're rather fragile. I hope you don't mind me saying. I can see you don't feel like talking about it. But the last thing we need is a displaced adolescent trying to find himself around the place all day, for God's sake.'

She'd told Kenneth that her friends had to come first, she assured me. There were only four bedrooms in the building, and she certainly wasn't putting Danby on the sofa. Or me either. She put her hand on my arm.

'Kenneth's son ruined my marriage, you know? And he did it quite systematically too.'

She sipped at her glass. She didn't seem to like wine much, but drank it dutifully anyway.

'Yes. That's something I can tell you for nothing, as my cleaner likes to say. He's jealous of me, you see. Jealous that daddy liked me more than him, and that I sleep with daddy too. Or did for about six months.'

She was quite flushed by now, which suited her greeny-blue eyes. I wondered if perhaps Jamie might one day like her more than daddy, and if Danby would like her more than me. I realized that was possible as she shredded a crisp packet, then shredded the shreds.

'I should have walked out years ago, Chrissie. But it's too late now. I couldn't get anyone now. And anyway, there's no one around. It's not like London.' She looked into my face. 'I mean, how old are you?'

It was the first direct question she'd asked, and I felt rather confused, so I lied and said thirty to seem about the same age as she was, but she laughed and said, 'What a baby,' and that that's how old she'd been when she'd married Kenneth. But she could see I wasn't about to do anything silly like that.

'Except this Danby thing,' she said. 'Don't even think you'll get anywhere satisfactory there.' She stared at me again, then continued to tell me that Danby was a difficult man to be involved with, and she should know, which I was sure was true. But she herself couldn't be too easy.

'He's weird to be with, I'll tell you. He was obsessed with me once, you know?'

She pulled her hair back to angle her head up into the light, which was orange and dangling from a beam, like something from a Seventies Sunday supplement.

'Anyway, he's in love with his daughter now, I suppose. Or will be, as soon as he finds her. Best thing for you if she's gone for ever, if you're hoping to keep him interested. But then he'll just mope and be lovesick. Adolescents. They're the pits.'

Lily was actually eighteen, but I didn't mention that. Or that I only knew Danby because I was his girlfriend's friend. I could see she'd think that was not very convincing. It was beginning to seem hollow to me, now I thought about it. Geraldine certainly wouldn't like to think of me here right now, no matter what I told myself.

'Do you think he's very attractive?' Sarah asked then, coiling heavy blond hair round a ringed forefinger to balance on the top of her head.

'Danby?'

'Yes, Danby. What do you think?'

I didn't have to answer, because he came back into the room just then. But I watched her watching him move into a chair and decided that she thought he was.

'Whose nose is that anyway?' she asked the room rather loudly. 'Where did he get that wonderful nose?'

Then she burst out laughing and said she didn't know what she was saying and who was it on the telephone anyway? What happened? Tell us something exciting.

'Geraldine happened.' Danby looked at me. 'I think I need a serious drink. Either that or a pistol.'

He said he thought he'd get the bottle of Scotch from the car.

'Not for us,' Sarah decided. 'We're drunk enough.'

She said she'd show me my room, which she did, while Danby went to his car. I heard them talking downstairs as I fell asleep in the wooden bed, which had sheets, not a duvet, and creaked whenever I moved, as if I weighed a lot, which I don't. I weigh about the same as Isa. Or did, before she got pregnant.

The next morning was wide with an eggshell-blue sky, through the stone frame of my bedroom window. My watch said three forty, but a man on a radio talking into the bathroom assured me that it was ten fifteen. I turned the radio off and washed and dressed in a silence which began to seem larger than it should have been somehow. Downstairs, the kitchen was empty, although more cluttered than the night before with things that small children use. A wooden trike under spilled sliced bread and a saucepan on the floor and an open Kit-Kat, which I fed to two dogs who seemed pleased to see me. I drank tea, watching hens stutter up a grassy track. They were black and white, which intrigued me. I looked at notes about issues pinned to a cork board along with party invitations for Daisy, and bills and nothing of personal interest. I let the dogs out, then wondered if I should have, so stalked them for a while through the pearled morning haze until they threw themselves over a wall. I went back inside and started washing up, then remembered the dishwasher, so stopped. I wondered where the telephone was, then realized that I was in the habit of expecting a telephone call wherever I was, like someone in a wartime drama. I listened to a chainsaw, dogs and the gestural noises of hens, until Kenneth came in to explain that Danby had gone for a long walk and that it was another marvellous morning.

Sarah was on call, he explained, down at the hospital. He'd been mending fences since six himself, but now he must go and collect Daisy.

'Can I come?'

He stared at me as if I'd asked him in Latin.

'I'm not doing anything. Just waiting for Danby to come back.'

Kenneth jangled keys in his pockets, said he'd buy the paper while he was out. I should put the kettle on, he thought. He'd be ten minutes at the most.

'Have a wander,' he shouted back through the door he left open. 'Get outside and explore. It's a glorious morning.'

Outside was empty, except for a smell. Hills surged away like a seascape. You had to look at your feet to remember perspective. Your feet or the walls of the farmhouse, which were green-edged and cut with wet black. No sheep were visible. Perhaps the vet was doing something with them. There were no buildings in view, except a church spire, like a Lowry person, miles and miles away. No cars in the drive, so who had taken Danby's if he'd gone for a walk? No shops and I needed tobacco. I wondered how long Sarah would be and whether Kenneth disliked me. He'd been gone for an hour when I next went to the bathroom and the radio informed me that there'd been a bomb on Regent Street. I found myself sweeping the kitchen floor, hoping that Nick and Isa weren't dead, that they had been safely in bed or on the Underground. They were my two favourite people, I realized, but I couldn't ring them up. I'd have to wait for a message if Isa'd been injured. My mother would let me know.

I seemed to be emptying the swing bin next, and was dragging the black sack towards the gate, thinking what a nice photograph I would make out there, when I saw Danby's red Mini driving past the end of the farmhouse drive. There was someone in the passenger seat. I waved. Danby waved back. The car swooped on up into the hills, so I followed its journey, on foot for a while, thinking of my mother and Christina Rossetti, because she named me after her.

'Does the road wind uphill all the way?' she used to ask the general environment from time to time.

'Yes, to the very end,' I assured a stream to my left, which was running down, as streams must do. I crouched to watch the shapes the water made swirling over a log until it seemed time to go back to the farmhouse.

The Land-Rover was parked outside again. Sarah was in the kitchen with a tangle-haired girl with a round plump face. The child was banging at the piano, so Sarah had to shout at me, which she seemed to enjoy.

'Chrissie. Thank God. Look, can you stay put for a while? Ken's stormed off and Daisy's got a party I have to drive her to now, and someone's supposed to ring me here very soon about a bed in Halifax General. Some woman needs a section. God. I don't know why I bother. She seems to have only just realized she's pregnant.'

She was buttering toast as she explained these facts to me, laying fingers of it across the black keys for her daughter, who pushed most of them onto the floor.

'Do you mind, terribly, Chrissie? I know it's a drag, but there's no one else I can ask. And at least you don't have to stay in this kitchen for ever.'

She made it sound as though I might, in fact. I asked where Danby was.

'Danby. What an angel. He's doing someone I know a huge favour. I hope you don't mind. He offered late last night. I was rather upset.'

She smiled at me in such a way that I had to smile back as she explained that Danby was driving her locum to Manchester airport because she had promised to do it herself but really couldn't face it.

She went on that in return for this she was to make enquiries about Gabriel for Danby. She'd be passing near that dreadful bookshop the man was supposed to have something to do with, because Daisy's party was in Hebden Bridge. It all seemed rather complex. I'd have liked to ask more about the man in Danby's car, but Sarah obviously considered the conversation closed.

'We're liaising back here at five thirty. I must get some gin. Remind me, Daisy.'

She lifted her daughter and left by the door to the stairs.

'That's OK then, is it?' she shouted back. 'I'm sorry. Blame Ken. This is all his fault.'

I called after her that I'd be glad to stay here, if it would help, but she can't have heard. She was telling me how lucky I was.

'You're so lucky,' she yelled from up the stairs. I didn't hear why she thought that was.

By two thirty I'd found a cellar full of coal and lit a fire in the room next to the kitchen, which was low-ceilinged and upholstered with sofas. There was a desk piled high with bits of things which I looked at until I realized there was nothing really to look at, except the fragments of other people's lives. Prescription pads and birthday cards, phone bills, text books. A framed photo of Sarah and Kenneth getting married in July 1979. The glass was smashed but had been Sellotaped together.

By four o'clock the phone had rung to say the pregnant person had a bed in Halifax hospital, was fairly comfortable but that Sarah should try to get down there. There were forms to be filled in. I said I was sure she'd be there as soon as she could. It seemed to me that Sarah's movements for the rest of the day might well depend on Danby, though I couldn't think exactly why. Nothing depended on me here any more, though, so I started to take the dogs for a walk, but they didn't want to go. They sat firmly beside the dustbins at the end of the track that led into the farm.

'OK,' I said. 'We'll all sit here then.'

I clambered onto an abandoned gate post and watched the daylight fuzz. I watched a field of static cows inside a lurching low black wall. I watched the hedge along the blown-thread road fade into the ground as a translucent fingernail moon moved onto the violet space of the sky. I watched a man walk across a field and was surprised at how long it took him. Then I watched a lone figure curling in and out of view, winding up towards me. The man was wispy, but bulked up by a rucksack, wearing fringed suede, I saw, as he got close up, and the dogs rushed to his khaki legs to nose and wag and whine, ecstatic. He squatted to touch the animals. I watched him fondle their necks and heads, with his knees apart and busy fingers, kneading ears and scruff. He didn't notice me. He went on caressing the dogs, smiling and more or less silent until I said hello, too softly, so I said it again and he looked up.

'You must be Jamie.'

I knew he was. He had a nose exactly like Kenneth. A nose rather like my own.

'That's right. Are you expecting me?'

I realized I was in a way, which made me slightly embarrassed as he looked up, with his fine face in line with my watermarked boots, one of which had come undone. I fumbled with the laces as I told him I was Chrissie, and I was a guest.

'A visitor, I mean. I came with a friend of theirs. They didn't invite me.'

'They never do,' he said, and held up a hand to help me down, where he was about six inches taller than I was.

Then we were walking side by side towards the farmhouse door, with the dogs leaping at his fingers, and I was explaining that there was nobody home, although I couldn't quite say where anyone was.

'Just us and the dogs then,' he said, and stooped to touch one. I walked on a few paces, watching my footprints, but he hadn't caught up by the time I got to the door, so I turned back to see him sitting square on the mud now, sort of hugging the dogs to him, with his backpack leaning up against the revolutionary sky. There was a whine in the air which I thought at first must be one of his animals, happy, but was really the sound of Jamie, so I turned back to stand nearer to him, then he looked up, surprised, and wiped his eyes, almost smiling.

Half an hour later Jamie and I were together in The Flag. We'd taken a short cut over fallen walls, under a fence and past a broken rope swing. The landlord said Jamie had just missed his father. Jamie assured me that he did not miss his father, or Sarah either. He missed the farmhouse, the skyline and the dogs, he told me over our leather-topped table. There was a brass bedpan hanging behind his head. He asked about my father, who was living in the States, then we talked on through his childhood and being unhappy at university in Bristol, and on then about Isa and Nick, who I found it was easy to tell Jamie about. He enjoyed the story, and asked for details of everything as if he was preparing a documentary, which I enjoyed in a perverse sort of way, because it made it seem as if it had happened to someone other than me. Then he told me about a girl at Bristol who'd slept in his room for a while. I found myself not wanting to ask any questions about her at all.

We drank Guinness through the pink-shaded lights, glowing pinker as night arrived, and Jamie glowed through my roll-ups, which he lit gingerly for me because his lighter was fragile and we had no matches. He was puzzled that I should be staying at his family home, because he hated the company there so much, but I explained about Danby, who had mislaid his daughter, who was probably with someone called Gabriel, who worked in Planet Ten. I liked telling Jamie things, and was telling him more when he put down his pint, dropped a hand on my arm and asked what Danby's daughter was called.

'Lily. A nice name.'

'Mmm. And nice-looking too, if she's the girl having a scene with the Gabriel I know. Not sure about this Planet Ten stuff, though. Think someone's been having a laugh there. It's not Gaby's thing.'

'What? You know him? How amazing. We've got to tell Danby.' I laughed out loud. 'I've found Lily without even trying.'

Jamie said we hadn't quite found anyone yet, but he

certainly knew where Gaby was. He'd spoken to him a few days ago. And sure, he hung out with a Lily.

'What's she like?' I hoped she was perfect and worth all the trouble that Danby was taking.

'She paints,' said Jamie, as if that was good enough. 'And she's mad about Gaby.'

'Well, what's he like?'

Gabriel was all right, Jamie said. Lily would be fine with old Gaby, he nodded. He was a carpenter. Had just lost a court case to stay on in a barn, which he'd saved from dereliction.

'But how could he know Lily? She lives in Sydney.'

'Gaby travels a lot,' was all Jamie said, but it seemed enough somehow, in The Flag that night. I never did find out how the pair of them met, but since you couldn't imagine them ever having not known each other, the question seems superfluous.

Jamie was pleased to have a practical role in the scheme of things now. He decided he would take Danby round to Gabriel's place in the morning. That was where he was headed himself anyway, so it all made perfect sense.

'I'm thinking of taking up carpentry myself for a while, Chrissie, if it's all the same to the rest of the world.'

'Who is the rest of the world?'

He didn't answer, so I picked up his empty glass with my own and went to the bar, where I was patiently waiting when cold fingers touched the back of my neck. It was Kenneth. He wasn't smiling.

'So you're here to steal children not find them, my girl. Are you secretly rather wicked?'

He seemed taller than he had been that morning, though of course I hadn't seen him this close up.

'Sorry? What children? Is your little girl here?'

Kenneth took a moment to consider.

'Let me buy you a proper drink, Chrissie, my love. You have

to drink whisky with Guinness.' He took a Scotch from the bar top and downed it in one.

'And you shouldn't be buying my boy pints, anyhow. He has a weakness for drink, like his mother. Take a seat, young lady.'

So I did, next to Jamie, and banged my knees into his for a moment. Then Kenneth was there, all smiling and ostensibly glad, but insisting that I must go back to see Sarah. She'd taken to me, he said. She needed female company. She wouldn't like the idea of us all being here without her, he explained, and besides, there was Danby to think of.

'I can help Danby, Dad. I know where Gabriel lives,' Jamie said. We smiled at each other with our information, like a treat we'd secretly arranged. 'I could ring them up now at the farm. Tell them how to get there right now.'

Kenneth exhaled deeply, with a noise like a dog disturbed in its sleep. He said he thought not. The farmhouse was Chrissie's job, he thought. Jamie and he had some serious talking to do.

'I think my son understands me,' he told the table. He took out a biro and a very limp cheque book to draw me a diagram of how to walk home by myself. I ran most of the way to tell Danby my news.

In the kitchen Sarah was feeding Daisy, who was in a seat attached to the table. Neither mother or daughter seemed pleased to see me. Danby was taking a bath, Sarah frowned. They were thinking of ordering pizza. She had discovered nothing at the bookshop because it was closed, which was odd for a Saturday, but that was how these people were.

She unpeeled a banana and mashed it, glaring at me on and off as she did so, as if she was having to glue something together that I had quite wilfully broken.

'I hear you've met the prodigal son?'

She dragged Daisy from her highchair and sat her at the

piano, where she played the same note over and over. I was wondering how Sarah could possibly know I'd met Jamie as she carried on with her monologue.

'Well you are honoured, I must say, to have been taken for a drink. And that's the last we'll see of that pair, I can tell you. That's Kenneth down and out for the count. How did you tear yourself away?'

I couldn't work out how Sarah knew I'd met Jamie, unless Kenneth had rung her after I left the pub. I found myself wiping the table capably, as if I were in Temps Perdu, where I am mostly in control, and was just saying that Jamie knew Gabriel, so all our troubles were solved, when Danby arrived in the room, shoe-polish shiny and wet-haired from a bath.

'Let's drive round there. Let's go right now. Chrissie, you're a genius,' he said when he'd heard my breathless facts. He kissed me violently on both cheeks, then sat down to turn his socks the right way out and smooth them on.

'Let's get down to The Flag, pick up this Jamie and head on out to the hills. Let's see where these charmers have been hiding themselves.'

There was an open gin bottle on the table. Sarah replaced the lid, then stared at it, biting her nails. Daisy slipped from the piano stool and wept, and we all three waited for the other to turn her right side up as the phone rang and Sarah left the room. Danby flipped the wooden tricycle from its side and lifted the little girl astride it. She seemed to like the shock and levered herself off with bare feet. Sarah came back smiling widely.

'Chrissie, darling. I'm going to have to ask you a massive favour.' Her face sobered up. 'They need a second opinion on some woman who's been in labour for days. Ken's supposed to be back, but that's pretty unlikely, unless the pub explodes. Could you sit tight if I settle Daisy? I know it's a drag, but at least you've been out. Look on the bright side.'

I sat down in front of the gin. Neither side of the bottle looked particularly bright.

'Then, Danby, you can follow me in your car. I'll drive past the pub – it's only a mile or so out of my way – and you can collect Jamie from there. He'll take you to these people you want to see.'

Sarah must be used to organizing people. It was probably a skill. She unhooked a dungaree button, showing a shoulder bone over scoop-necked linen. She explained again that someone would really have to stay here, and that really it would have to be me.

'Unless Kenneth can be dragged away from his retirement home.'

She undid her other buckle so the denim folded down and lifted her hands to reorganize hairpins. Danby stared, so I did too.

'Don't look so shocked. It's OK. Daisy will go to sleep.'

And she lifted wide-awake Daisy from her scurrying trike, which was by now halfway out of the room.

'You won't have to do a thing, Chrissie.'

Danby lifted the gin bottle and unscrewed the top, holding it out towards me.

'I think it's coffee and Valium I need.'

He had a swig himself, pulled on a jumper, then asked if I minded being alone.

'I don't have to go, this minute,' he said.

'Danby. You'll have to move your car, so I can get mine out. Do you want to do that now?'

Sarah's footsteps followed this question into the room.

'Off you go,' I said, smiling as well as I could. 'Sarah's in a hurry.'

By eight thirty I'd discovered which of the knives of the house was most suitable for slicing cold leg of lamb, and had eaten a lot of it between slices of perfect toast. The kitchen was working well for me. I'd been and seen Daisy, on her back with a dummy, and pulled the covers up to her neat dimpled chin. I sat in Sarah's chair and drank weak tea to the comforting hum of the fridge, listening to the bubbles of sound that blew evenly out of the Aga. Before long it was nine fifty on the bathroom radio, where I was applying hand cream and reading labels. Three people had been injured by the bomb in London that morning, but no one was dead. Danby hadn't rung and Jamie hadn't come home, so I supposed they could both be still in the pub. It was friendly in The Flag. It'd be getting busy in London at Temps Perdu by now, of course. A Saturday night on the Shepherd's Bush Road with talk of the bombing and big tips, with everyone glad to be there and alive. Jake and house red and Mont Blanc mousse. Ella Fitzgerald calling the whole thing off, and the best regulars' eyes slowly clouding. I should ring in and re-book my Monday shift and stop being so paranoid about Isa's new life. I could be there tomorrow if they needed a hand. I still had fifty-five quid in my wallet.

'Hellooowaa.'

It sounded like a hunting cry.

'Helloowaaa. Where are the Guard Dogs?'

The dogs were at the door then, scratching hard against it, so I let them outside into Kenneth's bugle impersonation and stepped out myself, onto the spotlit landscape, and saw Jamie in silhouette, swaying through the stile, with his father looming towards me.

'Chrissie, my lamb. Keeping watch over the fold. Come in. Come in and drink.'

He put a heavy arm around me to steer me unevenly back through the kitchen door. Jamie followed us, very flushed, with fairy-light eyes. His cropped hair seemed yellower than it had in the pub. I was pleased to see him. He made me flushed too, which was pleasant and new. Kenneth took a plastic bag from his son very gently, as if it were flowers or a baby doll.

'Fine wines for the house guests. For all our lost children. For we are all lost children, are we not?'

He slumped into Sarah's chair and fumbled a bottle onto his thighs.

'Jamie. The honours. Chrissie, your health.'

He raised an empty wineglass. I felt slightly alarmed and moved to stand beside Jamie. I don't enjoy being with drunk men I don't know unless there's a good reason for us being together, like them paying me to clear their tables, for example, in which case it's possible to achieve a distant contempt. This one owned the house I was staying in. I rolled a cigarette, which Jamie lit, then he folded his lighter into my hand.

'Keep it somewhere safe,' he said.

'Where's Danby?'

Kenneth answered my question. 'At Gabriel's hovel, it seems. I arranged a ride for him with one of our drinking companions.'

He gazed sadly at the dishwasher for a while, then wine was opened then knocked to the floor as Kenneth stood up, with his chair falling backwards, and said let's all have a song. He nudged dogs away from the piano's brass pedals gently with his rubber boot and played the chorus of 'The Way You Look Tonight' in a tender way, still standing up, which surprised me. Then Jamie went over and played the same song on the high notes and Kenneth sang the words, then after a while Sarah came in.

The singing continued. Sarah surveyed the spilled wine, the teatime detritus, and the knife I'd been using which was on the floor by now. She said nothing, just stood very still for too long.

'I've just delivered twins,' she finally said, so I looked up into her face to hear all about it, but she wasn't looking at me. She was walking fast towards the piano with her right arm out. She slammed its walnut lid down onto the men's four moving hands. Jamie carried on looking straight ahead, into a picture made with matchsticks and tissue paper, but Kenneth roared and forced the lid back up with his wrists. No one said anything for about twelve seconds. There was only the sound of Sarah clearing the table and slipping things down into the dishwasher grid. Then Kenneth sang about breathless charm very loudly without the piano, and Sarah said, 'How was Daisy?' to me, but I didn't say anything back. She said I must be exhausted.

She must have known that Kenneth was staring into her head, because she kept it high and still while she spoke.

'I'm going to bed. You must be exhausted, Chrissie,' she said to me again.

I wished she'd say hello to Jamie, but she didn't. She walked out of the room, leaving the door open behind her. We heard water running in the bathroom above.

Jamie moved slowly away from the piano. He came and took his lighter from the pocket of my jeans without speaking. He sat down on the table and lit a cigarette, which he passed to me. I smoked some of it, listening to Kenneth singing the word lovely over and over, then gave it back to Jamie in case he might be going to cry. It's hard to cry if you have to inhale a cigarette, in my experience.

Long after Sarah had gone to bed and after we'd all had toast and Marmite and more wine had been found in the cellar, Kenneth was still singing the word lovely to himself. Occasionally he'd say how well I looked, or how good it was to see Jamie, or tell us both to be sure to relax and drink, but mostly he just sang that one word over and over again. He had a good rich voice, but it was a relief when he stood heavily up and almost fell through the door of the next room, where the desk was, with his wedding photograph on it and the glow of the fire I'd made and all the couches too. Within minutes we heard him snoring.

'Do they ever sleep together?' I asked.

Jamie said he hadn't a clue.

When I went to sleep about an hour later, I found myself in Jamie's bed. Kenneth stayed sprawled on his couch. We passed him there when we walked through together to a door at the back of the house, which Jamie unlocked to take me down through cool fields to a stream he thought I should see. He said we would see fish, but we did not. We weren't really looking for fish anyway. We were seeking something else which we found when I wet my face with the razor-blade water and he wiped it dry with his hand without asking, then kissed me and I kissed him gladly back and it didn't remind me of Nick, but only of the rest of myself, that no one so nice had been so near for months. We were pleased to be kissing and it lasted some time, then we walked back through the windy soft black, holding hands until there was Jamie's dipping soft bed with slightly damp sheets and those small high sounds I'd forgotten I make and his warm face very near mine.

When I woke up the next day I was alone. The birds on the wallpaper were blue and green in the daylight, and the room looked down over the fields I had trailed over short hours before. I wondered not where Jamie was, because I had a feeling he wouldn't be hard to find again, but more what had happened to Danby and vaguely what Gabriel would be like and whether finding him would have found Lily too, and when I would go back to London. I decided it would be today, one way or another. I was glad to be glad to be going back to work again and went down to the kitchen to tell anyone there my plans.

The kitchen was empty and tidy too. Low sunlight made a bunch of thistles on the window sill glow a deep mauve-grey against the sandstone tiling of the surface they were on. I filled the kettle, opened the window and saw Danby and Jamie moving slowly in front of the hen house, with Daisy stuttering along between them, her little blue shoes touching the ground below her feet with uncertainty, as if it might be about to dissolve. As I watched, she must have tired of walking, because the men swung her up between their arms while a dark-haired young woman came into the frame. She was holding a wicker laundry bag, with bread sticking out of the top, and as she smiled hello, she looked very like Danby. She took his arm. Jamie lifted Daisy up onto his shoulders and they moved together towards the house, like a group of people just off a boat, perhaps, like a band of weary travellers, joined suddenly by Sarah, who appeared from the left to shake Lily's hand, touch Daisy's foot and smooth hair away from her sleepless face.

I was about to shout hello, but decided not to distract them. I waved. They didn't see me, but I didn't mind. I left the window swinging as the kettle boiled to click itself off. I opened the piano and played some scales over the throb of the dishwasher's surge, then I made some toast and opened the fridge, where there was a huge new bleeding leg of lamb and some gold-topped milk for the tea, which I made in the largest pot, in case everyone else wanted some too.

Six Lunchtime

I DIDN'T WORK IN THE WINE BAR FOR A WHILE AFTER I'D GOT back from Yorkshire, because there was so much designing to do and because I didn't want to run into Isa. I didn't see anyone for about a week, except Danby once, who brought Lily round. She was looking for somewhere to live. We decided Temps Perdu would be good place to put up a notice, so when Alison rang from there one Thursday morning I thought it must be about a flat or a room to rent, but she was leaving me a message to ask me to go back to work. Isa hadn't been in for three days and they needed someone for lunchtime. I said I'd be there at twelve, had a lukewarm bath and put on some long white shorts. You have to look like a waitress if you're doing a lunchtime. At night you can look like someone giving a party, as long as the party is for respectable guests.

By three o'clock we'd jammed the door half open to get rid of the smoke. Tables were strewn at odd angles to each other, with splayed spaces in between. Drink-limp legs of languid diners were mostly swathed in pressed denim – ending in immaculate trainers – or were female, slender and evenly tanned; well-oiled, shiny, waxed and smooth.

'I want something sickly and sweet that will make me fat,' my least favourite luncher told the handsome face straining into hers, across the lobster-pink of their tablecloth, rather than me, although I was the one taking her order, breathing in her body lotion.

'Let's share something naughty.'

His fingers slid over her Rolex into the sleeve of her blouse.

'Let's be gross. Let's have a sticky toffee pudding.'

I looked away in case they kissed. They'd already been feeding each other king prawns, and she'd slipped off her sandals to put her feet between his. They were always like this at the end. She wouldn't eat something sweet if he paid her. He would be paying, of course. I decided there wasn't anything left for dessert. We'd run out, I said flatly. Did they want coffee or just the bill. She looked at me then with something like hatred, but I chewed the gum we affected and smiled, sickly and sweet.

'I'll bring coffee, shall I? And a sugar bowl too?'

She knew I didn't like her. If she'd been with a woman she could have turned nasty, but her companion said how nice and the bill, if I would. He'd had enough foreplay clearly. Back at the dull wide sweep of the bar, Alison was lounging into Jake, who was spilling complimentary peanuts over the cutlery. Alison was supposed to be wrapping napkins. Their arms were intertwined. She must have realized she was irritating me because she offered to take over the lovebirds' bill, and one for Mary too, although she was in no state to pay at present. Mary came every lunchtime and fell asleep about halfway down her second bottle of house red, by which time her cheeks were finely veined with the same colour as her glass. We usually let her snooze on through the afternoons. She'd only be back at five twenty-five if we woke her up to go home.

I turned Ella Fitzgerald over and gave Jake a drink, which I asked him to pay for to show there was nothing between us, then I went over to have a cigarette with Suzanne and Jasper. They were slouching at table three by the open back window, where they always sat at lunchtime. Suzanne was finishing up her second apple crumble, scratching at the plate with a tea-spoon, complaining that it was her birthday and she'd only got two cards.

'I'm forty-three,' she told the room. 'I might as well be a hamster for all the notice anyone takes.'

Jasper put his arm around my shoulder, and his hand on hers, and his mouth against my ear to whisper that I must bring some champagne.

'Forty-three. I'll probably have a hot flush in a minute. Forty-bloody-three.'

She thought she'd have more apple crumble if there was any left, but I was needed by a man in red braces at table six, so I went over to the messy remains of steak and cigars to smile, curious, determinedly eager.

'I need more sex,' the one who hadn't called me explained to his thumbnail. 'My energy levels are all messed up.'

Then he looked up to me and said, 'Cheese?' and I caressed the whole of his face with, 'Of course.'

I lifted two empty bottles of Chablis by slipping my fingers into them and smiled widely at the space I'd made.

'Of course,' I indulged us. 'I'll see what we have.'

We had Stilton, Brie and Cheddar, of course, which was what we had every day, but it's sometimes worthwhile for a waitress to seem confused by the choices her customers face, to give the impression that the plenitude awaiting them is vast and terribly complex. Isa was best at this fictional bewilderment at what might have been available because she always knew exactly what was in the fridge at any given time. She has a photographic memory, our father used to say. But she hadn't been in for ten days, had disappeared some people said. Some people were worried, but I was not, partly because she always knew exactly what was in the fridge, and partly because if Isa wanted to disappear, she'd make sure I knew so that I'd tell our mother, who would then blame any disaster on me. If Isa wants our mother to be worried about her, she does it in a methodical way. Not coming to work was not disappearing. She was being naughty, was all, as far as I could see, and Suzanne agreed, so that must be right.

Ella sang that she still had a song in her heart and I whistled along like waiters in films do, and skimmed a full ashtray away to the bar top that belonged to me for now, like these last replete customers did too. Through the polish of our gold-lettered front window a bus was jammed, roaring in traffic. A child stared out from the top deck, with its palms pressed white to the glass. I dropped pound coins into the till and ran the taps. I had a gulp of my Côtes du Rhône, replaced the Chablis men's ashtray, was asked for two glasses of port and blushed out, 'Of course,' again. I found the champagne Jasper wanted and an ice bucket too, and I gave the lovers more coffee and said I did hope it was hot, then I took Mary's newspaper out of her uplifted hands, because she'd once set a Sunday supplement alight from a candle. I took smeared glasses to the kitchen, where the washer-upper was sitting on a counter sliding with dirty plates, eating cheesecake with a knife. He was new and Italian and handsome, but he'd just heard that his father was dying, so he was flying back to Rome the next afternoon. I asked him if he wanted a drink and he did, so I went to find one, collecting money from tables as I travelled. I assessed the sturdy porcelain tip jar, which was a satisfying weight. I poured myself a fresh drink, along with one for Antonio, and watched the rust-coloured geraniums in the window box quiver to the vibrations of the Shepherd's Bush Road.

'Three thirty,' said Jake. 'Lock-up time, Chrissie.' So I reached the long brass keys from the cleaning-cloth cupboard where we hid them, as Ella decided that this couldn't be love because she felt so well. She sounded as if she really did too. The woman who hated me left with her man and her sling-backs and her miniature rucksack and I went to round up the necks of their empties. They'd left four pound coins under a saucer. Alison must have admired his tie. She was good at that sort of thing since she'd been in love. I nudged tables into symmetry along the grubby sanded floor that was puddled with September sun. I picked up damp fragments of green paper napkins and someone's address and telephone number, which was folded and soft, like flattened warm grass, then I took the worn rubber wedge from underneath the plate-glass door. I was twisting the dangled cardboard sign to the side that said Closed when I found my face in front of a checked shirt I'd bought at a jumble sale about five years before. It was Nick's, and his face was above it, which I hadn't seen for months, unless you count dreaming. The door was half open. It was twenty to four.

'Isa's not here.'

I should have just said hello and not mentioned her name, because it was there then, in the room like a broken floorboard you have to step over.

'I'm doing Isa's shifts all this week.'

Not looking at him at all, but at the air outside, as if it might be about to rain something strange, and with the door handle still in my fist like a knife. The same bus was stuck in the traffic, and there was a siren out there now too, with a flashing light, frenetic and blocked. The child I'd seen before was still in the top of the bus, still staring and pressing the oblong glass. It was three forty and Nick was here at the wine bar and there was suddenly nothing to say. If it was a dream we'd be kissing. I must not look at his mouth.

'She's not here, if that's what you wanted.'

My face was probably sweaty and red. I hadn't washed my hair for three days. I must have smelled of grease and smoke and meat. He smelled the same as he always did, like a launderette with maybe a bread oven in it.

'Are we too late for leftovers even?' A girl behind him stepped forward to ask. She was taller than us and she knew my name, because she was Lily, I realized now. I looked past her, hoping Danby was maybe there too, but there was no one else on the pavement.

'I know it's late, Chrissie.'

She put a hand on my shoulder, smiled in the way she has, as if there's nothing to smile about really, so you might as well smile at most things.

'But I wanted to buy this hungry man something to eat, and we couldn't think of anywhere else we wanted to go. He's been lifting boxes onto a boat for me all morning.'

She has a soothing voice, which makes you want to hear more, whatever she says, like some people's mothers did when we were small. The music in the room behind me stopped. I held the door and listened to traffic and a police car and laughter. I waited for Lily to say something else, but Suzanne's voice was the only one I could clearly hear. She was getting cross with Jasper, saying, 'You can't be. You were older than that when we met. Don't lie to me on my birthday,' and he was telling her that he was forty-one and that was the truth, then he was over beside me, with his bleary breath and his arm around my waist, as if I was a bus stop late at night.

'Nick,' he said. 'Nick, for Christ's sake. Now we really do need a drink. And Lily, my Australian angel. It's Suzanne's birthday, Nick. More drinks all round. More drink for the birthday girl, Chrissie.'

I couldn't say we were supposed to be closed because Suzanne was beside me now too, going on about being forty-three and how there was no need to tell everyone, and Jasper saying he thought she wanted attention, he thought she wanted people to know.

'I'm not a child, for god's sake. I don't want attention. A

card would have been nice, that's all.' She stared at Nick as Jasper insisted that we must all have a drink.

'Forty-bloody-three, Nick.' Suzanne had her hand in his now, pulling him into the room. 'Say I don't look forty-three, Nick. How old are you?'

'Same age as Chrissie, however old that is.'

I dropped the door handle and went to the Ladies', where I stared at the mirror and seemed swollen and pink. I drank some water from the tap, but that made it worse because my mouth came out a different shape. I took my pulse, which was eighty-three, and I thought of climbing away through the window to the garden next door, but that would not be reasonable. I should go back and be polite but distant and leave. To disappear would seem hysterical, as if I just wanted attention.

When I came out the small birthday party was installed at table three, which was oval with a flat end where a drop-leaf was missing. Jake was leaning into the wall behind Lily. A bad painting of a French seaside resort was now hanging at a strange angle because his shoulder had banged it. Alison was over by the bar, filling her purse with tips, explaining to the room that she'd got an appointment with her dentist in Hammersmith, but would be back by five to open up again.

'Leave it a mess when you leave,' she said. 'I've been useless. Jake kept me up all night.'

She called to him that he had to go with her now, but he said he'd hang around and catch her back here later on. She went and took his hand and had a word in his ear. He decided to go after all.

'Putty,' said Jasper as I closed the door behind them and turned the key. 'The Jake we knew is no longer. That man is changed, I'll tell you.'

'It's love,' said Suzanne. 'You couldn't understand.'

I went down to the kitchen with the wine I'd forgotten to

give Antonio. I stayed there for a while, being gesturally helpful while he talked about his father, but I couldn't listen because of Nick being upstairs and wanting to go there, but not wanting him to have me there, in case that was why he had come. In the end I asked Antonio to come up with me for a drink in the bar. I could always pretend I was in love with him if the worst came to the worst – if this wasn't the worst already.

'I dwell in possibility,' I said to myself for some reason. I asked Antonio if he'd heard of Emily Dickinson, as if I were indeed in love with him, and then I told him that this was his last lunchtime here for a while, which he seemed to find confusing.

'I mean, it's your last lunchtime,' I said again, more loudly, although his English was perfect. 'Leave the kitchen for the night shift to finish.'

And I took his arm, which was skinny like a loaf of French bread, and led him up past the others to the back of the bar and asked him what wine he'd like me to open. He chose Montbazillac, which threw me, because it's expensive, but the owner was in France for three weeks, so I thought I might as well. Isa would be around to explain everything by next week, most likely. She took things she shouldn't all the time. She stole Nick from me, for a start. I don't know how she explained that to herself.

At table six Mary was snoozing with one hand on a half-empty glass. The yellow cardigan she never took off was rising and falling on the gentle swell of her front. I dropped empties into the chute that smashed them down to the bins and thought how nice it must be to be able to fall asleep sitting up. You wouldn't ever have to face the emptiness of bed. Ella had started to sing 'Nice Work If You Can Get It', and Jasper was singing along, then he suddenly stood up, as the piano strained into the strings. He took Suzanne's hands and there they were dancing together, she clutching a wineglass stem along with some of his fingers, and he with a dripping cigarette in his mouth. They were quite good together. They looked like a birthday. Like a dodgem car making little jerky paths across the darkening floor, banging tables and knocking the bar front, then finding a space again and swinging round inside it. He had a knee between her legs to direct her, and a hand on the small of her back. She danced, singing on about how nice some work was, if you could get it, and if you could get it, tell her how, as I noticed that she was tone deaf, which Jasper must have been aware of too, because he stubbed his cigarette into a saucer in front of me and whistled loudly over her voice for a while. Then he stopped whistling to kiss Suzanne's mouth, and they weren't dancing any more then, but leaning into the bar front about a foot away from me, and I didn't know what to do exactly, so I turned the music off. It was four thirty-five. They carried on kissing in front of the bar, and I should have cashed up by now. Perhaps I should leave it for Alison when she got back. Alison would probably be sober.

Suzanne untangled from Jasper at last, and went back to the group at the table to rub Nick's shoulders, talking loudly over the back of his head to Lily, who'd just got the keys of a houseboat she was renting till Christmas. Danby had met the owner in here at the weekend, Lily said. The rent was cheap because he didn't know how long it would be free.

'Why's that?' Suzanne asked. 'Is he a criminal?'

'It's not criminal not to have long-term plans,' Jasper said. 'Jesus. Give a guy a break.'

Nick was smoking, drinking the sweet wine that Antonio had taken over and put beside him, but they weren't talking to each other. Nick was looking at the clock on the wall behind me, and the Italian was looking at him do it rather apprehensively.

I opened the till and stared at the notes folded round each other there and the coins in all the wrong places. Then the phone rang to my left and Nick stood up as I answered, but he didn't come over, which was a good thing, because it was Isa, ringing from a telephone box that didn't seem to work. The little beeping noises went on through her saying hello, then she hung up. It rang again. I turned my back to the room to answer and said no, he wasn't there. No, Nick had not been in. Just the regulars and Suzanne's birthday.

'But he said to ring him at half three there today. Is it much after that?'

I said yes, it was nearly five, but nothing else. Jasper arrived at my side with a £20 note from his trouser pocket and asked for more champagne. I jerked my head towards the fridge. He swayed towards it and stared at the crowded bottles, very puzzled, not pulling any out. The phone beeped and Isa inserted more money.

'I don't understand. He said he'd be there.'

'Perhaps he changed his mind. He's been known to do that.'

Silence. More beeps and another coin forcing through.

'Has that girl Lily been in? Is Danby there?'

'Are you still pregnant?'

I shouldn't have asked that: it made me feel sick.

'Not really. I mean no, I'm not. Tell Nick that if he comes in, will you? Or don't tell him. Just tell him I rang.'

'I wouldn't speak to Nick if you paid me, Isa. Or you either, in fact.'

I put the phone down. It rang again, so I picked it up but unplugged it with my left hand and kept it to my ear for some time in case anyone was watching. Then I replaced the receiver and slid a bottle of Veuve Clicquot out from under some water and handed it to Jasper.

'Let's get drunk. I'm clocking off.'

I took down a cluster of champagne glasses to spread them

on the table, where they glistened like useless bits of fallen chandelier. I sat between Nick and Lily on the chair that people don't sit on because it has one short leg. Antonio was telling Suzanne that his father might not die. He said it reassuringly, as if it was her parent at stake rather than his. She told the smeared glass in her hand that her father had died three years ago in Ireland in a caravan, but she didn't care because she hated him.

Jasper said that was stupid. Nobody just simply hates their father. Although his mother had certainly hated his, but then he was the man she'd married, so that wasn't the same. Suzanne said that was dim. Nobody hates their husband unless they hated their father. Which was why she'd hated her last one, if she thought about it properly.

'He wasn't worth hating in himself,' she explained, drawing little round faces with smiles on them on the table with spilled fizz.

'He was fond of me. It wasn't his fault we didn't get on. It wasn't just his fault at all.' As if I had said it must have been. It seemed to be me she was talking to now. 'But I wouldn't let him be nice to me. Do you see what I mean? He was nice, though. Really he was.'

She had her hand on Jasper's leg, playing with the soft grey fabric there.

'And I was fond of him too. He was kind, you know? A very kind man. Good with children.'

She took a full glass of sweet wine, which was foolish, because she'd been drinking champagne until then. Jasper crossed his legs away from her hand with a jerk.

'He'd have had to be good with children to get along with you,' he said. He was slurring his speech. 'All men have to be good with children if they want to get laid.'

Lily stopped lighting a Marlboro to stare at him. She looked like she'd just seen someone being mugged. He went on regardless: 'What do you think, Nick? How are you with babies?'

'Nick's having a baby. Didn't you know?'

Suzanne's eyes glinted. Her dress was off her shoulder. She had a black bra on.

'He's not,' I said.

It was the first thing I had said, and I said it directly at Nick, who was buttoning his top button up, looking down, giving his fine chin lots of little underneath wrinkles. He seemed to not be listening, so I said it again.

'Nick is not having a baby,' I said.

'Thank God for that,' said Jasper. 'What's happened to the music?'

He fumbled up, focusing on the bar, where the cassette deck's little blue light seemed exceptionally bright. I wouldn't have thought you could see it from table three, but you could.

'Who was that on the phone?' Nick was talking into my eyes now. 'Who rang this place just then?'

I told him it was a customer. Two customers, I said. Two men who wanted big tables. I touched the top of his head while I talked to him because I was drunk and he said I should have some juice.

'I'm not a child,' I said. 'I'll drink what I like.'

And then there was Aretha Franklin very loudly going to knock on his door and tap on his window pane, with the back-up girls sighing in time, and Mary was awake and humming along. I'd never seen her do that before. She still had her eyes closed, but was holding her glass up. I hoped Jasper wouldn't ask her to dance. I felt like dancing myself. Then there was a real knocking from across the room, so we all turned to see Jake with Alison outside the door, holding hands, pressing their noses to the glass, squashing a bunch of flowers between them.

It was five fifteen. Jasper swayed from behind the bar to let them in, saying, 'A bouquet for the birthday girl,' and then Suzanne was weeping all at once, wishing her mother was here again between sobs, but nobody took any notice because something else happened at about the same time. The door banged open. Jasper hadn't locked it, of course, and a woman was suddenly moving into the room with a bleeding-faced baby and a purse in her mouth and a half-unfolded pushchair. She needed a phone, she was saying. She had to use the phone. She'd slipped off the bus, she shouted over the music, and the baby had hit the pavement. The baby was screaming and Antonio was behind the bar, soaking napkins with tap water, which he left flooding into the sink as he rushed to wipe the child's smeary face, which it was rubbing little fists into. Alison tried the phone, which of course was dead, since I had unplugged it, and she kept saying, 'It's broken,' so I stood up to go over and noticed a moment when everything seemed to stand still, with a gap in the music and Jasper holding his flowers and the sun making some sugar that was on the floor shine, and then Lily was on her feet and out through the door and back again, taking the accident with her.

'There's a taxi outside,' she shouted back to us all. 'We'll take the baby to Charing Cross. Forget the phone call. We'll get this cab.'

Then she'd gone, with the woman, the baby and the pushchair, and the middle of the room was empty. Alison started moving empty bottles from our table and nobody said anything, until Nick said he couldn't go anywhere now because he had Lily's houseboat keys in his pocket. We didn't quite know why Lily had gone, or if she would ever come back. Suzanne and Jasper said it was nicest here anyway, and Antonio decided to stay and wash up some more.

Jake had a brandy. The sight of blood made him feel faint, he said. Alison's mouth was numb from her dentist, so she decided she needed brandy as well. Tuesday nights were quiet as a rule, but I laid some tables anyway. Then I bulked up the high fridge with white wine and water, although I wasn't due to be working. I could have gone somewhere else whenever I wanted. Alison gave me my wages and most of the tips. She must have felt guilty, or sorry for me maybe. I bought a bottle of house white with my new wealth, and put it down in front of Suzanne and felt somewhat blurred, but took a full glass. It was unexpectedly cold against the top of my mouth. I took one of Nick's cigarettes.

'You see,' Suzanne was telling the table. 'You see, anything can happen. People can fall off buses. I nearly died when I fell off my bicycle once. People die, you see. People have babies.'

'You're a long time dead,' Jasper said.

Then he said Suzanne couldn't ride a bicycle, and she said she could – she'd been riding bicycles since she was four – and I noticed that Nick was looking at me in a fond sort of way, so I asked if he'd like to be married.

'Shall we get married?' I said. 'In case.'

'In case what?'

But he didn't say no, so I took his wrist and kept it for hours through the changing light, while we drank as the night arrived. Through talk about bicycles, birthdays and painting I held Nick's wrist. And about fathers too, and caravans and my mother's house, with the room that Nick and I papered the summer we met, with the ladder that wobbled, and stories of Suzanne's long-ago homes and Jasper's plumber in France. Through discussing each other and everyone else, and people we saw but didn't know, I held onto Nick, and when he left, at nearly midnight, I went back all the wavy way with him to his front door. And then he did say no.

'You can't stay, Chrissie. You know you can't.'

'But I can't get home.'

'I'll call you a cab.'

We went in together, through rooms that I used to live in,

and we stood side by side as he rang for a taxi. There were three messages flashing on his answering machine. It didn't seem worth touching his familiar body while I was there, but as soon as I was in the taxi I wished I had, so when I got out, I paid the man and ran all the way back to where I'd just come from, which took about twenty minutes. It was a foolish thing to do, because Nick seemed scared rather than impressed with my need and called another taxi right away. I wouldn't get into that one, though. I said I hoped he died sorry, which I took back the next morning, and I walked away in a different direction, towards the shine of the Fulham Palace Road. I moved quickly along the glossed pavement, walking near the kerb, before I changed to walk along by the wall to be more safe. After a while I turned off to the left, along past the noise of a party to make a short zigzag to the steps that went down to Suzanne's front door, which she opened. She was wearing her coat and toasting bread, and glad to have someone to share it with since Jasper was asleep in a chair.

'That's the trouble with men,' she said, putting a cigarette between buttery lips. She smoked instead of explaining it to me.

'What is?'

'What?'

'The trouble with men?'

'Well, they don't want enough, do they? That's why we live longer, you see. They just don't want enough.'

and we could ask to [illegible] if we [illegible]. There [illegible] fishing or [illegible] much in the [illegible] nothing [illegible] about what I was [illegible] with [illegible] that [illegible] I wouldn't [illegible] when I [illegible] back the next morning and I walked away in a different direction towards the shore of the [illegible] River [illegible]. After a while I turned off to the left [illegible] to the [illegible] that went down [illegible] which she opened. She was [illegible]

[illegible] with [illegible] me.

'That?'

'Yes.'

'The trouble with grass.'

'Well, they don't want money, do they? That's why we like [illegible] you see. They just don't want any[illegible].'

Seven Connemara

ONE LATE SEPTEMBER AFTERNOON, AS THE STREET LAMPS were turning to glow orange from red, Danby arrived to see me and said he'd come to say goodbye. He was on his way back to Lisbon to start teaching the autumn term. I was surprised. I thought he'd be staying in London for ages.

'Well, I have responsibilities there. I can't let people down. I'll have to see how it goes for a while.'

'You mean see how Geraldine goes?'

He almost laughed and said no, that had already gone, as far as he could make out.

'She's seeing a man called Emmanuel now. Drop-dead handsome, she assures me. Wants dozens of kids.'

'Nice,' I said. 'For her, I mean. Do you want a drink, or something?'

He explained that he couldn't stay. He was having dinner with his mother at seven. He walked to look at my goldfish, took a soft pack of uncorked cigarettes from inside his roomy tweed jacket and suggested I take a holiday in Ireland, where his father's family came from. I realized I'd been expecting him to invite me to go to Lisbon with him.

'Why on earth would I go to Ireland?'

Danby inhaled, raised his shoulders, exhaled blue smoke.

'Because you can. Because it's there, if you like.'

'Well go to Ireland yourself. I've got no reason to.'

He told me not to be so dismissive and flicked his Zippo shut.

'But it's true,' I said, 'I don't know anyone there. And why would I go away now anyway? I'm helping Lily with the houseboat.'

The river down by Hammersmith Bridge, where the houseboats are, had been a large part of my days lately. Lily's flaking but roomy boat was a compelling combination of wet paint, cut chrysanthemums and frying bacon to breathe in. The fact that Gabriel and Jamie had arrived to stay there the week before made long afternoons in its tongue-and-groove interior even more attractive. I was hardly ever at home.

'Besides, I've got my new friends to think of. What will Gabriel and Jamie do without me? And Lily? Why would I want to go away just now, by myself?'

Danby smoked and explained that Jamie was part of the plan, which surprised me. Jamie wasn't part of my plans, pleasant though his company could sometimes be. I didn't have any plans, except to work harder at my designing, which was being bought at an unprecedented rate by clients in Italy, it seemed. I'd stopped doing lunchtimes in Temps Perdu.

'What plan?' I sat down. 'There isn't a plan.'

Danby said that was his point entirely. He had been thinking about me a lot, he said. He said it as though he knew something I didn't, which made me think of a few days before when I'd rung Nick's and Isa had answered the phone. I'd put the phone down and rung Lily, but Nick had answered her telephone. He was with Gabriel on the boat, which upset me somehow, and I think I was crying by the time Lily arrived to see me later on. Everyone was in the wrong place, I'd told her. I couldn't bear the chaos. I'd probably said too that I'd like to be away from it all, which I would in a way, and she had probably told that to Danby.

'Yes, Chrissie. I've had a long think about your situation,

and I don't see why you don't go away for a bit. You might as well.'

This was said as if 'my situation' was worse than I had imagined. Maybe there was something to know that everyone knew except me. Isa had been leaving strange messages on my machine, and so had my mother, but I didn't ask Danby what anyone knew about my sister because he was still talking. He was saying that everyone had had a talk about me on the boat, and that Jamie was keen to take me away from London.

'Take me away.' I moved to the other side of the window. 'Take me. I'm not a child to be taken places.'

I asked for a cigarette to underline my grown-upness, and he tossed the packet at me. It spilled onto the carpet, so I took one but left the others to roll under a chair.

'And why would I go anywhere with Jamie?'

Why had Danby been talking to Jamie anyway, when he could have been spending time with me?

I'd only seen him twice in the last week, I realized then. Realized too that I had been counting.

'He's kind,' said Danby. 'He likes you a lot. He'd be good to be away with.'

'I don't want to go away. I've got to know about Nick. About Nick and Isa. I need to know what's going on.'

'Chrissie, you don't need to know. Honestly. You need a break.'

I resisted the urge to ring Nick right away and find out exactly what it was that I didn't need to know, but decided not to. Not with Danby there. I lit my cigarette to consider Danby further, as he told me that his father had a cottage on the west coast of Ireland. He collected cigarettes from the floor at my feet, then stayed standing close to me. He needed a shave and looked handsome.

'But I don't know your father. Does Jamie?'

'He died three years ago. The place is partly mine. Anyone can stay there now, if I invite them.'

He smiled, the way he did. He said again how good it would be for me to get away. Everyone thought so, he said, and sat down so I stood up, but he took my hand, so I sat down again. I like to sit down to make a decision.

'Give it a go,' Danby said. 'If you don't like it you can come home.'

He let go of my hand. If he hadn't done that, things might have been different, but since he did, I stood up, threw my cigarette out of the window and said all right then, I'd go to his father's cottage with Jamie.

'Anything to make you happy,' I said.

He didn't look too happy, but he did kiss me very warmly goodbye.

Jamie had never been to Ireland before. It made him think of pictures of the moon, he said, as our bus laboured through seagull-coloured rocks that shouldered swirls of rough purple aside, then threw themselves back into the thick green sea.

We weren't sure where we were going but we knew we'd be there soon because it was five forty and we were due to arrive at Tully Cross at six. From there we must walk about two miles along the road to the west and visit a woman called Bridie in the first cottage on the right. She had the keys to Danby's father's cottage, which we had been told was a thatched building with a fireplace and running water and several good dry mattresses in the room at the top. Danby had drawn a map, which Jamie had in his drawstring khaki pocket with our cigarette lighter and a torch, which he thought would be useful.

There were fuchsia hedges squeezing out flowers that looked almost black on either side of us now and the mountain tops were slipping casually into the darkening sky, which was slithered with pink and something like lime. Jamie was holding my hand in the crack between our seats. He did that sometimes and sometimes I liked it. I didn't mind it just then. We were on the seat in front of the long one at the back, with our bags above and a woman in front whose hair was so thin you could see flesh through it.

She got off with us at Tully Cross, where there was a petrol station and a bar called Murphy's which was long and narrow inside, with bananas and nappies and bags of stuff in lumps and shelved groceries to pass by before the drinks began. Two men in old loose suits were there, watching their turn-ups, nursing glasses of Guinness. Jamie ordered some of the same for us and carried the glasses over to a black-topped table, where we drank through the scent of a bale of hay at our backs. I rolled a cigarette and wished I was somewhere else, but by the time we'd finished our drinks I could see how pleasant it was. I bought another round and carried it back to where Jamie was talking about Kenneth, who'd sent him £50 last week. He was half Irish himself, it seemed, with a Tipperary mother. I went to a wedding in Tipperary once, I remembered, and the bride was outraged because she couldn't buy Tampax in the only store. Jamie mustn't have liked the story, because he said we ought to be walking along. That's the trouble with men on holidays. They always want to be somewhere else just when you've decided you like it here.

'But we're on holiday,' I said.

'Exactly,' he told me, so I picked up my rucksack from the dusty boarded floor and went out into the emptiness without waiting for him.

It was half-past eight and blowy. A damp night, with a half moon and white buildings with thatch, which looked like slumped hairy animals, nestling gently here and there. We walked left, along the narrow hedged lane beside rustling noises and below occasional flitting shapes which Jamie said were bats. My new boots hurt my feet and my bag was steadily heavier. We didn't talk, just listened to our feet on the crunchy way. We could hear the sea after half an hour or so, and then there it was, a long white line against shimmering space, with the moon's reflection on it like it's meant to be. Jamie took my elbow as we stood to look, and then we held hands for the rest of the journey, until we saw a low shape, with lights in symmetrical patches, and knew we must have arrived at Bridie's.

Jamie went and knocked, while I sat on my bag and watched the sea make its silver edge roll haphazardly in, then out again. I heard an Irish accent growing insistent. I moved in closer to hear what Bridie was saying.

'George has the key,' she was explaining. 'It's George is there now, since Saturday last. Only where he is this evening I couldn't tell you at all.'

I went to Jamie's side. Bridie had a baby attached to her front, and was clearly very sleepy. She seemed pleased to see a female, as I'd hoped she might be. I explained that Daniel Boyle had said we might stay in the cottage and that she would have the key. He hadn't mentioned George, I said. Did George know Daniel's father?

'He did.'

She frowned into my face, as if I were asking something rather untoward, then she looked past me to sigh that indeed he did.

'They broke that gate together, the pair of them now.'

The three of us studied a horizontal collection of wooden slats on a gatepost by the side of her dwelling. She explained that we could get through that way to the cottage if we wanted, rather than going back onto the road. She looped up a blanket that had trailed from the baby and backed away into the lurid wallpaper of her room.

Through a thicket of flower heads that felt slightly wet

then, and a spiralled smell of burning turf, onto a path of sorts which led to a door in a bulging whitewashed wall. Jamie walked ahead and I followed his hunchback shape. He was carrying our sleeping bags. I watched him try the door handle a few times, then there was light flowing at my feet and he wasn't in front of me any more, but framed by a window with panes of cobwebbed glass. Then back silhouetted in the doorway again, waving for me to come in.

Inside was a good-sized reddish room with a couch and a fireplace filled with smoking lumps of soft black. There was a table with a litre bottle of wine on it, of which about a quarter had been drunk. By the fire was an upright chair with two shoes on it, not matching. A faded photograph of Piccadilly Circus hung above the table and there was a bookcase there too, with a few books on the middle shelf and a roost of empty bottles on top. The room was lit by a bare bulb in the corner, beyond which was a half-open door. There was a salty smell, which was fresh rather than stale, as damp cottages sometimes are.

Jamie poured wine into a mug which said Dad on it. He came to stand by me and we passed the cup between us with our backpacks still on. The hard light made Jamie's face look unfamiliar, so I walked to a mirror on the back wall to look at myself. I looked different too. Jamie kicked the fire and put more turf onto it from a pile next to some magazines. The top one was *Country Life*, September 1978.

I took off my rucksack, but not my coat, and went into the next room to find an electric ring, a sink and another table, on which was an open tin of corned beef and half a loaf of brown bread. There were nests of empty paper bags, a wineglass with cigarette ends in it, a frying pan on a single electric ring and a saucepan in the sink, floating with spaghetti. George must be used to a housekeeper/cook, or a wife and mother I decided. Or maybe he didn't mind squalor. He was on holiday, after all.

I went back to Jamie, who was drinking more wine. We sat on the couch together and I took my jumper out of my bag and spread it over our knees. After our third shared cup of alcohol I decided to make toast on the electric ring. There was a jar of peanut butter on the hearth rug. Jamie stirred it up with a fork and we were spreading our first burnt attempts when we heard boots on the mud outside. I threw my toast onto the fire, feeling instinctively guilty for our unexpected intrusion, and Jamie stood up and flattened his hair. He's at his best saying hello to strangers. Perhaps it's because his mother wasn't there when he was a child and it was up to him to make himself liked.

George was plump and bursting out of a yellow jumper, wearing a hat like Christopher Robin that framed his open round face. He looked about twelve, but was probably sixty. He spoke with a slight Dublin accent in a stammering way. He was holding a large carrier bag, which he unpacked as we explained who we were. It was filled mostly with egg boxes but had some seaweed at the bottom, which he hung on a nail by the window, where it trailed like a burnt-out lace curtain.

'I've been down to the seaside,' he beamed.

He smiled at everything he said and held his mouth the same through any reply, while his eyes moved blue around the room. He didn't seem to mind that we were there. He asked if I could poach eggs without using a poacher. I couldn't, but Jamie said he knew how, and George was delighted and rushed through to the kitchen and there was water running and banging pans, then he came back through with a beer mug and filled it with wine.

He sat on the hard chair near the flameless fire and explained that Mammy was dead. Two months ago tomorrow, he said. Passed away in the night. It was her car outside that we would have walked past on the way here. She'd left all she had for himself, he said. The house in Bray was all his now. We should visit Bray on our way home, he thought. He'd drive us up whenever we wanted.

'Do you drive at all, the pair of you? Do you not drink? Give your man a drink there, Chrissie. I've plenty more in the boot.'

Jamie said he'd see about poaching the eggs, but George said not at all, sit down now and drink. The eggs could wait till morning. It was breakfast he missed without Mammy, he said. They'd always eaten breakfast together.

'Even at the end,' he said and as 'the end' filled the room he smiled even wider and stared into my face, nodding slowly up and down. I passed him the wine. He took a trickle, then handed the bottle to Jamie. George liked Jamie more than me, I could tell. I suppose he sensed that he was more of a mother. I myself was hungry, with a desperation that he must have been almost able to touch if he'd been used to wanting anything physical himself. I watched my toast burn in the back of the grate as George talked on about Mammy and how he'd come here to get out of himself for a while. His neighbour had told him a change would do him good. He thought she was right. She generally was, he went on. Indeed, he didn't know what he'd have done without Maureen these past few months. He couldn't have gone on without her. Maureen was the neighbour, it seemed, and George had always told her everything, even at school, where he couldn't manage playtime.

After an hour or so I felt greatly for Maureen, who was selling up now and going to her sons in Liverpool, although she'd always lived next door to Mammy and himself. She was Mammy's oldest pal. Mammy herself was Ruth.

'My grandmother is called Ruth,' I interrupted.

Then, having a moment of smiling attention, 'Where would you like us to sleep? We were on the boat all yesterday night.'

He looked puzzled, so I was about to say something about Jamie and me, although I wasn't sure what, since we'd never said anything specific ourselves, but I assumed we might share a bedroom. We'd done that before, and it was clearly going to be cold upstairs in the cottage.

'I mean, we're rather tired,' was all I came up with.

'Was your granny Irish?' George said. 'Ruth is a lovely name.'

I kicked Jamie's leg, so he too asked about a possible bedroom, which horrified George. We mustn't think of going up now. We'd hardly got started. As if we'd let him down by arriving late for Christmas, or he'd just got back from boarding school with a term time of apple-pie beds to tell. He threw turf firmly onto the fire. He found a firelighter under his chair and threw that in too, although there was nothing to ignite it. We stayed up until a quarter to two, which was when George fell asleep.

The room I woke into had wallpaper with lilac sprigs and patches of damp like a child's wet sheet. Grey electric cable hung all about and there was a window with a curly clasp that looked out onto a blotting-paper sky. I could hear the sea and a donkey, which sounded in pain, but Jamie said that was the noise donkeys made. He had his hand on my upturned tummy, through my clothes that I mustn't have taken off because I'd been asleep before we left the couch. I had a headache that I pressed into his neck, which was my favourite bit of him, and then we made love, which surprised us, since we hadn't done that since the farmhouse, and I thought we wouldn't again somehow. We were quite pleased, though, and I felt fonder of him then and happy to be there on an uneven mattress underneath unwashed blankets with my knees between his. I said I wished I had a house and he said, 'I'll get one for you,' which we both knew wouldn't be true. It was seven o'clock and I never woke up at that hour, but there was thudding from downstairs and the donkey louder as the banging front door of the building took George out then back in again.

Jamie unnerved me by rolling onto the floor, then getting

briskly up and about, tucking shirt into waistband and jerking the laces of his boots into shape. I was annoyed.

'Why are you getting up now? We're on holiday. Aren't you tired? Haven't you got a headache?'

'I had but it's gone now.' He kissed the inside of my arm. 'And I've got eggs to poach.' He tried to ruffle my hair, but I did it myself and stayed annoyed at everything until I fell back asleep.

By mid-day, when I went downstairs, both Jamie and George were out. The room with the couch where we'd sat the night before was filled with a light that made me glad I had it to myself. An end-of-year sea-glaze that made all the darks darker and everything white hard to look at. The door was ajar onto a sweep of mountains outside, their tops tingling like the shadows in Impressionist paintings and then to the left there was nothing but sea.

When I got down to the waves I found there was sand before the sea began, of course, but you couldn't see that from the cottage. The beach was empty, with rippling brown weed blown across it and clean waves that broke far out then grazed in in an inquisitive, cheerful way. The emptiness was a shock, but there could really only have been Bridie there, or her children or man, because hers was the only other dwelling to see. I paddled and picked up shells and weed, then moved around the space in an aimless way, like a dog that's been let out of a car.

Back again at the cottage I found the note the men had left for me and I opened all the windows that weren't painted up. I made toast and ate it slowly. I read a book called *In Search of Ireland*, written in 1934, which was dedicated 'to the raking of the fire, and the new flame in the morning', and described the long-legged girls in scarlet dresses who crowded this western coast, who were pretty and giggled and spoke only a musical Irish. Perhaps Jamie and George would be meeting some of these delightful creatures now on their shopping trip to Clifden.

I raked the fire. I looked in George's room. He was reading *Piccadilly Jim* by P. G. Wodehouse and drinking litre bottles of wine through the night to judge by the empties shining and stained around the floor. Leaning on the dusty dressing-table mirror was a photograph of a woman in a hat holding the arm of a plump child, wearing his smile, who must have been him. His eyes were exactly the same. Mammy looked as if she was in love with whoever was taking the photo. George hadn't mentioned a daddy so far.

At a quarter to two the car came back. My fondness for Jamie had melted somewhat by now and I felt unfriendly at best towards George. They were flushed and boisterous, after lunch in a pub, where the barman had taken a liking to Jamie and wanted to know all about him. I said there must be a lot I didn't know, to judge by the time they had taken, and I took the cake they'd bought me to eat on the doorstep with my back to the room. Jamie came to crouch nearby and asked if I'd like to go for a walk. George had suggested a nice afternoon plan. He would drive us to a good place to start, then collect us at the end in a different village. The man in the pub said it was beautiful up there, and George thought we'd like it.

'I'm surprised George can bear to let you go,' I said through cake with bitterness. 'What if he needs a poached egg?'

Jamie stood up, saying it was up to me, as you might to a sulky child, so I felt foolish and wished I'd said yes. It would be nice to go for a walk. We were on holiday and that was the sort of thing people on holidays do.

Then George was over, saying we should be away and was Jamie warm enough and what about socks? His all needed washing, he said, but he couldn't get the water here hot.

'I'm sure Jamie will fix something up,' I said.

Then I went upstairs to put plasters on yesterday's blisters and force my own socks into the constraint of boots. I decided to enjoy the walk.

Jamie walked beside me for the first half-hour of cliff-top, over grass with leaves that were different widths all the time and threads of white undergrowth, like an old person's hair, which burst into fluff as it brushed our legs. We had our eyes on the mauve skin of headland ahead that seemed always the same distance away, but that we knew must come to us before swinging round for the last stretch of our journey. We were to meet George by a stile at the end of the track at five o'clock.

By half-past three the weather had changed. The sea to our left rippled more brown than blue, then a blood-grey as the sky seemed to join the rocks, and the ground we were on grew lumpy and tough. It was called sheep grass, Jamie told me. Clinging to high, tight knots of earth that would suddenly dip six inches or so and were impossible to move over properly. It was like having to walk with one leg longer than the other. Jamie was in front of me with his head down and the back of his neck in his wrinkled hood, turning sometimes to see how far I was trailing and waiting a while, which was meant to be kind but soon came to seem a reproach. I told him to stop watching me. He went on ahead too fast then, until I stumbled and twisted my ankle. I had to call to him to wait while I sat down and rubbed it. He tried to rub it too, but I pushed him away.

'We could have got there by now if you hadn't been so long in the pub,' I shouted, which seemed to make sense. 'Then this would never have happened.'

I felt splats of rain, which made perfect sense too, given the colour of the sky.

'George must have known it was going to rain. He shouldn't have made us come. You shouldn't have agreed to be driven to this wilderness.'

Jamie took my arm silently to help me up. I hobbled along

with him at my left elbow now, on the edge of the cliff that fell down to the sea. He watched our feet and said nothing. He should have been agreeing with me that George had meant all this to happen. They both must have known that we never could get where we were meant to be in the time they'd arranged. It was almost five already, and it looked as if we were exactly where we had always been.

By five thirty the headland was still the same long way away and it was raining steadily. My ankle was swollen and Jamie was trying to help me walk faster and I was hating Ireland. I made us sit down for a rest and we tried to light cigarettes, but the flame wouldn't stay on the lighter and the damp air on our fingers made them useless and bent. It would be dark in half an hour, Jamie said. He said he wasn't sure what we could do, which frightened me.

'We'll have to keep walking,' I told him. 'That's all we can do, isn't it?'

So we moved on through a wind now too, and held each other's arms and said nothing because there was nothing at all to say and the noise of the wind was tiring.

I was beginning to feel tearful and was trying to imagine what would happen if we were in an Enid Blyton story to cheer myself up when there was a noise slowly growing above the uneven weather, then something that could only happen to the Famous Five really did arrive. A little boat was chugging steadily across the inlet below. There were two orange-clad shapes down inside it and Jamie was taking off his jacket suddenly, which seemed crazy until I saw him rushing down the hillside shouting, 'Help! Stop! Help!' waving his arms madly up into the misty air.

'Help! We're stuck,' he was shouting, turning back to me with his eyes very wide, waving his jacket above his head, moving fast away and down so I lost sight of him as I dragged my jumper over my head to wave as well. I shouted, 'Help!'

repeatedly too, like Jamie was, but mine came out as if I didn't mean it at all. I don't think I'd ever actually had to say the word 'Help' out loud before.

On the other side of the bay, where the men in the boat dropped us from the cosy instability of their slippery craft, there was a track which had an abandoned bicycle lying across it, as incongruous as a scar of graffiti somehow after the emptiness of the mountain. We'd been assured by the fishermen that we would get to a pub if we walked for ten minutes or so, but it took much longer than that with my injured ankle and the glowering silence between us. We weren't in possession of glasses of Guinness until ten to seven, by the tall grandfather clock of Mallory's bar, where a fine-featured red setter slumped under one of the only three tables in the place.

We were starving, so Jamie bought peanuts which had no salt on them, although the packet insisted they had. I complained until Jamie told me to shut up, which amazed me. I was pleased in a perverse way that he was as annoyed and tired of me as I was of him, but then I realized it was George he was preoccupied with rather than my bad mood.

'We'll have to let him know we're here. He'll be incredibly worried.'

Jamie was stroking his nose, like he does when he's upset. He explained that George would be waiting for us by the stile and assuming we were dead. He might have got the rescue people out. He'd be panicking and thinking he'd killed us.

'He'll be desperate,' he assured me, as he finished his drink. 'He already thinks he made his mother die.'

'Most people's mothers die,' I replied. 'Especially if they're into their nineties.'

Jamie said that wasn't the point.

'You're being obtuse,' he said, and the word surprised me, so I was silent as he continued that he understood George very well by now. George would be worried, he insisted, which was bad because George thought he couldn't take care of people, which was why his mother was no longer alive. I emptied my glass and agreed that George did not seem particularly careful of the lives of those around him. If he'd set out to murder us he couldn't have done much better. George couldn't look after a donkey, I said.

'He's probably drinking in Tully Cross by now,' I went on, 'or getting Bridie to help him heat up a can of soup. If he hasn't gone back up to Bray that is.'

I finished my drink and banged the glass to the table.

'He obviously wanted us out of the way. Well, he wanted me to not be there. He made that quite clear. I'm not obtuse enough not to have noticed that about your dear friend George. Why didn't you go for a walk with him instead of me, since you're so concerned for his welfare?'

Jamie stood up, fumbling in various pockets for money and said I was being childish. Couldn't I stop thinking of myself for once in my life? The man's mother was dead. Did I have no proper feelings for people? He was surprised at me. I said since he hardly knew me that wasn't surprising. There are other griefs besides death to be dealt with in life, I said. If he'd had any himself he might not be being so sentimental.

'People's mothers die. People learn to look after themselves,' I said, and he said I didn't seem much good at it so far.

'Shall I get you another drink?' he asked, with what was meant to be sarcasm, and I said I'd do it myself and went on my uneven legs to the bar and waited for attention, wondering why I'd left London and if Nick was looking after Isa, bringing her tea to bed in the morning. He used to bring me tea in bed. He didn't mind looking after me sometimes. I looked after him as well. But we didn't expect each other to take care of everyone we met.

I bought Jamie a pint, although he always drank halves. He

asked if I was trying to make him sick. I said there would be little point in that, since he was the one looking after the world. He was the one who cared, after all. The one with proper feelings. Then I sat down and watched his eyes. We hadn't had an argument before.

He asked me then what I cared about, anyway, scanning a photograph of Bobby Kennedy on the wall to our right, smiling and carelessly handsome. Taped country music started up, too soft to hear but too loud to ignore. I pushed peanuts into groups of three and remembered asking my sister what she cared about once, when she appeared not to care about me.

'Myself,' I told Jamie, 'like everyone else does.'

Then it was Tammy Wynette suddenly much too loud, singing 'Stand By Your Man' in her raspy way. I listened for a while, then continued that I cared mostly about my ankle just now, and Jamie glared into me across the cigar-box gloom as if I'd said I liked to stub cigarettes out on the clean firm fronts of plump babies.

'We're on holiday,' I reminded him. He said I made him sick. Someone turned Tammy down and I went to the telephone, which had buttons on the front that shone like policemen's whistles in Buster Keaton films. I asked an ancient lady operator if she could arrange for a taxi to be sent to where we were. She knew it by the phone number, which was Illaunmore 17 and she was reassuringly concerned about the broken ankle that I insisted must get back to Tully Cross tonight.

'You rest that now,' she advised. 'You take care of yourself now, so.'

She would send himself, she said, right away, now so. Himself drove the local taxi cab, and drove it very swiftly too, because it was at the door of the pub before the speakers' next muffled tune was through.

*

Danby's father's cottage was full of smoke and a pea-green blur of steamy canned food, along with the low droning noise of Bridie's baby, which she was cradling, pacing slowly about the room. On the couch a small girl was doggedly eating from a large bowl of mashed potatoes, and beside her was a man in a cream woollen cap, nursing a glass of red wine. Nearest the fire was George, bleary and staring, unaware for a moment that we had arrived. When he noticed he rushed to hold Jamie to him. Jamie hugged him vigorously back. After that George patted me on the back, then he patted the man in the hat. He was visiting Bridie, who was his sister, I was told later on that night.

Having satisfactorily expressed his pleasure at our safety, George resumed his seat to continue with a story of a bar in Letterfrack, where he'd sheltered, hoping for news of us, when the storm had started up. A man there had had his groceries stolen from the back of his bicycle, which he'd left leaning against the selfsame pub. Bridie's brother was shocked at this information and refilled his glass to steady himself. George nodded and drank and smiled at the random facts of his travels. He explained that he'd bought the poor man a drink or two and shared with him the end of Mammy and how much he missed her now. The amazing thing was that the man had known Mammy, from Molly's bakery up there in Bray, where he'd gone often as a boy. Bridie's baby stopped crying at this coincidence. Bridie herself stood behind the couch, rocking slightly, smiling apprehensively at me, holding the handle of a saucepan in her substantial free hand.

Jamie helped himself to another drink and sat down on the couch next to the child with the potatoes, which caused her to stop eating and stand up. She rushed to cling to her mammy's leg, which caused the pan Bridie was holding to slip to the floor. I was given the baby to hold then, along with the little hand of the whimpering girl, while Bridie went to the kitchen to get a cloth to wipe up the spilled slop from the pan. She thought it a shame that her dog was not with her, and I agreed, but was able to reassure her that there would be no stain on the much-marked carpet.

George remembered how good warm doughnuts had once tasted, and opened another bottle of wine. Jamie laughed at something and looked about twelve, like he did sometimes, and the man in the hat slapped more turf on the fire.

'I'll be taking the children away inside then,' said Bridie, repossessing her infant.

'Will I now, George?' Neither George nor the other man answered. She looked at me as if I might know what she must do next, which I thought I did. She must take her children home, so I offered to carry the baby there for her and she smiled and looked about ninety and glad, which made me glad too as she passed her child back to me. It was nice to have a baby to hold.

As Bridie and her little girl and I with my warm lump of baby made our way from Danby's father's cottage to hers, the donkey brayed from wherever he slept. He was the only creature to mark our departure. He must have been woken by the scrape of the gate that Danby's father had broken, that Bridie rarely walked through and that I myself did not pass through again until the next wet, salty morning, when I took myself back to find all the men still asleep just as we'd left them in their various chairs. I decided to teach myself to poach eggs without using a poacher. When I'd learnt how to do that, I learnt how to walk on a twisted ankle and I took myself down to the open sea. I had some plans to make.

Eight Monkstown

WHEN I TRAVELLED FROM THE WEST COAST OF IRELAND TO Dublin, I went by myself, with a biography of Constance Markievicz to read, because hers was apparently 'an independent life'. As I stepped down from the soporific heights of the coach I looked up at a clock to find that it was half past five, which was just as it should be, and the street was full and warm with noise. The darkening light smelled of wet newspaper, peat and cigarettes, which I had run out of, so I went into a shop and chose a packet that had a line from Robert Burns across the top. Outside again, I bumped into a man with a half-up umbrella and we stood together, like an illustration from Dickens, as I asked where I might find a number 8 bus. He directed me to North Baggot Street, which sounded suitably sturdy and was along by the green, he said, so I turned through the closing of office hours, through the glitter of windows and scrawling gulls, through door-step voices and the comfort of municipal litter, to find myself obstructed outside the door of a pub, by a man with a suitcase battling through large children with pushchairs.

I stepped through swing doors into the bar and ordered whiskey in an independent way. Now I could telephone Crystal and let her know where I was. Crystal's name was actually Christine, like mine, but Danby had said not to call her that. She had been his girlfriend a long time ago. She was the mother of Lily and had lived in India and Sydney and the Dingle Peninsula, but was now temporarily resting in the suburb of Monkstown. Danby had suggested that I go and see her, on a postcard he had sent to his father's cottage from Lisbon.

'Why not check out Crystal on your way back through Dublin?' I'd read on the doorstep of my temporary Connemara home the day after I'd twisted my ankle. 'Forty-two Rock Road. She loves people from London.' Then, 'Telephone 427768, I think,' in different-coloured biro underneath. I did think Danby might have put something more intimate than 'See you, D' at the end of this communication, but I was glad to get it anyway. Jamie had decided to hitch-hike to Galway to see some cousin of his in a monastery there, and since George had departed for an aunt in Cork, Dublin seemed the best place for me to go next. It was in the opposite direction to both of them.

I lifted my whiskey from the bar and moved through the pub's eiderdown gloom to sit in an armchair next to the fire. I drank slowly, watching smoke pass into the beaten pewter of an art-nouveau fireplace and I wondered if Crystal might shape my life.

A long-haired dog came and slumped by my feet. A boy wandered in with the *Irish Times* spilling out of a sack almost as long as his legs. There were no women in the room, I realized, but I was a foreigner, so didn't feel out of place. I could leave whenever I wanted. Or I could stay there for hours if I wanted, because there was no one to please but myself. I could join the Communist party. Crystal had been a member once, Danby had told me. She'd been to the Soviet Union on a revolutionary holiday. But she'd be at home in Monkstown all tonight, I knew, because I'd rung her from the country to ask if I could stay a few days. Her accent was Australian and her voice very smiley. I'd explained that I'd met

Lily in London, but was vague about my connection with Danby. At six fifteen I finished my drink and went to the payphone on the corner of the bar. Crystal answered immediately and told me that I could be with her in under an hour, which was good, because she thought we'd go out again about nine. Her smile stayed intact through the directions she gave. She sounded as if she issued them every few hours.

A bus was waiting for me when I got to the stop and the driver called out to me when Kenny's Bar had been reached, as Crystal had promised he would, and number 42 was on the corner of Rock Road, next to the broken lamp-post she had described. I could smell the sea straight away, and assumed it must be at the end of Crystal's long sloping road, because there was nothing at all to see once the stately stone squares of the dwellings were over. The area must once have been well-to-do, but was ramshackle now, with milk cartons on window sills and ill-fitting curtains and beer cans rolling free down the wide steps that I walked up to press the second-but-one bell on the left.

I pressed the bell twice, then a light glowed above the door and the number four and a bit of a two was silhouetted in black against the white of the oblong glass. I prepared myself to greet Crystal robustly, but she didn't open the door. My sister did. She was dressed in one of my old jumpers and a pair of black jeans that bagged off her legs, which seemed endless although she's only five foot two, like I am. She'd had her hair cut short and dyed darker, which made her neck look almost transparently thin and her eyes enormous and unfamiliar, but it was Isa all right, although she couldn't really have been there. She couldn't know who Crystal was. She hardly knew Lily, as far as I knew, although Jamie had told me she rang the houseboat sometimes to find out if Nick was there, which he rarely was. Isa was supposed to be in London, in love with Nick. For a moment I wondered if he might be here too.

Perhaps they were on holiday together. But Danby would have known and told me not to come. Unless he didn't know.

Isa stood on the doorstep, not saying a thing. She stared at me as if I couldn't be really there either, so I asked her what she was doing here, which came out very high-pitched, and she said, 'I don't know,' and sort of jammed herself against me, like a large slab of cardboard, so I almost fell back down the steps.

'I'm on holiday,' she said then into my shoulder.

I would have asked why she had chosen to come on mine, but our hostess was suddenly with us. I had to smile over the boniness of Isa and seem relaxed to be hugging this stranger who was Crystal's guest and my sister.

Crystal had bare feet and a kimono with herons embroidered all over and a towel around her shoulders, on which the longest hair I'd seen for years was splayed out in a straggle of wet.

'Surprise, surprise,' she lilted in her Australian way. She was about six foot tall. 'Are you guys OK? Wow, you look so samey.'

She seemed pleased that we were a pair of guests now, and smiled down as if she'd just met our plane or was about to give us some coaching.

'Come on up. You find us OK?'

She swung my bag up under a spindle of chiffony arm as her towel fell to the floor. I picked it up and found I was stuck with it because she had her free arm around Isa by then; her hand a clutter of puzzle rings draped over where my sister had breasts the last time I'd seen her.

'So, Chrissie, you found us OK?'

Crystal kicked the door to slam it shut and adjusted my bag on her hip.

'It was simple,' I said into Isa's back as we started off in a line up the threadbare stairs. I watched my bag bobbing on up ahead, like something thrown overboard that I had to rescue. I noticed that the back of my jumper on Isa's narrow back had moth holes all over it, which I had never seen before.

'That's just what your sister said,' Crystal shouted back at me. 'But some people end up all over.'

The flat was filled with drifting incense and bacon-sandwich smells and had a stainless-steel rail of slippery garments just inside the hall door. I knew Nick wasn't there as soon as we got to the top of the stairs. I could tell if he was in a house I'd arrived at. There were bits of stairways in three different places and the narrow corridor with its scuffed scarlet walls had undulating floorboards that creaked like a ship as we made our orderly way to a room with bare windows that was cooler than outside. Our hostess did something to a free-standing gas heater and told us to sit down, but I didn't want to. I didn't want to commit myself to anything just yet.

'You guys catch up while I dress, why don't you?'

Crystal picked up a Siamese cat and caressed its concave frame, watching my face, then dropped it onto the couch next to Isa and lit a cigarette from a pack on the marble mantelpiece, which had bits of lace draped along it. My cigarettes were in my bag, which had been left in the hall, so I went to collect them, and when I came back Isa was smoking too, which I'd never seen before.

'Did you paint all these?' I said to stop myself watching my sister.

The walls were covered with crudely done paintings, with the same indeterminate animal floating towards all their tops, seeming alarmed to be in them. I hoped Crystal would say she had not.

'That's the first thing your sister asked too,' she said, blowing smoke at the ceiling through smile.

'I guess if you paint, then it's paintings you see first.' Her hair dripped onto the cat. 'I notice pots in a room. I'm a potter. Or used to be. I'm kind of buying jewellery now though.'

I looked around for pots, then instinctively to Isa, to give me a clue where there were some, but she was engrossed in picking at the fabric around a tear on her knee.

'I don't really paint. I'm a textile designer. Isa's the painter,' I said and she looked up at her own name and took a drag on her cigarette in an off-hand way. I was struck by her fingers around it, which looked like something in a child's drawing. I wished she wasn't there. She looked ill.

'How's the wine bar?' I asked, for Crystal's sake mostly. 'Is everyone back from the summer by now?'

I'd have liked to ask where she was living, exactly, how Charlie was, when she'd last seen Nick, how she'd managed to be here the same time as I was, and why, but there wasn't any point saying anything just then. We were guests. She was picking a scab on her trousers.

I said, 'Does anyone want a drink?'

I had a litre of red wine in my rucksack, which George had given me before we parted at the cottage. No one answered, so I explained the wine in more detail and how I happened to have it and Crystal frowned, which suited her narrow features, and asked if Danby's father's cottage was still the same. She used to stay there with Danby before Lily was born.

'In fact, Lily was conceived in that room at the top. Is that where you slept, Chrissie? That room with the window?'

I watched Isa drop her cigarette stub into a cup of tea, then glance up guiltily to see if Crystal had seen her. It seemed a healthy sign of social responsibility.

'Are the urns still there? Did you like them?' I wasn't sure what urns she meant, but said yes they were great and where would I find a corkscrew?

'It's good for sex that cottage, isn't it, though? I mean, Danby's practically impotent, as I suppose you're aware?'

Isa looked up at the mention of sex. The word seemed to scare her. She left the room, which made Crystal guess that she must be having a scene with Danby, but I said she certainly was not. The idea annoyed me, I noticed.

'She's a bit jumpy around me, either way.' Crystal repossessed the cat. 'I guess she needs a drink.'

She left the room too and I looked out of the window and watched a woman inside the opposite house holding a baby, and a man come and hand her something, then move out of sight again, rubbing his head, then come back and move his mouth through words to what looked like laughter. His shirt-sleeves were rolled up and there was a towel over his shoulder.

'Yes, Lily was conceived in that cottage.' Crystal's voice came into the room before she did. 'I know that for a fact.'

She fingered an elaborate corkscrew and smiled right into my eyes, as if she liked me a lot, which made me feel awkward. The wine I had with me was still in the hall.

'Yep. Looks like Georgie Porgie's all right,' she said when I came back with the bottle.

'Does he still drink a litre of this junk every hour?'

I laughed at that and said more or less.

'But he's in grief just now, so I assumed that was a contributory factor. Mammy died a few months ago.'

Isa came back and sat where she'd been and took a cigarette from up her sleeve.

'Who is Mammy? How did she die?' she said, as if there was something suspicious about it, and Crystal said pills and whisky and a flight of stairs would be her guess, then the telephone rang and the cat crawled under the couch and Crystal told the phone about George's mother's death and I felt as if I'd told a secret that I'd promised I wouldn't. I'd be a hopeless Communist.

'Mammy was George's mother, and George is a man who

was staying with Jamie and me in the place I've just been,' I explained to Isa to put the situation into perspective.

'He drinks all the time. He liked Jamie a lot.'

'Does Jamie still like you?'

I stared at her. It wasn't a question I'd asked myself.

'Everyone still likes you, don't they?'

Crystal stopped talking on the telephone.

'We're hitting the bright lights, girls. Doheny and Nesbitts at ten,' she smiled. 'We're retrieving a hat there. So how about this glass of wine? Do you guys want to wash?'

Isa went out of the room again.

When Crystal and I left the house we left by ourselves. My sister had decided to watch TV. She was expecting a phone call, she said, which I didn't really believe. I know when Isa isn't telling the truth, but I was glad she was staying behind. She'd drunk two large glasses of wine and her face had gone red, like it does, before it goes a startling white if she follows her drinking through.

'Are you going with Crystal?' she'd asked me as I applied my lipstick, which was now oval in shape, having been in my back pocket all the way from Connemara.

'Why not?' I said, although I could see why partly from her face, pulled over its bones, and her eyes in it, needing, and her fingers working her thumbs, but I hadn't asked her to come here. She should have stayed in London. She shouldn't have done whatever she wanted for as long as I could remember.

'You'll be fine. You've got your phone call to wait for, anyway.'

'Sure. My phone call. I've still got that.'

She laughed in a way she used to, which wasn't like laughing at all, then Crystal came through and told Isa to remember not to let Lucky out. Her hair was now plastic-wrap dry and stacked up above the weight of her earrings. I lifted the cat onto Isa's lap and wrapped her arms around it, which felt like sticking down a parcel.

'See you later,' I said, and stroked Lucky's nose bone, which was easier than touching Isa goodbye.

Crystal's shoes were velvet, so we had to walk in careful zigzags so as not to get them wet. She took my arm sometimes, to steady her progress and also to consolidate our shared concerns. Was Isa always this way? Should she be travelling right now? Was I planning to shape her up? She'd been weeping when she'd arrived, she said. She could've understood it if she'd got lost or something, but she had a perfect map with her that Lily had drawn, although how Lily knew it, Crystal hadn't a clue. Her daughter never bothered to cross the Irish Sea, she said. Only phoned every other blue moon. She'd brought her up to look out for herself, she said. She liked independence in a woman.

'I mean I can handle it, you know. Don't get me wrong, Chrissie, but I was kind of expecting it to be you at the door there when Isa arrived.' She took my arm as the pavement scooped itself into a pool. 'I mean, I like surprises, but not if they're howling. Know what I mean?' I nodded and made an Mmm sound that came out as a growl. She dropped my arm.

'I mean, I was in the bath when the doorbell rang, on the phone to some guy whose wife's just got cancer. Then she arrives and gives me this hard time, you know? I mean, I thought she was you. So what? Why bawl about that?'

'When did she arrive exactly?'

'About this time last night, I guess. I mean, I was in the bath, you know. I didn't check on the time.'

Crystal stopped talking to drag up the collar of her blue leather coat. I'd had one like it once, but Isa donated it to one of her friends.

'So how's Lily shaping up anyhow? How's my little girl? Has she got some OK friends over there in London?'

I wasn't sure how to answer. I was one of Lily's friends myself, as far as I knew.

'So what are your sister's plans, anyway?' We had stopped on a crumbled kerb. 'Does she know anyone in Dublin?'

Crystal shouted above headlights and tyres on mashed leaves. I had no idea what Isa's plans were. I hadn't had a conversation with her for over two months, but I didn't tell Crystal that, although there was really no reason not to. I said Isa would most probably be going down to see some friends in Galway.

'They live in an old monastery,' I explained. 'Artists and people. Potters. That sort of thing.'

'Cool,' said Crystal.

We crossed the road. We waited in silence, as cars driven by men with moustaches passed by until a number 8 swayed towards us in high yellow-white, and the orange of a bus became clear through the rain and then I said I thought I'd changed my mind. Crystal better go into Dublin without me.

'I've got my period,' I explained as I helped her onto the bus. I watched the lights of its back until they weren't there any more, and then I watched the black shine of the road for a while as I realized for the second time that day that I hadn't had a period for too long now. It could be the travelling, I decided, and all the troubles I'd had.

Back at number 42 Isa opened the door wearing Crystal's dressing gown. She had a towel around her head and a cigarette in her hand. She didn't seem surprised that I'd come home alone. There was still some wine, she mumbled, so I poured myself a glass as she dissolved herself into the couch. She was paler than even she could have become. She struck a match and watched it burn down to her fingers and said she knew I'd be back. She said it as you accuse someone of stealing your passport or locking you out of their house.

'I knew you couldn't bear me to be here by myself.' She struck another match. 'You had to talk to him, didn't you, once you found out?'

'Found out what?'

Who is 'him'? I could have asked, but did not. I knew who 'he' must be, although not yet why he'd be ringing Crystal's house. If he was coming to see Isa, she might as well say so, since she'd already been to Greece with him. And if he was coming to see me, he was mad. He'd been to Greece with my sister.

The wine had flaky bits in it that could have been metal, which stuck to the back of my teeth. Isa blew at her flame and stared at the television, where there was no volume but someone eating on a riverbank. She said nothing for a while, then mumbled what I already knew, which was that Nick was going to phone.

'Well, it might be tonight or it might be tomorrow, but he'll be telephoning this house very soon.'

'Why's he doing that? He doesn't know Crystal. Have you got plans you haven't told me yet? Isn't London enough for you and Nick? Do you need to be everywhere I am?' How typical of her to ruin this for me. Now I'd have to find somewhere else to go.

'Stupid,' Isa said. 'He's ringing to talk to you. He doesn't know I'm here, does he? As if you didn't know.'

I stared that I had no idea. I didn't know what she was talking about, I said, so she started to tell me. Nick knew where I was, she said. He'd heard about me going to Ireland with Jamie and he'd been on the phone to Danby in Lisbon and he knew I'd be here about now and he was coming to Dublin to find me, and he'd be bound to be calling tonight, and could she answer it please?

'Let me speak to him, Chrissie. Please. Just once. Just let me say something to him.' She swerved towards me for a second with her war-zone-photograph eyes, and I felt slightly frightened, so I said all right, she could.

'OK,' I said like Crystal would. 'Answer the phone if you want to.'

I couldn't believe it would ring anyway, or that it would do her any good if it did, if Nick was really ringing to talk to me. But I didn't know if I believed that, either, as she said, 'Thanks, Chrissie. I love him, you see,' she said then, and she picked at her trousers as I watched, and thought maybe it could be true. She could love Nick, after all. He could have made her love him. He might have wanted her to. And if he had, then he had only himself to blame for the fact that she loved him back after he'd changed his mind.

I sat opposite her at the other end of the couch for the next hour or so, as if we were just people on a couch at home, as if we were often in this room together, absorbed in ourselves, not saying something sometimes. Isa smoked and studied her legs and glanced at the television set and occasionally looked at her watch. If she looked at me I pretended to be watching television, which I'd made so you could hear it. I didn't want to ask anything specific to provoke her into shouting, which I could see was a distinct possibility. Although maybe it wasn't her shouting I was afraid of, but rather the lack of it. She didn't look as if she had the strength to do much more than whisper. I wished she'd be normal. I wished I was in London, or Russia perhaps. I wished I had some independent plan and I wondered if you could be independent without people thinking you were selfish. I wondered if I wanted to talk to Nick. I thought that I probably didn't, any more. I thought of ringing Danby in Lisbon and asking for advice, but realized that my using the phone would make Isa nervous. She was looking at it every other minute.

About ten thirty she got out some duty-free whisky, from her old bag, which was once our mother's. She said she'd bought the Scotch for Nick, but it looked as if she wouldn't be seeing him now that I was here.

'I suppose I'll have to go home when he comes to see you,' she said as she opened the bottle, using an old piece of lace to get a grip on the metal.

'You can give what's left of it to him from me.'

She poured a large glass for herself, then started to cry, then stopped. She drank most of her glass down in one. I had some myself as we both watched the phone, which I began to wish intensely would ring so I could make him talk to her. I tried telepathy to Nick, but no one rang that night except for Crystal, and that was long after Isa had passed out, which was just after she'd decided to talk to me.

I woke up at eight thirty the next morning with an immediate panic inside me, as if it was an exam day and I hadn't revised, or I'd smashed someone's car up and driven off without stopping. Something had gone wrong last night, and I must have done it. Isa wasn't right, anyway, and it was all my fault. I lay still and tried to calm down. I looked at the leaves intertwined around the moulded ceiling's central rose, which would be good to use in a design some day, and I thought about Isa and Nick. Mostly it was Isa I dwelt on. She was in a very bad way, which was not my fault, of course, but perhaps it was my responsibility now. I thought I must do something, but I couldn't see what, as the cat scratched at my dark pink door, meowing pitifully. I was supposed to be feeding her, but there was no food. I wasn't quite used to being badly needed. It seemed to require more thought than being needy did.

Isa was asleep in Crystal's room along the hallway. One thing I could do would be to get up right away and leave before she saw me, but that would mean missing Nick and not telling him what he ought to do. It was me he was coming to see, Isa had told me, although she was here to see him too. She seemed to think somehow that she was here instead of me, that she had simply to take my place here to set everything right. She'd made it all sound very straightforward before she started being sick. Like the plot of a magazine story, with myself as the central character, ruining lives and winning through. She wasn't exactly the heroine, though. She was bad, she explained, because she'd had an abortion and stolen a man from the woman he'd loved all along, and she didn't know why she had come, except that it had seemed the obvious thing to do after she'd heard Nick on the phone, trying to arrange to fly to Dublin.

'Trying to get away from me, you see?' she explained, and I nodded blindly, while she found a pill in her trouser pocket and washed it down with whisky.

'Sorry,' she said. 'It'll calm me down.'

I asked her how long she'd been taking pills. It came out in a motherly tone of voice, which I hadn't exactly intended but was reassuring to hear.

'A while,' she said. 'Since the abortion maybe. Since Nick told me to go back to Charlie's. Since I stopped going to bed. Since you stopped talking to me. Since I got them really.'

She might be going to cry again, but she took some whisky and sniffed and looked firmly back at me. I smiled, like the nurse in our local surgery. She looked green by now. I hoped she wouldn't throw up on the carpet.

'Nick said I could stay on in his house if I wanted, though. Till I'd sorted everything out with everyone else.'

She spoke into the floor with her knees pulled up, like the bits of a chair that she couldn't fold flat and had to hold in place. I wasn't sure who 'everyone else' might be, but didn't feel like asking, like I didn't feel like saying I knew how she felt. I wondered anyway if I did.

'Nick wasn't unkind. He just doesn't like me being with him any more. He says I'm being silly. About the baby, I mean.

And he's never home when I'm there now. He left me a spare set of keys, but he never comes back any more. I waited up all night to see him before I got on the boat-train. Before I came to see Crystal. He left me the keys. Do you think Crystal likes me?'

'You've got my keys to Nick's house now, you mean,' I said without thinking.

'What day was that?' she said. 'How long have we been here?'

I didn't like the way she and I'd become 'we', but she chose that moment to start being sick, so I took her along to the bathroom, running, like people who've just escaped from a car crash, and she told me to leave her there, so I did, although she probably didn't want me to. I heard her going to bed some time later, but didn't go to say goodnight. I imagined she might not let me leave her alone. She might decide to murder me, for all I knew.

It must have been about midnight when Crystal rang. The television had ended. I was drinking hot chocolate, made mostly with water since there was only a dribble of milk. I was wondering how Isa had got in such a bad way. If it was Nick or the baby she didn't have, or me or my mother, or something else entirely that no one could wonder about. Then Crystal rang to tell me about her own spare set of keys, and how I must use them from now on throughout the weekend because she was not coming home. The keys were in the top left-hand drawer of the chest in Crystal's bedroom, where my sister was deeply asleep. Our hostess had met some old friends during the course of the night and been invited back to their place in the Wicklow Mountains.

'I need some space,' she explained. 'I need to breathe.'

As if we were married and she was tunnelling out.

'Is that cool with you?'

It was, I said warmly. Of course it was fine. Trying to sound the right mixture of envy and unselfish pleasure at her plans. I hoped she wouldn't ask me to go too.

'Make yourselves at home.' She'd smiled through the hum of the phone line and pub-closing-time voices. 'Make yourselves right at home till I get back tomorrow.'

A hint that it would again be her home after that, which it wasn't, in fact, but for now I could do her some favours. There was a fern in the bathroom that needed to be sprayed once a day. There was a shop on the corner of Rock Road that sold cat food. Lucky liked chicken flavour best. I should take a look at the ocean, which was left out of her door, then over the footbridge. The ocean would do me some good, she'd decided. I agreed that it would.

'Great,' she said. 'Great. Thanks a lot, Chrissie. That's cool.'

She didn't mention Isa. She didn't mention Nick, either, although if Isa's story were true she should have, since she must have known he'd be arriving here sometime today. He must have already been in touch with Crystal to know where she lived. Or perhaps Lily had told him and he would simply ring from the airport. Maybe he hadn't bothered to warn anyone at all. Isa only knew what his plans were because she listened outside the door whenever she heard him making a phone call when he was at home. Otherwise she wouldn't know what he was doing, she explained. He never told her what he was doing any more. He didn't seem to want her to be doing it too.

The cat was by now doing something violent outside my bedroom door. Something which involved its whole body, by the sound of it. The clock on my bedside table said it was nine o'clock, so the shop for its food would be open, but I needed the keys to the flat from the room where Isa was. She was lying on top of the bed, not under the duvet, wearing my jumper over Crystal's kimono and some socks I recognized slipping off her feet. She was in the foetal position. She looked more like my mother now she'd cut off her hair. She looked too small, but rather lovely when I got close up. I couldn't believe that Nick didn't like her any more. He couldn't simply not like her. It couldn't be as simple as that. I took a patchwork blanket from the shipwreck of a wicker-work chair, and folded it round her legs, which were thinner than mine now, but still nice straight legs, like they always were.

Outside the day was grey. At the bus stop there were raincoats and huddled women with children. Above them some scaffolding was being erected to the sound of Percy Sledge from the open back door of a lorry. The shop smelled of fresh bread, so I bought some with the cat food and milk and a Crunchie bar too, because Isa likes them and it might fatten her up. Back in Crystal's wood-panelled kitchen I made coffee and tried to decide what to do for the best. Across the street the woman I'd seen in her house the night before was walking along the footpath with her baby in her arms. She unlocked a green car door and strapped the child into a car seat. Then she folded herself in and the car started up with much blue smoke and a loose exhaust banging and she circled it round in a five-point turn. Then her man came running out, holding a large white envelope like a flag above his head. She rolled down the window and he passed it in and leaned down for a kiss. He seemed to wave at the back of the car for a long time before ambling slowly back inside their shared front door.

I realized that Isa must go home to London, and probably to Nick as well. That was what she wanted. But I didn't want to take her. I couldn't bear her on the boat with me, being sick, most likely, and wanting something and thinking I had it. Although of course if I was on the boat with Isa, I couldn't be with Nick, so that should please her somewhat. Except that she wouldn't be with him, either. And that was what she wanted.

I went to the hall and found Isa's jacket hanging against a ballgown of Crystal's. Isa's wallet was in her pocket and her Access card was there. I found Aer Lingus in the telephone book and was told there was one seat left on a flight to London at five thirty-five. Check-in was at four, in theory, but if you only had hand luggage you could get there later. The ticket would be at the airport.

I was on my way to the kitchen to make more coffee, which I was planning to drink while I waited to see if Isa would wake up or if Nick would ring, when the phone rang, and there he was. I pretended at first to be Crystal. She'd find it easy to talk to any man.

'I'll take a look,' I said in a vaguely Australian accent when he'd asked if I was up yet. 'I think she may be taking a bath.'

I should really have said I'd gone out to get cat food, or to look at the sea to be independently reflective. Should have said I was still out from the night before. Made him wait, like Isa and I had waited last night.

'That is you, isn't it? That's Chrissie.'

He lit a cigarette as I agreed that it was. We were talking to each other already. He smoked as he explained that he was coming to Dublin today, unless I was coming to London.

'I need to see you,' he said. 'I want you to come home. I can't explain on the phone, but I need you to be here. I'm sorry, Chrissie. Sorry for everything. OK?'

I almost said, 'So am I,' but that would have made it too easy, for me as well as for him, so I said, 'How's Isa?' instead.

In the opposite house the man had a towel on his shoulder again. Washing up the breakfast, perhaps.

'How should I know?' Nick said.

That's what he'd said to me a few months ago, on the doorstep of our house, when I'd wept and asked him what could I do.

'I can't do it for you, Chrissie,' he said to me then. 'You've got to make out for yourself.'

That was when he'd said he was in love with Isa and he couldn't help it but that was how things were. She meant a lot to him, he'd told me. It was important.

'You mean a lot to her,' I said into the phone.

I wondered what he was wearing and where he was and where he'd slept the night before, then decided not to wonder. It was nothing to do with me. I said, 'She's had a hard time, I've been told.'

I listened to him breathing, and was glad he wasn't in the room.

'Isa is a hard time,' he said flatly. 'Look, I'm coming this afternoon. I'll be with you tonight. Don't move till I get there. I'm coming there if you won't come home.'

I heard a thud in the hall as the cat attacked a shadow. It often did that. It was jumpy. Two children appeared on the road with a ball, but couldn't decide what to do with it, so they shouted for a while.

'No, don't come here. I'm coming back today,' I told Nick then, which was true, although somewhat misleading.

'I've just booked a flight. Aer Lingus. It leaves at five thirty. Why don't you meet that at Heathrow since you're so desperate.'

See what a desperate person looks like, I thought to myself as he said yes, he'd be there. He'd be there at the airport whenever the plane arrived. He'd ring and find out the times right now.

'Do that.'

'I will. That's great.'

We said goodbye.

I left a note for Isa, propped up against Crystal's alarm clock, which was set to ring at two thirty, with the Crunchie bar just in front of it. I explained that she was booked on a flight to London, and that Nick would be meeting her plane. I thought it would mean a lot to her, and I hoped it would mean something to him as well. I hoped he would see what had to be done for now, which seemed to me to be something only he could achieve. But when I was on the boat at twilight, eating chips while the rocks of Ireland trailed like dropped clothes from the shore and the empty horizon spanned like heaven ahead, I did wonder if sending my sister to Nick had been the best or the worst thing I had done so far.

Nine Moscow Road

IN EARLY NOVEMBER I HAD A BAD TOOTH, WHICH I LEFT TO ache for a while, thinking that perhaps I deserved it. Or ought to keep it, at least, since Isa was in pain too, which I couldn't share and which would take more than a dentist's attentions to solve. It was good to have toothache in a way, because it made it hard to dwell on anything else.

After one Thursday night, though, when I couldn't sleep with the stinging in my jaw, I made an appointment with my dentist on Westbourne Grove. My mouth was examined and mended the same afternoon, and I left the surgery to emerge into a snow scene as flurried as those plastic transparent domes that souvenir shops sell which you have to shake up and down. There was a double-decker bus in it naturally, shuddering to a halt at amber traffic lights and a man in a Burberry with a dachshund on a pavement full of wellingtons and sludge. There was a young woman standing near my bicycle in a Cecil Beaton sweep of a hat. She was tall, with a sheepskin jacket and not much else except leather boots up to her knees. These buckled in square brass clasps at the beginning of the shapely length of her thighs. I unlocked my bike and tried not to stare.

I decided not to cycle home in these arctic conditions, but to walk round to Queensway and wait in the café there until the snow calmed down. As I passed the woman with the legs I noticed that she was peering into a plate-glass window to stare at a couch, and as I was leaning over my bicycle to see how much this couch cost, a man standing next to the woman said hello to me. It was Charlie. He was holding the woman's hand, I realized, as he said hello again. He said it about three times, like you do when you're pleased to see someone but wish you hadn't met them just there, and then he introduced me to the woman. Her name was Cathy. I said the couch was a nice one and she said yes and we all looked at it for a while, then Cathy said she'd better be getting along. She was due at the dentist's at eleven fifteen.

'There's no rush,' I said. 'I had to wait half an hour, if it's this dentist here you go to.'

That was her dentist, she said, and how strange that we shared him, but she hated being late, so she'd go in now anyway. Charlie kissed her cheek and she squeezed his arm.

'Don't forget the fish. By five thirty. And soak it right away. I don't want to be eating a salt cellar.'

She kissed his cheek rather reproachfully. Maybe he was meant to go into the waiting room with her. Maybe that's what they'd planned.

'See you at seven. Nice to meet you, Chrissie.'

She had a wonderful smile. Mine felt quite deformed after the filling I'd endured.

'Nice to meet you too, Cathy. Good luck with the butcher.'

She didn't smile again.

The café I used to go to after seeing my dentist was on the way to Charlie's flat, so we walked along together through snowfall, with our heads down and my bicycle rolling between us. I asked if he was playing much these days and he said he was leaving for a Munich gig in three days' time, but hadn't been that busy lately.

'What does Cathy do?'

I asked that to stop myself asking if they were sleeping together, if she was using our dentist because she was living with Charlie, like Isa still could have been if everything hadn't gone wrong.

'She sings. She's coming on the German tour with us. You could say she's an old acquaintance.'

His face seemed substantial and red against the thick white world. He might have meant they were just good friends. We arrived at the door of the café.

'Why don't you come for a coffee with me, Charlie? I haven't seen you for ages.'

It was suddenly important to continue a conversation with Charlie. I hadn't really talked about Isa to anyone yet and Charlie was the obvious person to discuss the whole catastrophe with. He probably knew more about her than anyone else in London. I brushed snow from my saddle as I asked him into the café, then found a lamp-post to chain it against when he said yes, why not? He'd love to. Lily was at his place, he explained, with some people, otherwise he'd ask me back there.

In the patisserie I chose a lemon tart. It tasted strongly of rust. Most things I ate that month had a metallic flavour. I envisaged the food I swallowed as a browny-red shape, entering my intestine. I was aware of what this meant, along with my aching breasts and ongoing lack of menstruation, but decided not to talk to Charlie about these self-evident symptoms. I didn't want him to think me hormonal and unbalanced if we were going to be talking about my sister. Perhaps he wouldn't want to talk about her anyway, but I was fond of Charlie's face and unreasonably glad to have it there near me again, across a table, about to drink tea. Charlie had a way of always looking as if he'd just woken up, which I find reassuring in a male. And if he'd got as far as putting a coat on, he rarely took it off, which made you think that something else and probably better was just about to happen.

‘Are you feeling any better about things these days?’ he said, hosing sugar into the maroon and gilt-edged cup that a white-wrapped waiter had slopped between us. The sugar shaker had a napkin stuck to its base.

‘Better than what?’

I gulped some washing-up-liquid tea into the side of my mouth that had not been drilled. He looked at me uncertainly. I must be more straightforward.

‘Well yes, I suppose I am. I’m feeling better, in some ways, but not about Isa. Have you heard from her yet?’

I was better than her, that was certain. It would be hard to be worse than she was then, in a psychiatric hospital in Scotland.

Charlie explained that he’d had a letter from my sister the day before. He paused and I waited for him to tell me how she was, where she was, how long she’d be there, but he went on to say that he’d had a letter from his father as well. It was handy that we’d run into each other just now, he explained, because otherwise he’d have had to ring me up. We stared at each other as if that would have been dreadful, then Charlie told me that we had to clear the attic of the flat where he lived. His father had arranged for people to come and insulate the loft there, because the tank had burst in January and then again in March. I remembered the last time the pipes had burst very clearly. Isa had arrived at mine and Nick’s in the middle of the night with a hairdryer and a pint of milk, saying there was water all over her bed. She’d stayed for two weeks and worn all my clothes. That could well have been the time when she and Nick decided to fall in love. They could easily have fallen into bed at any rate, because I was working every night at Au Temps Perdu. It was before I got Isa a job there. Before she arrived in that part of my life.

Charlie was watching me over the rim of his cup, waiting

for me to say something about his father's attic, presumably. His father was in Rome, where he bought and sold art and wrote books about painting and long letters to Charlie about not letting the flat in Moscow Road run to seed.

I'd never met Charlie's father, but I had spent a lot of time in his attic, one way or another, and left a lot there. A lot of Nick's stuff was still there too and almost all of Isa's. Her chaise longue had been in the much-flooded loft ever since she'd moved in. We'd have to find somewhere to put that if the place was supposed to be emptied.

'You'll have to do something about Isa's couch, I guess,' said Charlie. He looked at me, not asking but telling, then started to finger his fine, long nails.

'I mean, you can ask Nick if he wants it, or knows someone who does. Could he use it in his studio?'

I didn't think Nick would want to be dealing with anything of Isa's just then. Certainly I wouldn't want to be the one to ask him. He'd made it quite clear that I'd asked too much of him already, since I wasn't prepared to give anything back, he said. I didn't think that was fair, because I'd given Nick plenty – of time, at least – but Charlie wouldn't want to hear about that, so I just said that I'd heard Nick was painting every hour he was up. His show was in three weeks and he'd lost a lot of time in the summer.

Charlie and I sat then in silence, thinking about the time we'd all lost in the summer, through Isa's having such a wild and full one.

'Yes, well that's nothing to do with me, Chrissie.' He sounded like my father. I said I thought it was, in a way.

'I mean, it's obviously something to do with you, because you still have Isa's stuff in your place. Which is because she used to live there, with you. Which is because you liked her being there, I assume. It's not my fault she moved in with Nick. It didn't exactly make my summer either.'

'So it was my fault, was it? I'm the reason Isa's fucked up, am I? Is that what you and your friends think?'

He stood up, so I asked him to sit down again. He did and picked at his nails while I explained that I didn't blame anyone. It wasn't a simple issue, I said, but he went on defending his case.

'Isa was seeing half of London last June and July. I mean, she screws around, gets herself pregnant, doesn't even know who the father is, and you're blaming me. Was I supposed to sit still for that? What am I, St Francis, for Christ's sake? You can't just have any old baby and expect me to want in on it, Chrissie.'

I wasn't planning to ask him to. I didn't want to talk about babies or fathers or Isa and Charlie or anyone else any more. I wanted to discuss the chaise longue, I decided, because that was something we could do something about. Clearing the attic at Moscow Road might be a good way of passing this overwrought time. I could organize Isa's possessions, and when she came home the chaise longue would be somewhere pleasant, where she could sit and tell me everything. She'd have to have somewhere new to stay now, and she'd need all her things around her. Nick might help. He had some of her stuff. I suggested that Charlie telephone him. Maybe he'd know someone who might want a chaise longue and a fragile woman in their home for a while. Charlie said he'd rather hang himself than talk to Nick about anything, thanks. I left a moment to show I could see that was what he would say in the heat of the moment, but went on to ask if he really wouldn't talk to Nick. They were supposed to be friends. And friends of Isa's too.

'I mean, you must have spoken to him about her going away? Didn't you talk before she went off to Scotland? She was at his place that afternoon.'

'Yeah, well you'd know all about that fiasco. And no, I did

not ring. Lily rang for me. Look, I don't want to talk about this right now. Do you? Are you talking to Nick?'

I was unsticking the green paper napkin from the base of the sugar shaker bit by bit.

'Not exactly. You couldn't really say we were talking just now.'

Nick and I had certainly shouted at each other a lot on my return from Ireland, when we were trying to work out who we could blame for Isa's breakdown, but that wasn't something Charlie needed to know. I said I would talk to Nick if I had to. If it would help anything.

Outside the snow had stopped. On our table the ashtray was filled with fragments of napkin. My stomach was gurgling alarmingly.

'Well look, Chrissie, I don't have to do anything except check out a guitar in Clapham later today and get the crap in the attic moving before I leave the country.'

'You've got to buy some fish for Cathy.'

I smiled. He didn't.

'So I think you should talk to Nick. Isa's stuff's not my concern any more. Besides which, there's loads of your stuff up there too. All kinds of crap. And my dad wants it empty. Ring Nick, Chrissie. You can do it from my place now if you want.'

Some feeling was coming back to my jaw. I took another bite of my tart and listened while Charlie told me that Lily would be glad to see me, and why didn't I go round right away? It was best to get things moving. Telling Nick to shift the couch was the best idea.

'We can get it over with then. You can get him to collect it when I'm gone next week. He and Lily can sort it together. She needs loads of gear for some place she's moving into up in Yorkshire anyhow. But she won't take the couch. I've asked her twice.'

My tongue negotiated a lump of tart that was suddenly chewy as floorboards between my teeth. The waiter brought a sausage roll to a man at my side. Grease from its centre oozed yellow and fat. It would never get through his moustache.

'It's not *the* couch, Charlie, it's Isa's. And what's Lily got to do with anything? Why's she taking whatever she feels like? Those are my things and Isa's. You should have rung me up. You don't own those things, Charlie. They're nothing to do with you.'

I imagined Lily bent over one of our dust-creased bin liners, tipping out intimate garments and photographs and trying on the samples of perfume that Isa took from Boots. Charlie stirred sugar sediment then licked his spoon, like a girl would, and said he was glad I could see it his way now, but I ignored that.

'Isa'll be mad when she finds out, you know? You shouldn't give people's things away, Charlie.'

He stared over stainless steel at me then, in something like wonderment.

'Isa is mad, Chrissie. She's in hospital, for Christ's sake. She couldn't care less if she has hair on her head or not just now. You should see the stuff she sends me. Jesus.'

He put his receding hairline into his perfect hands and said it was outrageous that I was arguing about this. I should be trying to make it simple.

'It's just stuff,' he almost shouted, so the man next to us stopped eating and watched. 'It's old stuff that no one needs, and Lily's going through it because she's kind and she wants to help. I don't want to see it, Chrissie. It's like the inside of somebody's head up there. Come on back now and see.'

He slid his hands up flat, not quite over his face.

I did not go back to Charlie's with him that afternoon. I sat on in the café for some time after he'd left, listening to the melting snow slide off the awning to hit the pavement in uneven splats. I watched a pair of women across the room from me almost eat a chocolate cake. They were overwrought for some reason I was too far away to hear about, but I could sense their intensity from their stretched red mouths and wide eyes and the tumbling glossy hair they pushed frenetically back and the cigarettes they didn't have time between words to inhale. They would be sharing some resentment, some outrage, presumably. Isa and I used to do that in this warm steamy room too, before it was she I resented.

I'd told Charlie I'd be going along to his place in a bit, but I knew it wasn't true. It wasn't the phone call to Nick I couldn't face so much as Lily being capable and kindly and taking charge. And Isa not being there, where she'd been last time I went, when we'd argued and I didn't ask her enough or tell her what she ought to do. When I had told her she couldn't have my boyfriend's baby, before she'd had time to explain herself. But how could she have explained herself? I wished someone would explain to me what I could have done better. I decided to go home. I didn't want to be near Moscow Road any more.

I was waiting to pay the plump lady at the till with my last £10 note when a familiar coat arrived at my left. Lily put her hand on the sleeve of my old red jacket.

'Chrissie. Could you stay a bit longer?'

Her hair was greasy and her face rather drawn. I took my change and explained how long I'd been there already.

'I know. Charlie said. But I want to ask you about something.'

'Is it about the things in the attic?'

'No.'

'Is it about Isa and Charlie? Or Nick?'

'No.'

Lily was smiling now, showing a gold crown to the left. My visit to the dentist seemed a long time ago. The excitable women squeezed us to one side so they could pay and leave to be excited somewhere else. Lily and I were jammed together against the plate-glass-screened cream cakes.

'I'll buy you a cake,' Lily said.

I chose a doughnut this time. She chose an éclair, and we didn't talk about anyone we knew in London at all, because she wanted to know about Monkstown and Crystal, which I would have told her more about than I did, except that I had to leave before it got dark. My bicycle had no lights.

When I got back home it was almost twilight. I sat and watched the street lamps burst on and become the brightest blue they ever achieved instead of taking my coat off or opening the letter that had been lying on the hall floor as I'd landed my bike there. There was a message on my answering machine, which flashed from across the detritus of my floor, but I didn't listen to that. I just sat, not even smoking until I found a pack of S.G. cigarettes, which Danby must have left in the cushions some time ago. My fingers were almost too cold to flint a lighter that had slipped into the upholstery too. The drips outside my window were icicles now. I hoped the pipes wouldn't burst, and realized that was the first thing with words that I had thought. 'Your thoughts don't have words every day,' I said out loud. Emily Dickinson wrote that and I find it a consoling notion. But my thoughts were really that I wanted Isa to be herself again, and I didn't dare open the letter from Scotland because it would confirm once again that Isa was not here and she was not well and nothing was as it ought to be. I wanted Isa to be with me there for what seemed like the first ever time. I'd never had to want that before, of course, because Isa had always been practically there. Even when I'd hated her she'd been with me in my head. I had a lot of conversations with her then.

The phone rang twice as I missed my sister and started on missing other things too, blowing smoke at the halo of a lamp-post a few feet from my head, which was reflected in my window pane. My face was rounder than it had been a few weeks ago. I heard the answering machine click on, then off, with another person leaving a message. I'd stopped having the sound of the thing in the room about the time Danby left London, which was when Isa had stopped ringing me too. Now I preferred to be in silence. My mother was ringing a lot. She wanted me to tell her why Isa was in Scotland and I'd sort of tried, although nobody knew precisely why she'd gone there, not somewhere in London, when she'd got back from Dublin. She had a Scottish friend who was at school with us both, but I didn't know her address and neither did Nick, although he'd told me he was making enquiries. He shouted rather than spoke to me these days. I didn't blame him really, since I'd told him he was the most selfish person in the world. When I phoned him the day before I went to the dentist, he put the phone down when he heard my voice. We hadn't shouted a word at each other since.

I opened the letter from Isa, but only read the first five lines, in which she explained that she knew I'd wanted her baby to die, which was why she would never forgive me. There was no address on the paper. The letter was five pages long, the writing very large. Loopy was a good word for it, I thought, and slid the whole thing into the side of the couch and wondered if Isa's chaise longue would fit into my flat. It probably would not, and anyway, Isa wouldn't want it there. I'd have to find a nice room for her. I could ask at the wine bar. Alison always knew someone.

The first message on my machine was from my mother. She

hoped Nick and I hadn't had words, she said, and that he had asked her to ask me to feed his cat.

'He's gone up to see Isa, dear. She rang me. She wanted to see him, so Nicholas has gone on up there. We had a good long talk. His keys are in the usual place, and he'd like the cats fed until he comes back. Why he can't tell you himself I don't know. Give me a ring when you come in, Chrissie, would you?'

She never says goodbye to my machine. I suppose she thinks it would be a waste of her politeness. I was relieved that Nick had gone to Isa, and pleased he was speaking to my mother too, although I doubted that there had been any 'good long talk'. You don't have good long talks with my mother. I wished Nick had told me where Isa was before he went off to find her. I'd have told him, if I knew. The second message I heard was from Danby. I crouched near the phone to hear him say he was coming back to London the following Thursday. In six days' time.

'Can't make contact with Lily. Assume she's alive and well, but can you get her to ring me? I'm thinking of renting that boat she's leaving. I think you have my number, but it's 0035818866005. OK. See you. Soon.'

I resisted the temptation to ring Danby right then. I might do it later, if I couldn't sleep. I listened to the messages again, deleted my mother's, then I fried some sausages and ate them listening to a radio programme about Torvill and Dean. Isa had been to see them for her birthday treat. The programme was ending in embracing music when the doorbell rang. I ignored it. It rang again, so I went down and it was Lily. She was wearing a leopard-skin hat that I hadn't seen since New Year's Eve some years ago, when Nick and I went back from a party to sleep at Moscow Road. She lifted the delicate object from her fine-boned head and said I must wear it and come for a drink with her. She'd been thinking about Crystal and

Danby, she said, and I was the only person she knew who knew them both.

In the Brook Green Hotel bar she talked about her mother, who had fallen in love it seemed. She'd told me this already over our cakes, but not that the man was penniless and that Crystal was planning to marry him.

'Did she mention someone called Milo when you were over there? I mean, how could she marry someone we've never heard of?'

'Well, why shouldn't she?'

I couldn't see what the problem was, but Lily explained that Crystal was planning on supporting Milo for ever, and thought her daughter's allowance must be cut from now on.

'She says I can't go to Yorkshire, for a start.'

Lily was to have started a fine-art degree at Leeds that autumn term.

'She wants me to go to Dublin and meet Milo. She calls him "your father" in her letters now.'

Lily thought she ought to tell Danby. The whole thing was disturbing.

'But what could Danby do?'

I didn't want Danby to be upset, or to have to find more money just then either. He might not be able to move back to London. I suggested she talk to her paternal grandmother, who was wealthy and fond of Gabriel.

'But my allowance comes from Crystal's parents, not Danby's.'

That seemed fine to me, and I said so.

'Why don't you just write and say you're glad she's happy, but you'll have to discuss your allowance with the rest of the family? That should do for now.'

I was glad Crystal had something to fill her time. It would stop her reflecting on the fact that I'd left her flat in Isa's hands, and Isa had left it to go to Nick.

'You don't understand,' Lily told me. 'It's upsetting having a mother in love.'

She drained her glass of lager, as I gave her the news about Danby coming to live in London.

'I'm sure he can rent the boat if he wants to.' She was frowning, rubbing the studs in the table top. 'But why can't he live in Dublin? He could get to know Crystal again.'

'Why would he want to do that?'

'Well, they might fall in love or something. Do you think they'd get along?'

'No, I do not.'

I was embarrassed then at the way I'd said it so loudly, so I laughed as she looked surprised. We said we'd talk about it all the next day, again. I was going to rescue the things in the attic, I told her.

'We must find you a warm hat of your own,' I said, and I put mine on to walk home.

The following morning at eleven thirty Lily and I met in the café on Queensway, then we watched each other's footsteps through the red-grit shiny pavement and I found my much-thumbed keys to let us in through the sun-stained door on Moscow Road and up to Charlie's father's flat. It looked just the same as it had on the afternoon I'd last been there with Isa, except that the corridor walls were lined with stacks of records, so there was only about a foot of carpet still exposed to walk along. On the kitchen table was a note from Charlie, addressed to myself and Lily, saying that he couldn't get in touch with Nick but had arranged for the records to be moved the following week.

'If there's anything you don't want up there, throw it away,' the green writing went on. 'I don't need any of it.'

'Well, that's pretty decisive,' I said to Lily.

'It's not how he feels. He's not himself, Chrissie.'

Since I'd known Charlie for ever and Lily had not, I felt I would be the best judge of how himself he was, but I decided not to go into that as we made our way up to the top of the house.

Lily seemed to know the attic very well. She avoided the gaps in the floorboards to plug in the electric fire that was shaped like a liner, which I'd once found in a skip.

Isa's couch was almost hidden by piles of plastic bags that you had to climb over boxes to reach. There were shoes all over the floor. Lily picked up a slipper which had lost a sole and placed it carefully onto an upturned orange box which was painted in yellow gloss. It had been my bedside table once upon a time. I turned round a large piece of hardboard, getting cobwebs all over my front, and saw my painted self, looking worried with a mouth that was wrong. I recognized the blouse I was wearing more than the face, and I couldn't remember who'd done it or when. Perhaps it wasn't me at all.

There were rolled-up posters and birthday cards and maps underfoot, and dull beer bottles lining the walls and a box of candles that I knew had no wicks. I remembered the night Charlie brought them back from the market and the row he'd had with Nick, who'd told him where to buy them. It was Christmas or Hallowe'en or something, and Isa had flu and wept every day because she thought it must be something worse and she ought to be in hospital.

Lily suggested we go through the sacks piled up on the couch, so it would be ready to leave if we found somewhere to take it. Cathy had rung her already today to say her brother might know of someone. We must make piles of people's possessions for now, Lily thought, and have a bag for rubbish which we'd put on a skip another afternoon. The boxes were mostly full of books, she said. She'd read half of *Zuleika Dobson* the day before, which was why there was still so much to get through today. She thought she'd like to go to Oxford with Gabriel at the weekend. Crystal had a friend who lived in some sort of commune near Oxford and Lily wanted to see her. She could ask her about this love affair maybe. Crystal would have told her all about it. She was telling everybody. She'd put an announcement in the *Irish Times* last weekend.

'I don't know what to do. I've got to make her see sense,' Lily told me as I lifted a page of grimy newsprint from the curve of the cluttered couch.

'What sense is there for her to see?' I said. 'I mean, how do you know she's not really in love? She seemed quite sensible when I saw her.'

Compared to myself and Isa, I could have said, but didn't bother to make the comparison then. I found some more newspapers. I read that Nureyev was very ill and would not be dancing in Paris, then I struggled with the creased dust of a council bin liner, which I thought must have some of my clothes inside. We should have got some rubber gloves before we started on this, I realized. Lily was OK because she was wearing dungarees. She usually wore some sort of workmen's clothing. She felt that artists should look capable and ready for action all the time.

'Crystal doesn't believe in love. Love is for losers. She thinks good sex is more important. She used to go on about it all the time.'

'Well perhaps the sex is so good this time that she's fallen in love.'

It wasn't something I'd normally say, but I was preoccupied by a jumper I'd just pulled out from the soft inside of my bin bag. It was something Isa had knitted. It had a tiny neck, and no one had ever been able to wear it, but we'd had it on the back of a chair in the kitchen for years. As I unrolled it now, I saw it had been eaten by moths. The sleeves were in rags and the rib looked like lace. There were tiny white trails of lava, like cat fluff, all over everything that came out of the bag after that. Nothing was in one piece. Bag after bag had been devoured by moths.

The rich geometric design of the couch's upholstery was uneven when it finally appeared from underneath everything else. In places it was completely bald. The moths had liked the yellow bits of the fabric best. Fragments of the unwoven pattern came away in my palm as I smoothed my hand across into the crease where the arm met the seat. It was ruined. Everything was ruined.

Lily stopped sorting through the sacks after I'd discovered the jumper and shown it to her. She sat on the floor and watched me tussle with one knot after another and tip rags down beside her until she was surrounded by softness. Sometimes I'd pull at a particularly large hole in the front of something familiar, seeing how far gone the fabric was, or if I could further destroy it perhaps. One cardigan had almost no front left at all. It was a garment that my grandmother had given me when I was sixteen and wanted to astonish the sixth form. I have a photograph of her wearing it with my mother in her arms.

Isa's silk bedspread was in shreds, like tissue-paper seaweed on a child's collage. Nothing was wholly intact. A bowler hat's lining shredded like a leaf skeleton under my fingers. I looked at Lily as I dropped it. The hat she'd brought for me to wear to the pub last night had been fine. Where had she found that to tempt me here? Either she had taken all the good stuff already or it was all a plot to upset me. A scheme to get me here to see this mass destruction of things I cared about and had neglected. It was probably Charlie's idea of revenge. They wanted to punish me, I understood then. This was a punishment for me and Isa for having all these things and leaving them here. For expecting other people to care after we had stopped caring. For not taking care of ourselves.

Lily hadn't been trying to help at all. She'd probably spent the afternoon before with Cathy and Charlie, after she'd left the café, and worked out how to lure me here with the hat and histrionics about Crystal.

'You're having a great time, aren't you, Lily?' I said as I threw the last bag up and away and towards her. 'It must be fun watching someone else's things fall apart. It must be really nice to know that Isa and I have nothing left here but a load of crap.' I threw something else at her, a shoe maybe.

'No wonder your mother's new boyfriend annoys you. You can't stand the idea of people having anything they care about, can you? You hate Isa, don't you? You and Charlie can't stand her, and you've got me here to make me feel as bad as she does. Well I feel very bad. Are you happy? Happy to see we've got fuck all between us? Happy now everything's ruined?'

She stepped back as another bag landed near her. She put her hands into the pockets of her dungaree bib, which made her look much younger than she was. She asked me what I was talking about. I started talking about something else.

'How come that hat of mine you brought round last night was OK? Where did you get that from?'

She must have gone through some cupboard downstairs. She couldn't have found it up here. She hadn't been sorting anything, clearly. She'd been snooping for things she could steal.

'I want to go to your boat right now, Lily. I want us to go to your houseboat.'

She must have stacks of our stuff stashed already.

'Who was here with you yesterday when I was out having tea with Charlie? I need to see what you've stolen. If you've taken any of his records Nick'll kill you.'

She moved towards me and picked up the bowler hat. She shook out a sack and placed the hat deep inside it, then started pushing other things that I'd tipped out in there with it. She squatted onto her heels and did it slowly and with care.

She looked soft and consoling, like a Bonnard peasant, which annoyed me. She should have stayed standing and explained herself. She must have known about the moths. She and Charlie must have known. There was nothing to sort out here at all except rags. It was all a joke, and they'd planned it, and Isa's chaise longue would never be the same again. I tried to nudge it along the uneven boards, away from the piles of jumble. I pushed my whole weight against it.

'Why don't you help me? Help me move this couch.'

Lily stopped squeezing shoes together. She dropped them and put her hands in the air.

'Why can't you do something useful and get this couch over there for me?'

'Why do you want it over there?'

'Because that's where it goes.'

She stayed where she was and stared at me, as if I were a child that wanted to stamp on a snail and it was her job to dissuade me.

'This is where we put the mattress down if anyone needs to stay. You have to have the mattress in the middle here or people get cold. There's a draught.'

'But the workmen are coming on Monday.'

She started packing things together again, methodical, serious, intent. She had my grandmother's cardigan in her hands and was folding it into a square.

'Leave that alone. Put it down. These are my things, do you understand?'

I could feel my breathing shaky and my underarms wet. I wanted a cigarette but I wouldn't ask Lily. I wouldn't want anything from her sturdy blue pockets and her strong stubby hands.

'Just leave it alone and go home. Nick and I will sort everything out.'

I knew she knew he wasn't in London, but I could get him

back if I wanted. He would come and help with Isa's things. He cared about Isa. And about me too.

'We don't need your help. And Isa doesn't either, thank you very much.'

She looked as if she might be going to cry, which was how I felt. I told her to go away again and she said she didn't understand and the moths were not her fault and we should go downstairs for a cup of tea and come back when we were calmer. We were both hungry, she said.

'We need some lunch, Chrissie.'

'Well go home and eat some lunch then.'

'Do you want to be by yourself?'

'Yes I do. That's exactly what I want.'

I sat down on the couch and picked my fingers.

'I'll go then. I'll call you later.'

She made me sick and I said so and threw a padded coat hanger after her back.

'I won't be in later,' I shouted down after her. 'I'll be out, so don't ring me.'

I waited for her to shout something back but she didn't, which made me want to weep suddenly, but I bit my nails instead. I heard the door slam beyond the stacked records, then I looked around and slowly came to wish that Lily had not left. I was hungry. I should have gone somewhere else with Lily. We could have gone to the café together. I could still go there now. She might be having a sandwich. I must go and say I was sorry. I'd over-reacted. Lily was only a teenager, and she was trying to be nice; and no one else had offered to help and she hardly knew Charlie and I don't think she'd ever met Isa. She must think I was deranged, that the whole of my family was mad. I would go and find her in the café in Queensway. I badly wanted a sandwich. I needed a conversation too.

*

Half an hour later I was still inside the building Lily had left because I didn't have keys to get out with. The keys were in Lily's pocket, where she'd put them when I left them in the door to check the post on the window sill in the hallway downstairs. You needed keys to leave Inverness Mansions because the downstairs door was always double-locked. Tramps came in and slept there in cold weather otherwise, and the residents didn't like that.

I could have asked the people downstairs to let me out, I suppose, but I didn't think of that at the time. I thought of Nick being miles away with Isa, most likely, who was so far away no one could count the miles, and Charlie being with Cathy somewhere, and Lily on her houseboat, with Gabriel there for her to have lunch with, probably kissing her hello. Everyone was somewhere else, involved with someone other than me. There was nothing to do but have a cup of tea with skimmed milk and caster sugar in it and go back up to the attic and stare at the couch.

I'd have to wait for someone to come back, but I had no idea when that might be since I didn't know where anyone was. If Lily had still been there she would have been putting the stuff on the floor back into plastic bags, so I started to do that myself. It was exhausting and soon my arms ached as much as my alarming breasts had been lately, which was one of the things my toothache had made me forget. I sat on the floor and felt like something clockwork that had wound right down and needs to be horizontal and absolutely still. I often felt like that then in the afternoons. I wanted apricot juice intensely. I should have been ringing my doctor's surgery, like I should have done the day before too, to discuss my condition, rather than putting these bits of the past into bin liners.

I decided to leave the attic alone. I must look after myself. I'd go to the bedroom to lie still on what had been my sister's side of Charlie's wide bed, with its swooping green wrought-iron frame. The pillows there were old and deliciously sinking and I lay down and slept for two hours, until the clock by the bed said three thirty-five and the blue walls of the room were seeping to grey. I dreamt that Isa and I were sitting at a table in the wine bar with a tall narrow bottle between us, which had a picture of someone who looked like Danby on the label. She was telling me that she'd written a novel, which she was going to call *Half Left*. She looked like she used to when she was at her best, and she was eating toast with anchovy paste, which I too wanted as soon as I woke up and tasted the red-brown lining of my throat again.

In the kitchen cupboard above the gas cooker I found a dusty tin of anchovies, but no key to open it with. No tin-opener either, although there used to be one hanging above the sink. I ate crackers from a crumpled pack on the table and searched every drawer in the room, every shelf, then every cupboard, including those at floor level. There was nothing for the anchovy tin, but in the cupboard under the sink, with the bleach and the tent pegs, I found something unexpected. It was a spray can of moth repellent. There were line drawings of giant moths and other insects disintegrating under a blast of spray-paint orange, which was meant to represent the killer product in action. The bulk of the can was coloured a sinister blood red. 'KILLS MOTHS IN MOMENTS', it said on both sides in a disturbing shade of blue. Too late now, of course, for the repellent effect, but I decided to take this find up to Isa's couch to protect it from any malingering moths who'd been wintering there and would wake up hungry, like myself, and tuck into whatever was left to ingest. I would make that gesture for Isa, for myself and for Nick perhaps, for anyone who had ever cared about the couch and the people who sat on or near it.

The attic was dark so I groped for the lamp switch, sat on the floor and read the cluttered instructions. It all seemed quite feasible until I came to the words 'Do not use if pregnant', which caused me to replace the lid, which I had worked very hard to twist off. It was strange to see the word I hadn't yet said to anyone amid lots of other words on this somewhat violent can. You could not kill moths if you were pregnant, it said. If you were pregnant, you must put the can down right away. I put the can down. I sat on the couch, amid plastic sacks of moth-eaten clothing, and could think of no words at all until the phone rang downstairs.

Lily's voice said my name.

'Chrissie. You're still there. Are you OK?'

I said I was pregnant. It sounded odd. She didn't speak.

'I'm locked in here and I'm pregnant.'

The phone went dead, so I put it down, then it rang again, and Lily said she had no more change, but she'd come right now to set me free.

'I'm at the café round the corner,' she said. 'Do you want a cup of tea?'

I did want a cup of tea, I told her. I wanted tea and toast and anchovy paste, and I would go downstairs and wait and see what happened next, which would include Lily somehow, which would be for the best.

It was snowing again when she opened the door. She took my hand in hers, which was warm and firm, and we walked out into Moscow Road through the blurred white wet softness and the hard shrieks of children throwing snowballs at passing cars.

Ten Brighton

IT WASN'T UNTIL I FOUND MYSELF IN CHARING CROSS Hospital on the last Friday of November in 1985, about to have an abortion, that I properly realized I had to have the baby. It was seven forty in the morning and I watched the frail red minute hand of the grey-faced clock at the end of my ward, with two nurses chatting underneath it, and I decided I couldn't not have a baby. Not one that was already inside me anyway. The only reason not to have it was that I'd never had one before, which was a perfect reason to have one. Of course, I had no washing machine, no father to hand, no experience of nappies or breastfeeding, but everyone said this wouldn't matter. Most people thought Isa wouldn't mind what I did either, which I wasn't sure was true, but I lay in my bed in the day ward under a cellular blanket, under cellular strip lights in an angel-like garment that you all had to wear, and made up my mind to have my baby after all. Then I got up and dressed and went home.

The first thing I did when I got back was ring Danby, because he was supposed to be collecting me from the hospital after the operation had been done. We'd arranged it all the day before, when he'd offered to take me there as well, but I knew he liked his sleep, so refused that exceptional kindness. I couldn't remember his telephone number when I was back in my flat with the phone in my hand, so I rang directory enquiries. Then I forgot the number the woman had told me and had to ring back and ask again. I almost told the operator about how I was having a baby but didn't quite get that far. I saved the news for Danby.

'I'm having the baby after all, Danby, so there's no need to go and collect me later because I'm home already by myself, you see.'

Danby coughed instead of reacting, which I knew by then meant that he'd just woken up. He'd stayed on my floor for some days the week before, while the stove in his houseboat was being replaced.

'Is that OK?' I thought he might not have heard me. He was blowing his nose. 'I've changed my mind, I'm having a baby.'

'That's great. I thought you might. That's really great. What time is it?'

'About half past eight. So that's OK then is it?'

He couldn't know, but I had to ask someone.

'It's great.' He laughed, and I did too, then he said, 'Amazing. That's amazing. So look.' He blew his nose again. 'So look, let's go to Brighton. A girl I know's having a party there. Come with me. Some travel will do you good.'

'I've been travelling since seven.'

'Well have a nap. Go back to bed for a bit. We're not setting off till after lunch. Go on, Chrissie. I'll buy you afternoon tea. You and the baby, I mean.'

I said I'd have to think about it and ring him back. I still hadn't had any breakfast.

Danby was living in London, doing a course on teaching people to teach people to speak English as a foreign language. He had Lily's houseboat, which she'd left to go north, where she was renting a cottage with Gabriel in a village near where Jamie came from. She'd had her goodbye party in Temps Perdu at the end of November. Jake and Alison had a row. I was sad that Lily was going, but not as sad as I would have been if I hadn't been pregnant, which seemed to make me indifferent to most things, except the potential fate of the foetus. Having to decide what to do about that made me not mind that Nick was still in Scotland with Isa and had sent a card saying they were trying to sort things out. I didn't mind either that Jamie was unconcerned about any possible baby, and would be living in Galway for the following year. He was building a house there, and didn't mind what I did as long as I was happy, he'd written on a postcard. The postcard had a donkey on it. Jamie wrote that motherhood would do me good, and he'd help in any way he could, which I believed for a while, at least.

Most people said motherhood would be good for me, which I didn't quite know how to take. Did they mean I'd been bad at most things so far, or that I had an obvious maternal talent, which was as yet untapped? I didn't care much, either way, once I'd decided what I was going to do. Suzanne explained that a certain indifference to the outside world was nature's way of conserving a mother's resources. You don't have energy to waste considering things that won't affect your unborn baby directly. She may have been right. Certainly, when people started to give me things, later, like cots and pushchairs and baskets of blankets and sterilizing units and cumbersome car seats, I didn't mind that I had no car or that these accessories took up the whole of my hallway and were mostly in duplicate and offensive in colour.

I didn't mind that Alison thought I was mad, or that Geraldine rang and said not to visit her ever again because she blamed Danby's move to London on me. I suppose it was my having a baby that really annoyed her. But I wasn't planning any trips to Lisbon or anywhere else, once I'd started planning for my new infant-oriented life. Trips were the last thing on my mind at that woozy time, and I didn't make any, except one with Danby at the start of it all, on that hospital morning, when he said I should go to Brighton with him and I must let him know by noon if I would.

'Let me know by twelve,' he'd instructed, having suggested a good long nap.

I slept from nine until half eleven. When I opened my bedroom curtains for the second time that day, the holly bush outside was leafed in mirror slivers and the window sills opposite were licked with an astonishing white. The sea would be good to see, I could see, so I ate an egg mayonnaise and anchovy sandwich, then rang a woman called Judy who used to work in the wine bar, and had moved to Brighton some time ago. I hadn't spoken to her for months, but she was pleased to hear my voice, she said, and that yes, she would love a visitor in the early stages of pregnancy.

'I'd love it, Chrissie,' she shrieked, and wowey, a baby. And she knew that I would love Brighton. I hadn't seen her since she'd moved out of Cambridge Gardens with her little girl, who'd been about one at the time.

So I rang Danby, after the call to Judy, and said I would go to Brighton. But I wouldn't go to the party, I told him later, as I sank into the low seat of his Citroën, with its heater that hummed like a hairdryer. I wasn't interested in a party. I was interested in seeing a two-year-old girl. Children, rather than parties, were my future now, I said. Danby said it wouldn't have to be either or.

'How would you know?'

'It's just a feeling I have.'

He pushed the button of the tape machine. Bob Dylan sang that he wasn't sleepy and there was no place he was going to, as we sped through undulating countryside, and I was happy to be going somewhere different now, in Danby's car, with a small unknown creature inside me, to take everywhere for a while. I stayed unprecedentedly happy, even after it started to rain.

*

Judy's house was one of a hunchbacked row of terraces that stumbled up the side of Victoria Place, away from the grey sea and towards a grey park, with two grey pillars to mark out its entrance. She'd explained that she wouldn't be at home until about six, because she did a writing class on Tuesdays, then had to collect Rosie from the other side of town. The lady next door on the left had a key to her place, though, so I must get that and let myself in if I got bored or cold.

But I wasn't bored in Brighton when Danby and I arrived. We had a pot of weak tea, with dense and satisfying carrot cake in a health-food emporium just up from the sea. He didn't say much and neither did I. He stared at me a lot, so I kept looking down at myself and wondering if I had visibly swelled since the morning. I hoped I had.

'How does it feel?' he asked, and I said it felt fine, but I was worried about telling my mother.

'Don't be silly. Doesn't she like babies?'

'She likes Isa. And Isa won't like this.'

'How do you know? From what I've seen of your sister, she's one of life's perfect dotty aunts.'

'Don't say that. Nick thinks she's better.'

'Are you in touch with Nick? You didn't say.'

Danby stopped eating cake.

'I had a card.'

I didn't want to go into details but Danby asked what was what, so I said Nick was trying to work it out with Isa, and Danby said he'd give that a week, unless Isa really was insane.

'I suppose it'll all come out in the wash,' I said, which is something Lily likes to say, which I felt went well with my pregnancy.

Danby said he was too hot. He wanted a walk.

So we walked along the smooth-stoned beach for a while, watching the laborious wash of the sea, and he took my arm and said he was glad I had come, so I said I was too, then we went for more tea in a different place and talked about names we thought a baby could have.

'Anything but Geraldine,' was his final decision, which made me wonder if he still liked that name a lot, but I didn't ask. I tried to avoid that subject.

When the café closed Danby drove me slowly to the side of the park where he'd be staying that night, and showed me the house in Parkside View where his party would be in case I changed my mind.

'You never know, you might feel like dancing.'

Then he wrote the telephone number of his friend on a cigarette paper for me to put in my pocket, in case an emergency happened. He kissed my cheek goodbye. He rubbed my head, said have fun, leaned across to open my door, and I turned then to wave from the pavement before I walked away through tossed trees and loping dogs and the abandoned shapes of a children's playground to reach the top of Victoria Place.

Judy's neighbour was cheerful and was expecting me. By the time we met, Judy had already rung her to say she might be slightly late, but that I must make myself at home at her place.

'She never has a minute to herself, that girl,' the aproned figure explained, strapping a wailing child into a high chair. 'She doesn't have time to turn round.'

Her small boy craned around just at that point and knocked his face into his high chair frame, so she lifted him into her arms and the three of us moved back through to her hallway, where there were labelled keys on hooks and a knife hanging next to the door.

'For emergencies,' she explained, noting my stare. 'There've been some goings-on lately.'

Her eyes swirled up to the ceiling then back into mine. The

child in her arms was crying, despite her haphazard kisses. I didn't like the noise much so I said, 'I'll let you get on,' which was a phrase I'd heard recently on a radio play. It seemed to satisfy her, so I got on myself and let myself into Judy's, where I dropped my bag onto the floor of the blue-painted front room, which smelled sweet and expensive, like the cosmetics department of Barkers in high summer.

At the back of the cluttered main room there was an entrance to a long narrow kitchen, where the rich smell of the place grew painfully strong. The source of this pungency was a glass bottle, lying in pieces on rush matting on the floor in front of the sink. The bottle's label was intact, holding two fragments together: Miss Dior eau de toilette. I left it where it was, thinking it might be there for a reason, then I looked at the stove where there were pans of crusted porridge, scrambled eggs and baked beans.

Plastic bowls were piled high on the red tiled work surface, beneath which were numerous half-open cupboards. I stepped over carrier bags and a small wickerwork donkey to reach through lidless pots of peanut butter and jams to the kettle, but decided not to attempt to disentangle its flex from the spilled contents of a sack of muesli.

Judy had never kept an orderly house. When she worked in the wine bar our shifts always lasted about twice as long as they ought to have done. She got orders confused, or customers' coats covered in cream or herself drenched with spritzers, of which the owner thought she was somewhat too fond. It was a relief when she got pregnant and sat down for most of the time. She couldn't do much harm folding napkins.

I mixed myself a glass of Ribena and took it away from the kitchen's cocktail of smells to the front room, which was dominated by a moulded plastic kitchen unit, which had dried haricot beans in every scooped surface. Miniature pans were filled with what looked like cold tea. Above the fireplace was a poster advertising a night-club called Off The Beach, and a glossy picture of Marlon Brando. Another man in a black T-shirt was in a silver frame that had fallen flat on the carpet below. I lifted the hollowed handsome face to lean it against the mirror on the mantelpiece. I read a postcard from Manhattan that said, 'Wish you were here too,' with a large 'O' drawn after the kisses.

There were no empty chairs in the room, so I slid crumpled newspapers and laundry from the cushions of the couch, and was balancing gingerly there when the telephone rang. A male American accent asked Judy's machine if it would be cool to swing round in a while, or if Rosie was still on her hands. The voice said to ring the garage sometime before eight and let him know what was happening either way. I didn't have a watch and the video clock was flashing a consistent two twenty-five, so I went upstairs, into the first room I came to, where a double mattress sprawled over most of the floor and a clock slid its digits to show six fifty-one. I watched the numbers slip neatly until six fifty-four, then I studied a photograph of Judy and Rosie on a beach. The background was empty and perfectly blue.

Outside the house I heard footsteps and someone young laughed, then headlights panned the room's drawn floral curtains, but the car didn't stop so it wasn't Judy coming back. I hoped she would come home soon. I wanted something to eat. Or rather something inside me needed feeding, which had the effect of making me feel slightly sick, but not uneasy like it had until now. I didn't mind it now that we were in it together. Now that my body was something I'd decided to share. But I couldn't imagine there would be any food worth consuming at Judy's. I should have listened more carefully when Danby was telling me his evening's plan. He'd be settled into some pub by now, where you could buy soup and crisps and soggy meat pies.

I stepped on a May edition of *Marie Claire* and took it downstairs with me to read on Judy's ungiving couch. There was a feature on getting the most out of Milan, where I'd once been with Isa. We'd both lost our wallets on successive days. I read a knitting pattern to see if I remembered how they worked and discovered I did not. By the time I'd studied an article on suburban witchcraft and another on virgin births, the telephone had taken two more messages from the American at the garage. He told the room that he wouldn't be coming round tonight after all because there was a party to go to in Parkside View. I dropped my magazine.

'Why don't you come too?' the glamorous accent enquired. 'Get someone to sit in with Rosie.'

He advised Judy to join him there, at number four, which was the house where Danby was planning to party. This information unnerved me so much that I knelt down beside the flashing machine, not quite able to make sense of what it had said. I think I was about to erase the man's voice, although I hadn't exactly decided. Maybe I just wanted to hear the message again, but the doorbell rang with an old-fashioned chime before I could do anything further, so I sprang back onto the couch as a key turned in the lock. Judy started shouting hello.

'Chrissie, where are you? Come and give me a hug. We're free. Come here. I need to see you now.'

Her voice always sounded as if she was pretending to be someone else.

'Hi,' I shouted back, sounding unlike myself. I could feel my face flush as she arrived in the doorway, so I rushed to put my cheek against hers and squeeze her hello, hearing my heartbeat guilty against her chest, as if I'd been caught reading her diary. She dropped a pile of grey papers onto the floor and clutched me to her, making small noises to express affectionate pleasure, which I wasn't sure I could match. I'd forgotten she liked long drawn-out hugs. Nick used to pretend he hated them.

When we'd disentangled I stepped back onto her papers, which I saw were a child's drawings, scrawled in flaking primary colours. I picked one up that might have been a dog, or a bear with three legs. It dawned on me that Rosie hadn't come home.

'Where is she? Where's Rosie?'

'You're different.' Judy smoothed my cheeks with cold hands. 'Your face is all smooth.' She made it sound as if I'd had acne for most of my life. 'I mean it's plump. You look lovely. Rosie's staying over at her dad's. We're free.' She stretched her arms to the ceiling and wriggled her hips. 'I'm starving, but I can't eat. I want to be thin. I got a bit thin already, didn't I? Rosie says I look like a witch.'

Her face was tauter certainly, with something anxious about it as she waited for me to approve, which made the clear green of her long eyes somehow unnerving. She watched me assess her then laughed.

'I know, I look dreadful. About seventy-three on a good day, I know. You'll look like this in a few years' time. This is what motherhood does to a hopeful face.'

She walked to the mirror above the mantelpiece and pulled her forehead up into her perm then down into a cartoon snarl. She dragged a snapshot of her daughter from the frame of the mirror and passed it over to me.

'But this is the face I see much more than my own. Unfortunately it reminds me of Mark. Or his mother, which is worse.'

'She's lovely,' I said. I'd looked at the picture already. The small face looked strained, very like Judy's to me.

'And how is Mark?'

Mark was Rosie's father, who Judy had lived with for a year or so, before their daughter arrived.

'He's teaching unemployed people to relax. But let's not talk about him. Let's have a drink. I hope this baby is nothing to do with Nick, by the way?' She made a face, so I made one back, which could have meant anything, I hoped, but she was already halfway out to the kitchen. 'Are you drinking? It relaxes the foetus, you know.'

'I don't know. I only decided to have the baby today. I wonder if I should.'

'You shouldn't have a baby if that's what you're asking. God. You must be mad. Have a drink and reconsider, Chrissie. I didn't know you still had a choice.'

She came back over the carpet to pat my tummy. I told her I didn't have a choice. It was out of my hands now, I said, and also that baby was hungry.

'That can only get worse,' she said. Then, still touching below my waist, she went on that she might have some clothes I could hide myself in if it was all going to be going ahead.

'But are you sure you know what you're about to do, Chrissie? Do you want a room that looks like this for the rest of your life?'

She gestured to the carpet, which we could barely see for plastic things on wheels and bits of dolls' bodies.

'God.' She picked up a toy lawnmower and shook her head. 'It puts the men off, I'll tell you.'

'So what?' I said, which I thought she'd like, and she did.

'Too right. Let's have a drink. Did anyone call?'

She was in the kitchen before I could answer, then she talked on to me through the door frame. Bottles bounced together as the fridge door opened. I sat on a small chair beside the tiled fireplace and heard her apologizing for the nauseous smell. She'd had a nasty row with Rosie that morning, she said, which was partly why Rosie was staying at Mark's tonight.

'I don't know what I'm doing wrong, Chrissie, but I can't

take much more,' she shouted through the sound of glasses touching each other. Rosie had developed this weird thing about messing with make-up all the time. Just last night the girl had smeared a tub of Clinique all over the bathroom then gone on to fill the toilet with talc. This morning Judy had found her trying to wash her hands with Dior at the kitchen sink, and that had been that, she explained.

'I'm surprised no one called Social Services. It was like World War Three, I can tell you. I had to arm-wrestle with her to get the bloody thing out of her hands, then she fell off the stool and the stuff went all over the floor and, well, this perfumed air is the happy result.'

She was now back in the same room as I was, with two open beers. She started on hers from the bottle. She decided she needed a cigarette and fumbled inside a red suede bag. She asked again if anyone had rung and I said I wasn't sure, although I wasn't sure how that could be the case. Maybe she wouldn't realize that she'd left the volume of her machine turned up. Or maybe I'd say that I must have been in the bathroom when it rang. I went upstairs as she bent to check her calls, so I wouldn't have to seem surprised to hear them. I locked the bathroom door behind me. The floor was sticky, and the basin full of something viscous that smelled of carnations.

'Are you interested in a bath?' Judy shouted up to me through the noise of a car horn somewhere. 'Let's dress up. Let's get out of here. We're free.'

I opened the window of the tiny room and bent over the bath, where something smelt very bad and was brown in the plughole. I turned away and unlocked the door, which slammed itself shut behind me. Judy was still saying, 'We're free,' as I stood on the landing, not knowing where to go next. I didn't feel free at all. I felt suddenly completely trapped.

*

By nine fifteen Judy had changed three times, taken two calls from Rosie, cut her thumb on a can-opener and left for the party.

We'd eaten bacon sandwiches at her round glass table, which had glitter stuck to it, and I'd explained that I'd like to stay in and watch TV, which she found hard to believe, but not impossible to accept. I told her I'd had a long day, but edited out my time at the hospital because she'd have gone on about babies and how awful they were and how only idiots or people on television were pleased to have them.

She was intensely pleased to have negotiated a night without Rosie, but then again, she seemed pleased to be speaking to her daughter when the little girl rang up from Mark's house. Judy's tone with Mark was terse. He hadn't wanted to have Rosie tonight, of course, I was told, but Judy had to see Otto this evening because she hadn't seen him for days and Mark had no right to complain because he didn't want to go out. And even if he did, he could go almost any other night. She had to deal with Rosie every day. The child was a monster but Mark didn't see that, because of course she didn't bother to wind him up. He was so wet there wouldn't be any point. He was living with a woman who loved children, so that made it easy for him. Mark's girlfriend was infertile, which was typical, of course. Judy would doubtless have had much more to say on the subject of Mark's inadequacies, but the phone rang and it was Otto asking how long she'd be. She applied careful make-up then, and talked about the MA Otto was doing and the old Porsche he was reconstructing and how he was the best man for sex that she'd met.

'And that's saying something.'

She did her hair so it was high on her head somehow, smoothed the top of my own head and left in the minicab I'd ordered for her while she was scraping Play-Doh from the heel of her shoe.

When she'd gone, I opened a tin of sardines, spread them on toast and washed them down with camomile tea. Then I lay on the couch and thought about Judy. She'd spent a lot of our time together folding Rosie's small clothes into squares and piling them up until they collapsed, then starting all over again. She'd looked at my tummy from time to time too.

'You'll be OK. You'll be good at it,' she'd said, as if having a baby was like learning the piano or tennis, then she laughed and told me not to buy it any clothes because you only had to find somewhere to keep them all.

I stretched out on the couch, pushed a small padded jacket underneath my head and thought that Judy should have had a boy. She liked boys once they were grown up at least. I thought mine would be a boy, I decided, and thought of boys I'd known and what they would look like if they were me, or even what I would look like if I were a man, and I must have fallen asleep somewhere in these imaginary transformations, because I woke up with a pain in my leg and a terrifying sense that I wasn't alone.

Someone else was in the room. I lay still, pretending to be asleep or a part of the couch in case this was the violent intruder the woman next door was prepared for, but the person turned out to be talking to me. My name was being said softly by the dark shape across the room. I rolled onto my side and saw a man's long girlish legs. I sat up and said hello. It was Mark, who was holding Rosie against him, with her legs wrapped around his waist as if she were a soft large bag on his front. He nodded instead of saying hello to me and said he needed some Calpol. Rosie needed a dose of this analgesic because she had earache. There was usually some in the fridge, he said, and wandered through, then came back explaining that Rosie wanted her mummy. She'd wanted to be here, at home with Judy, and he couldn't stop her crying so he'd brought her back. He hadn't expected to see me. He hadn't really expected anyone to be home, but the last person he'd have thought of expecting was me.

'It's been years.' He looked pleased, if tired, to be staring at me. 'What are you doing in Brighton? Why are you sleeping on Judy's couch? It's after two. Didn't she give you some blankets or something?'

I moved my legs, so he could sit down and tried to remember why I was there.

'I came to go to a party, but then I didn't go after all. Judy had to go without me.' She had to meet a man about a car, I explained, and Mark said, 'Sure she did.'

Rosie took her medicine. She looked stunned. Her eyes were pale blue and her lashes almost too long. She stared at me blankly.

'Mummy's out,' I told her soft red wet face as it lolled over her father's torn leather sleeve.

'Mummy's out, but she'll be home very soon.'

Rosie stared on.

'Mummy loves me,' she said firmly.

I stared at Mark.

'Of course she does, baby,' I watched him say.

He looked younger than he should. I'd last seen him at his thirtieth birthday party, when he'd moaned about fatherhood, of which he'd just learned, and obsessed about Judy all night. He was convinced that she didn't really love him, but had just used him to get hold of a baby. That had turned out to be true, although now she seemed to not want the baby much either, as far as I could see, which was unfortunate, because the baby was clearly obsessed with her. People were always getting obsessed with Judy, one way or another. Nick couldn't stay away from Temps Perdu when she was working there the same nights as I was. I was half in love with her myself, but I didn't need her to love me back like Mark did. I could see that would make anyone desperate.

Rosie's earache subsided, which may have been due to the medicine or simply to the fact that she was home again, expecting mummy to be here soon. She ate chocolate biscuits thoughtfully and involved herself with a pink furry cat that made a whining sound when its wire tail was dragged out. She said nothing to me but stared if I talked, so I said very little until Mark had put her to bed. I did kiss her good night when she was proffered to me from the safety of his shoulders and she said, 'You smell nice,' as I withdrew.

'So do you,' I said, which was true.

'Mummy smells nice,' she said.

I might have asked Mark about his daughter's preoccupation with smells, but he started asking me impersonal, interview sort of questions as soon as he came down from tucking her up. He asked where I was living and how the designing was going and how I was 'in myself'. I responded by asking the same things back, so nothing really was said for ten minutes or so, then he said, 'That poor kid,' which I wished he hadn't.

There was silence until he apologized for the mess.

'I'm really sorry,' he said. He looked it too, so I said there was beer in the fridge and he offered to keep me company until Judy got back, in case Rosie woke up again. She was now in her own bed, which I was to have slept in if I'd ever made it upstairs. Mark said he had a sofa bed at his place which I was welcome to. He'd give me a ride back there later when Judy came back. He offered me a cigarette, which I didn't accept, and some beer, which I did, to keep him company, and then we were there together, like babysitters on the couch with our drinks and biscuits and shared concern about Rosie, and our worry of when mummy would be back, and the Calpol bottle safe on the mantelpiece in case of further infant pain.

I remembered as we talked that I knew Mark better than Judy, and that he didn't have to say much for you to feel at ease in his angular presence. I'd seen at least as much of him as Judy when they shared a life in west London, because Nick and he shared a studio space, where I often arranged to meet Judy, who rarely turned up. I wondered if she'd turn up again tonight, and if she'd met Danby at the party, and if he might be getting obsessed with her in any way. I supposed he might, and she might like him back. He was bound to be nicer than Otto. In fact, he was bound to be the nicest man there and would probably stay in Brighton for ever with some woman he met. Probably Judy. I stood up, thinking I should make an attempt to get to the party, but was overwhelmed to be suddenly vertical, so sat back down again.

'Are you OK? You look green,' Mark observed, so I told him about expecting a baby, and he was pleased and held my hand and gave me a chocolate biscuit, broken in half, as if I was a small child myself, which was perversely reassuring.

'Thanks,' I mumbled through biscuit. 'I hope it's the right thing to do.' I looked around the shambles we were abandoned in. 'I mean, I hope . . .'

'You hope it works out better than this?' Mark lit another cigarette. 'Yeah, well that wouldn't be hard. I wish this had worked out better than this too. And I'm half-responsible for it all, I guess.'

'I doubt that,' I said without thinking. 'I mean, I know you're Rosie's father, but Judy's her mother, and well, she seems to want her . . .' It wasn't sounding very convincing. 'I mean, she's the one who's not here just now.'

I didn't want to sound disloyal to my friend, but I didn't want to sit on a couch all night either.

'Yeah, well. Don't worry about it, Chrissie. You'll be fine. It'll calm you down. Judy's not like you.'

He took my hand lightly. Everyone seemed to feel they could touch me more since I'd been pregnant. I hoped he wouldn't start talking about my personality.

'A baby will soothe you, Chrissie.' He kissed my hand. 'You'll be good at it,' he said.

'How is your mother?' I said to redirect his attention. I'd met her once or twice. She had a massive flat in Oxford Gardens, which Judy and Mark used to stay in to look after her cats when she went away.

He told me his mother had died the year before on his birthday, which he was sure was her final reproach.

'Why?'

'Why did she die? She had cancer. Why did she have cancer? No idea. All I really know about that woman is that she hated me. And I hated her back.'

I looked at the collapsed piles of Rosie's clothes all around us and the plastic kitchen-sink unit. I couldn't think of anything to say. I could see how hatred might come into it all.

I thought of Rosie saying, 'Mummy loves me,' and almost said it out loud, but didn't. Mark wasn't saying anything either.

At four o'clock I must have been fast asleep because Mark had to shake me to wake me up. He said he'd better leave. He had a class at eight thirty to make and if he didn't sleep soon he'd be chaos. He'd been thinking that I might as well get into Judy's bed upstairs and make myself comfortable, since she might not get back till she had to.

'When's that?'

'Eight fifteen. That's when I'm meant to drop Rosie back. Judy might just get back by eight twenty.'

'Does she do this often?'

'Often enough.'

He lit a cigarette and left it in his lips as he pulled his jacket round him to zip up. 'She smells nice, though.' He stubbed his unsmoked cigarette into an empty glass on the mantelpiece. 'And I should know. See you round, Chrissie. Take care.'

Then he left with a nod that made me feel I'd just said something offensive, as if I was now a part of the world that was here, and against, not for him. His goodbye made me angry, not with him but with Judy. I wished she hadn't left him. I wished she hadn't left me. I wished I wasn't there alone, looking after someone else's baby, while someone else was at a party she may not come home from. This disturbed night was probably not good for me or my baby, still curled up inside my insides.

When I next woke up for the third time that broken night, I was asleep upstairs on Judy's large soft mattress and the person calling into my sleep was crying and small.

'Mummy,' Rosie kept whimpering, more loudly after she'd discovered I wasn't that person. I sat on the edge of the mattress on the floor with the little girl between my knees. I rubbed her head and she clung to me, which seemed odd, since she hardly knew me. I felt bad that I was where mummy ought to have been, as if I was making her unhappy on purpose.

'Would you like to stay here with me in Mummy's bed, Rosie?'

No answer. Her quiet weeping continued.

'Would you like a chocolate biscuit?'

No, she wouldn't, she said.

'Mummy will be back soon.' I wondered how often she'd heard that lie. 'Shall we watch television until she comes home?'

It was six fifteen, so there might be something on, some flickering coloured shapes to amuse us. Besides there must be videos.

'Shall we go downstairs and find a video to watch?'

She didn't say no at least. I was terribly thirsty, and our crouching position was aching my back. Rosie was now making small animal noises into my shoulder, which expressed something of how I felt myself. I wished she wouldn't cry. I could see how men must have felt in the past when I got desperate and wept. If it had been me making the noise that Rosie was making, I'd have told myself to drink some water or go out for some air.

The air outside Judy's house was light by now. A pale line slipped through the cracks of the bedroom curtains to glint on Judy's dressing table, smoothing the shapes of her assembled cosmetics into shimmering things, like you see on a beach at eye level if you wake up on one at dawn. I had a sudden brainwave.

'Shall we look at Mummy's perfume, Rosie?'

She lifted her frail head to sniff, incredulous, slightly alarmed, perhaps. Her eyes in mine were wide and shiny wet. She nodded silently. We staggered to my feet as a top-heavy unit and prepared ourselves for forward motion. I'd never had to carry anything so awkward before, except perhaps wet, badly folded tents. My tongue was dry in my mouth. I needed liquid before we did anything else.

'We'll just go down to the kitchen and get Chrissie and Rosie a nice drink, and then we'll put some lovely smelly perfume on Rosie.'

I'd heard my mother talking to children like that. She said their names all the time, as if they might forget who they were.

Rosie wrapped her arms around my neck and we made our laborious way down the narrow unrailed staircase, which I couldn't find the light switch for since I had no free hands. I half expected to trip and have a miscarriage, like people in old films, but we arrived safely on the ground floor and stumbled through bulked objects to arrive in front of the kitchen cupboards, where I took out two plastic beakers, keeping my left arm underneath Rosie. Her underneath felt plush. Nobody had said anything about nappies, but she was clearly wearing one. Perhaps I ought to change it. I decided to think about that after we'd had a drink of something and come to some agreement about getting on.

I located the Ribena and unscrewed the lid, working by feel since the bottle was behind Rosie's back and she was in front of most of my top half. I should have made her stay in the other room, on the couch, while I organized this. With legs wrapped tightly around my waist and a small head pushed into my shoulder, it was hard to apply the necessary force to the tap, which was stiff and on the far side of the draining board from where we were. I stepped sideways to be more in front of the sink, and as I stepped the glass fragments of the Dior bottle on the floor sank into the flesh of my naked left heel.

I cried out, with a sound unlike any I'd heard myself make for years. Rosie and I fell back onto the floor, tearing a poster of London Zoo from the wall behind us as we slid. She shrieked and gripped my thighs as I bent around her body to see the cut, which was deeper than it should have been. I suppose I'd been heavier than usual. Blood streamed onto the matting and she screamed as I swore and pressed my hands against the cut, which would not stop flowing blood. My fingers were wet with it, so I pushed myself to a standing position, rinsed my hands in the washing-up bowl and pressed my foot again. Blood leaked through my fingers.

Rosie screamed and screamed, the word 'mummy' coming in frantic bursts, and I didn't know how to stop her crying, so the noise began to scare me more than the red of myself running onto my hands. The word 'mummy' had something chilling inside it as she screamed it right beside my ear.

'It's all right, Rosie,' I said again and again. 'It's all right. We'll go and sit down. We'll make Mummy come back.'

Because that was what I had to do now, of course. I must calm Rosie down and find my jacket and the phone number that Danby had written down for me. I must ring the house where the party was and make Judy come home as fast as she could. Rosie wouldn't stop crying because I wasn't mummy. I was a frightening thing that bled and cried, and since I'd been forced to be that, Rosie's crying began to annoy me. I found myself almost dragging her out of the kitchen and through onto the couch. I put her down.

'Stay there,' I said harshly, surprising myself. 'Stay there. Do you understand? I'm going to make Mummy come home.'

The gash in my foot was deep and leaking into the threadbare grey carpet. I took a cotton vest from the top of a pile of clean clothes and pressed it against the wound, but blood came through right away. I hobbled up the dim stairs to the bathroom through Rosie's howls and ran cold stinging water onto the cut and realized it would have to be stitched. It was about an inch long and flapped like a fish gill. I'd have to go to hospital. I must call a cab and make Judy come back. She should be here by now, in any case. Her behaviour was disgusting and I was beginning to hate her as Rosie screamed from down on the couch. I was shivering, with rage as much as the shock of my blood and the pain of the foot and lack of sleep and the fear of being alone with a noise I couldn't control.

I jumped back downstairs, the arms of the vest trailing from the foot I had swaddled it with. I rang the phone number of the party, smearing blood onto the answering machine and the receiver. Danby's sleepy voice said hello. He coughed.

'Who do you want? What time is it?' He coughed again as I said his name, and he took a few moments to hear it was me. I said I needed to get to a hospital quickly and could he meet me at Brighton Infirmary in half an hour's time and he said sure he could. He was on his way now. He'd just get his boots on, he said, and other slurred internal arrangements as he asked if I was OK.

'Is it the baby?' he said, but I didn't answer that question. I asked if he'd seen a woman called Judy. I needed him to find her for me, I told him, and he laughed and said he'd find that easy. I heard him say her name.

Through low music and laughter, Rosie's mother called to me down the phone, but at first I couldn't bring myself to speak. I listened to her saying that she was on her way.

'Chrissie, I'm coming. I was on my way out. What's happening? Has something happened? Is Rosie OK?'

'You've got to come home,' I said. 'Something terrible's happened. Come home right away.'

'Oh God,' she said. She said that a few times, between asking me what was wrong, and as I pressed another small garment against my foot, and Rosie was silent and staring and stunned, I felt a calm sense of revenge.

'There's been an accident,' was all I said to Judy when she asked me frantically what had gone wrong. It was cruel, I know, but I just kept saying that over and over, whatever she asked, until she too was weeping and I was glad. Glad to be so good at making her scared. Glad she was sorry for something, although I wasn't exactly sure what it was she was supposed to be sorry for.

When the phone went dead, when Judy was on her way home, I told Rosie that Mummy was coming.

'She's coming now. Mummy will be here very soon. Mummy loves you,' I said, and I held her as well as I could as I rang for a cab.

I hoped Danby wouldn't mind about my foot. I didn't think he would, and I didn't think my baby would mind a hospital either. We'd be in one together when I was in labour, after all, and then again, of course, many times after that if Judy's house was anything to go by. Life is full of accidental violence, I thought as my cab swept along past the pale dawn sea, past early-morning people going out and late-night people going home, on my way to meet Danby at a hospital – which I'd almost done the day before – just over twenty-four hours ago.

Eleven Teatime

MY BABY WAS A BOY AND I CALLED HIM BILLY, BECAUSE HE HAD a robust little face and a small deep cry, like Billy Goat Gruff's might have been if he'd wept. When the first winter came after Billy was born, my landlord visited one Tuesday afternoon to say we were to have new gas fires. He thought the bathroom window must be replaced too, and the kitchen one fixed. I was pleased he'd decided to improve my lot, but when the window man came to measure up for the job and explained the complex nature of his task, and when another man came to disconnect all the fires, I decided I'd better go away for a while. I would go to Yorkshire to visit Lily and Gabriel. Billy wouldn't like to stay in London, with the noise, the disruption, the moving male voices that new fires and windows would bring. He was used to routine, which involved mostly just me and the shadows of things we saw moving around our limited world. And Lily had been wanting to meet my baby ever since he was born in June.

A large part of my life with Billy in those first few months was the gingham-lined pushchair which went ahead of me whenever I went in the outside air, which would often not pass through the doors of shops and which seemed to make people not look at my face. People would generally talk to the pushchair, rather than to me or Billy himself, lying curiously inside. At first I resented the bulk of the thing, the way it labelled me from yards away as a person set apart from the carefree population, who could swing their arms as they walked, and carry umbrellas and handbags. Who could buy large objects in shops and bring them home easily, using both hands. I didn't like to be part of a recognizable clan, with smaller concerns than everyone else. But as the weeks passed, I came to see Billy's pushchair as a comfortable part of my whole new life, and like the regulation school shoes I hated at the beginning of each new year, it became less of a uniform and more a particular part of myself.

So when I rang Lily to say I'd decided to travel to see her, and she said there was no need for me to bring anything, because the woman next door had three children, I told her I'd bring my pushchair with me. I didn't want a borrowed one. To have Billy lying inside somebody else's pushchair would have been like wearing someone else's bra, or sleeping in another person's unwashed pyjamas.

I think she thought I had gone slightly crazy, like single new mothers are meant to. She spoke slowly and calmly as she explained where I must wait to be met at Leeds station, and asked me to take care on the journey, as if it was a matter of days rather than hours on public transport. I said I wouldn't talk to strangers. She didn't laugh. She told me not to leave Billy alone at any point in the journey.

'Otherwise someone might steal him.'

I looked at my baby, asleep in his basket, which Alison and Jake had brought when they first came to see us in Queen Charlotte's Hospital.

'Well he's so gorgeous,' I said. 'I'd steal him myself if he wasn't mine.'

'Don't be silly, Chrissie. You wouldn't.'

I said I'd let her know the time of my train the following

day. She was clearly in no mood for whimsy. People who had nothing to do with babies took the idea of them very seriously. And Danby had probably been on the phone to Lily, issuing strict instructions for my stay. He didn't like the idea of me going to Yorkshire much, but was going to Paris that week himself, so accepted that my plan was better than nothing, in terms of my being warm and safe.

'As long as you ring me when you get there,' he told me. 'I don't want to have to drive to Yorkshire to find you.'

'Well, since I found Lily for you, I'm hardly likely to lose myself.'

He gave me his address and phone number in Paris.

'Take a coat, remember. It's cold up there.'

I almost said I'd been planning to go naked, but decided not to bother. Some men are even more worried about women with babies than women who have no children are.

Lily and Gabriel were living in a cottage near Kenneth and Sarah. When I rang Jamie to tell him I wouldn't be at home for a few days – in case he should worry, which he never had so far – he suggested I take Billy to see the folk at the farm. That way, we might all be remembered in Kenneth's will. Lily and Gabriel agreed that it would be a good idea to introduce Billy to his grandfather, and I might have gone to the farmhouse if I hadn't met Anne in the post office on the second day of my stay. I had walked to the village post office with Billy and his pushchair to buy a stamp for my letter to Danby in France. I thought writing would do, to let him know I was safe. Lily and Gabriel had no money, so phone calls to Paris would be an extreme request. Gabriel wanted to walk with me, but I said I'd be fine and would buy tobacco for Lily – I'd been smoking hers the night before in the early hours.

I got back safely from my expedition, which seemed to surprise my young friends, who were watching at the window and ran to greet me before I was near enough to shout that I'd forgotten to get cigarette papers. As we huddled home I told them about the woman called Anne who'd invited me to tea that afternoon. I'd met her in the post office. Gabriel, Lily, my pushchair and I were arriving in a limbed bundle through to the oven-warm kitchen when the phone began its substantial ring. It was Danby, in a bar on the Rue St Michel, calling to see if I was OK. I immediately told him about Anne's invitation, as if it was a children's party I was dying to go to. As if there was nothing nicer anyone could want in the world than to have tea with Anne and her friends. He was pleased, as he was meant to be. He said that was great, it would do me good.

'You mustn't hole up with Lily there, Chrissie. You have to keep being a part of the world.'

'I'm Billy's world now,' I said back, and he laughed, but he wasn't supposed to because it was true.

The world for me was Billy at that time, and his smile to see me when I lifted him up from wherever I'd last put him down. I scooped him from the bed we were sharing after his nap, after my conversation with Danby, and tucked him into the pushchair to walk down with me to Anne's converted Sunday school, which I thought was near the post office. Lily lent me an enormous Kagool. She wanted me to take their van, but I'd dented it on a lamp-post the day I arrived, having gone to buy coal, so I said I'd prefer to walk, although it was pouring rain and they both said I was mad. I said they were mad not to have a baby, and also to be living in Yorkshire, because it was always raining there.

It had been raining when I'd arrived on Monday and had rained consistently since; a noisy uneven rush that spurted from scooped-out slate rooftops and hanging-off gutters and sounded like a washing machine emptying somewhere nearby, wherever you happened to be. The sound of the rain came the same through listless dawns, long mornings and sleepy afternoons and made the nights a part of the day, which was fine by me since I slept as little in each. The weather was company for me as I woke at one thirty, or four, or six, and slid up out of sleep to curve round for Billy and give him a feed. Gabriel and Lily weren't much company, although they were nice to be with when they weren't in bed. They were fairly absorbed in each other, and since I was absorbed in the private affair of my baby, we all got along.

They didn't mind about my denting their van, for example. It happened all the time they said. There were too many lamp-posts in this part of the world. Lily gave me sweet tea and biscuits after I'd had my crash, while Gabriel went to unload the coal, taking Billy with him in his corduroy sling, so I needn't bother myself. He did that to be kind, but it left me wistful, because there wasn't often a man to watch walking around with Billy. Danby used to visit and hold him, of course, but he was setting up a language school in Brighton and organizing the syllabus at another in Earls Court, which meant he was often too busy. My baby and I had other visitors who frequently arrived, but still it always felt as if we were somehow alone, whoever else was there in the room. And outside, we were generally alone with our pushchair, as we were on that wet Wednesday, when we walked down to the village together through low rainy sky on our way to have tea with Anne and her friends, when I decided we were lost. I'd been walking for more than half an hour when I realized that I had no real idea where I was, or where I ought to go next.

I should have asked Anne for precise directions when we'd met in the post office, but I was trying to leave when she arrived and called out my name, which was why I'd accepted her invitation as quickly as I had. Billy was hungry.

'That would be lovely,' I'd said, on being told that she and her friends with their babies would be meeting for tea that afternoon and would love it if I came along.

‘What time is everyone coming?’ I’d asked, but not where they’d all be exactly. Not exactly how to get to Anne’s house from Lily’s, because my pushchair got wedged between two other shoppers, both of whom had babies, and both of whom knew Anne. I had to concentrate on freeing myself from the place, and the greetings and urgent arrangements. I had to get Billy back to Lily’s.

‘See you about four then, Chrissie. Be sure to come, won’t you?’

‘Yes, lovely. That’ll be lovely,’ I’d called back, wishing I were more familiar with the sort of words that Anne easily used, and wondering what quite would be lovely now that my life was so entangled with Billy’s. It might have been lovely to sleep and not wake for days, with someone enormous curled round me, someone as big as I must seem to a baby.

It was not lovely, though, to be lost in rain on the way to Anne’s house, where I wouldn’t know anyone and where everyone would have babies. I’d never known Anne closely when I’d met her years before in a village near here, where I’d briefly lived with Nick. She had never offered me tea in those faraway days. But now we had babies to tend together we must naturally have tea. We must meet and talk about the men who did or did not curl round us, of course. Anne had assessed my wedding-ring finger in the post office and asked how Nick was with studied carelessness.

‘He was such a sweet man. Or was he, Chrissie? Anyway, I’ll hear all your news this afternoon.’

She might hear a version of some of my news, if I could ever get to her house, I thought, as the rain-clotted road I was struggling along became simply a wide rippled pool with nowhere further to walk. It was almost four, and almost dark, and I was standing at the edge of what seemed to be a small lake. Billy was stirring. He must be hungry again.

Across the expanse of water before me was a T-junction.

On my left was a telephone box with no door. On my right was the primary school, with its climbing frame like a spaceship, and a stack of wood ready for Bonfire Night. Moving between these two landmarks I saw a man on a bike with a large square shape strapped onto the silhouette of his back. It could have been a placard or a music case or a bit of wood for the fire. It was making his journey rather unstable. He stopped and put one foot on the ground and peered at the trees behind me, then started off again, so I shouted as loudly as I could through the noise of the rain. The rider put a boot to the ground and shook his head, then looked over towards the phone box, balancing himself at a slant. There was a moment's silence as I realized he wasn't going to dismount from his bicycle, so I'd have to shout, which might wake Billy up.

'Excuse me,' I called as shrilly as I dared. 'Can you help me? I'm lost.'

He wasn't looking at the phone box any more. He wasn't looking at anything anywhere in my direction. He was taking his cap off and replacing it with the peak at the back instead of the front. When that was done he hunched and unhunched his shoulders, rang his bicycle bell, then pushed himself off and moved precariously away with his flapping back and his bicycle chain grinding.

I thought of shouting again, and louder, but didn't want to scare Billy. I decided to check that he was all right while I thought of what to do next. He was only five months old and I knew that they sometimes stop breathing, but he was alive and asleep in his oxygen-tent rain hood, so I pulled the plastic contraption back down and wondered what to do. I could ring Lily if the phone box worked. I could ask her if she knew where I was and why the bicycle man had ignored me, although she'd be unlikely to know if there was a reason. Perhaps there was a reason. Maybe he'd had some bad experience with women with babies. I felt rejected and lonely. I seemed to be letting Billy down this week. First I'd crashed a van we were in together and now we were lost in the rain in the middle of nowhere.

I must try and do better, I was thinking, and not panic about being lost, when a green Renault 5 arrived from nowhere and stopped in our puddle and splashed us. The window scrolled down with a scratchy noise and a triangular face with lipstick leaned out and asked if everything was OK.

'You look a bit lost,' the lipstick said, and I asked if she knew where the old Sunday school was? Next to a disused chapel, I thought.

'It's Anne Livingstone's place. I don't suppose you know it?'

'I do. You're there. Turn left and you're there.' She smiled widely. 'I'd give you a lift, but you're almost there.'

She jammed into first to take a sharp bend and arrived at Anne's before I did, because she hadn't had to pick round the edge of an ocean, dragging a pushchair behind her.

She was sitting on a couch when I arrived, with her feet warm and dry in pale suede boots. She was frowning into a drip-glazed cup of steaming tea as I moved tentatively into a cream-walled kitchen with spotlights sunk into its ceiling. No one noticed my arrival, so I watched the gathering, immersed in itself. A lean woman in white jeans was cradling a baby with a dummy in its mouth as she stooped to talk to the woman who'd given me directions. The conversation seemed to be about men, as I had suspected it would be.

'But it's not a real desire, is it?' I heard as I pulled my pushchair's wet hood back into itself, trying not to wake Billy with splashes.

'I mean, he doesn't really want her rather than you, you silly. It's just an idea he's got about himself and sex, or something. It's normal. He'll be back. I wouldn't worry about it.'

I didn't know whether to lift Billy out or not. He looked so happy to be asleep by himself.

'You'd worry if it was you,' another woman said. 'If Harry was sleeping with someone. I mean, you'd mind about that, wouldn't you?'

She certainly would. Even Billy could tell them that Harry's wife would mind Harry sleeping with someone else.

'I would not. How could I? I'd diminish myself. It's meaningless.'

She was talking more loudly now. Her Harry probably was sleeping with someone else already. 'And anyway, with a mother like his, I mean, what did you expect . . .?'

I tried not to listen and felt suddenly too tired to be here. I knew this sort of talk by now, that they did over their babies on these tread-water afternoons. There was always something bad happening to someone else, some dissatisfaction to be discussed that would make for a satisfactory afternoon's conversation, but not make anything or anyone change. They wouldn't want any change. They'd have nothing to talk about.

'And anyway, she won't want him for very long, will she? Not from what I've heard. Then he'll be back and buying you underwear and minding the children, just in case you've noticed he's been a bit indifferent lately.'

They laughed as they could probably afford to. Their men would mind these women's children for them and be mindful of these women's affection too. They'd have taken care of that by now, I could tell. These were not desperate people. These were people who had afternoon tea and talked about their husbands, who wouldn't dream of bothering to discuss their wives. Their husbands were busy out earning the money that paid for their nice suede boots.

The last time I'd seen Jamie he'd minded Billy for an afternoon and asked me to lend him a fiver when I got home. He sent the money back to me a few weeks later, with some photographs of Billy he'd taken, and said be sure to take our boy to Yorkshire. He'd said he'd be in touch again soon, but that was six weeks ago. Jamie was living with a Dublin girl in Galway now. I didn't mind for myself, but it seemed hard for Billy to only have me to care.

The baby between the two talking women burped a spider's web of white sick onto a black padded shoulder, but neither of them noticed.

'You're over-reacting, Ruthie. That's what I think. But what's Anne's line on all this? Anne should know what to think about infidelity, for goodness' sake.'

I could have told them something about men leaving, if they'd asked me, but they wouldn't do that. They wouldn't want my opinion. They wouldn't want anything unfamiliar.

I stared at the walls with their paintings of flat hills. I remembered Anne's husband, Wolfie, who must have painted them all. He'd taught me on foundation, and taught Nick too when we all lived in Triangle, before this black chapel had been converted into a dwelling, when I was often afraid to walk past it alone. Nick insisted it was haunted and I believed him completely. I was in the habit of doing that then.

'I mean, they all go off for a bit sometimes, and then they come back. It doesn't mean anything. It's just what they do.'

I watched the taller woman take a tissue from her pocket to rub off her child's sick as she talked. She saw me watching and smiled, but frowned somewhere too, so I looked at the sanded floor that was lumped with crawling children, wearing denim and stripes with their socks falling off. I thought of Gabriel's smile when Lily came into the room every morning and couldn't imagine him leaving her, but perhaps he would. But if he did, then would he come back? My father left my mother once and we didn't see him again. Nick hadn't phoned me for months. Billy would be leaving me one day and might not come home for Christmas.

I studied a stack of wet pushchairs beside me, folded flat, like chairs were at school. I stood and dripped in Lily's orange Kagool and wondered if I should introduce myself. I would have liked a cup of tea.

'Well I just don't know quite where I stand, that's all.'

The woman with the unfaithful husband was sitting down in fact, as were most of the women there, but suddenly a large hand-knitted shape came swinging across the room towards me. It was Anne's cardigan. Her short legs stopped moving when she got to me.

'Chrissie, hello. Hello, hello.'

Her hand was on my shoulder, then the small of my back, as she hugged me into her felted breasts. I'd never been held so close by someone so plump before. I realized she was pregnant.

'You've got so thin, you little waif. You've got to eat lots of Mars Bars when you're breastfeeding, you know? Wolfie's mother says so.'

She bent to peer at Billy. I thought Wolfie's mother was dead, but he could have a replacement mother by now, I supposed. His father was very attractive.

'Bring that adorable baby out and let me see.'

Anne made the word 'see' remind me of 'glee' and *The Beano*. Then she made a church-hall announcement to everyone there except me: 'Everyone, this is darling Chrissie. A friend from London, by special arrangement.'

I untangled Billy's straps from his limp little legs and held him to my front for everyone to see. Everyone smiled and seemed to be walking towards me, except for one long woman at the back with a kettle in her hand and a large pregnancy to balance between her breasts and knees. I hoped Billy was smiling, or clean at least.

'Who *does* he look like?' Anne asked, watching my face, then someone said to have a seat and they were all separate from me again, clustering round a table that was narrow and low, like a tombstone. I followed them over with Billy and pulled out a chair which knocked into a child who started to scream. Everyone said not to worry. It happened all the time, they said, and one of the mothers bent from a wide-belted waist to collect the collapsed infant into the folds of her elbow. Then she straightened up and stared at me. She had a cup of tea in one hand and a crumpet in the other. She told me she was Mary, and passed me her tea so she could pat her baby's back. Someone else handed me another cup of tea, so I had to pass Mary's tea back to her, which I could see she felt was incapable of me. Seasoned mothers can hold dozens of cups of tea and several babies. They can hold a baby while re-stocking a supermarket if they have to.

Mary had a beaker of juice hooked onto a thumb and a biscuit somewhere too and the child and a dummy and some sort of cleaning cloth and a lot to say about being tired, which was why she was always eating these biscuits, which made her fat, which she hated. She was indeed rather plump, so I nodded to be sympathetic, but that was the wrong response, because she tried to put the biscuit back onto the plate it had come from, which meant she knocked a cup of tea over. I took the cloth from her shoulder and wiped the tea, with Billy nudging at my front. I didn't do a very good job of cleaning up, but I'm not sure she would have wanted me to.

I was then informed by Mary that my baby seemed hungry. He was rooting, wasn't he, she asked, to see if I knew what that meant perhaps, and I did, because I loved the word; thought it a perfect description of Billy's ruthless curiosity as he rooted for himself around my breasts.

He rooted on as the affair that Ruthie's husband was having was discussed in energetic spurts around us. Everyone gave advice and sympathy, while lifting sandwiches, cups, cartons of juice and stroking the small bodies fastened to their own.

Tea was poured and poured again, and there were occasional bursts of water spilling from drainpipes outside.

'Well I think you're over-reacting, Ruthie, I really do. What do you think, Mary?'

Mary was sitting firmly at the table now, sticking a fork through the hole in the teat of a bottle. Billy butted my front more insistently. I hadn't fed him since lunchtime. Someone named Isabelle, like Isa was really, suggested I give him a suck.

'Sit on the couch now, sweetness, and give that baby a drink.'

So I moved away from the table to a paisley chaise longue, not unlike Isa's, which was still in Moscow Road, and did as I was told. I fed thirsty Billy and drank the tea someone passed me and watched these women who knew each other talking. Taking biscuits from painted plates, and care of their babies and cakes to their mouths and taking stock of me from time to time, smiling when they saw I'd seen them. If Isa'd had a baby she could have been here with me now, I found myself thinking. But Isa didn't have her baby – she had Nick now instead, and I had Billy, who at least cried if I left him, which was more than anyone else had yet done. I was thinking I might send my sister a picture of my son some time, when Anne arrived to sit beside me and asked how I was coping. It would have been best to say badly, of course. I'd learnt that in London at post-natal classes. You were best liked if you told a sad story well. You could ask about sleep patterns and night crying and weight gain and baby books and Calpol, but that wasn't what was wanted in the end. You had to have a story, so they could tell you theirs, which would be like your own, but worse.

My story was the best kind to have, and I should have told it, but I didn't want to hear myself. I wouldn't be able to speak with the breathless passion required, because now it often seemed as if it had happened to somebody else. Although I could end up spilling my tea if I started on my autobiography, and then they'd take Billy from me and probably ask each other if I was coping.

My silence was filled by a confident voice from over beside the table.

'Well, from what I've heard he's not coping well with the situation. Harry said he's been drinking heavily lately.'

I wouldn't have minded drinking heavily myself. I wondered if they'd get out the gin when it got to five o'clock or so. Some mothers I knew in London did that.

'It won't come to anything, I'm telling you.'

Isabelle snapped a wafer in two and handed half of it to Ruthie, who turned it in her fingers as if it might have the weather forecast or her horoscope on it.

'I mean, I know it's easy to say so, but you mustn't take any notice.'

She bent to a little boy straddling a tractor and eased a sock back onto his foot. He pulled it off and she put it on again calmly. She could repeat that action for ever, I expected, and her pale plump face would always be almost a smile.

'Do we need more tea, everyone?' someone said.

Anne lifted the pot and tilted it back and forth carefully. The front door slammed and a 'Hi' came through, then 'Christ', then the 'Hi' got louder as something solid in clogs advanced.

'There's a maniac out there on a bicycle,' the voice was shouting as the new arrival approached the kitchen door. 'Nearly came through my windscreen. Could have killed us all.'

A Henry Moore of a woman holding two ovals of baby was suddenly framed in the doorway, making the whole room seem fragile and small.

'I'm not kidding. There's a maniac out there. On a bicycle, out of control.'

Anne put down the teapot and strode to take both babies

from this outraged guest, so the woman could unsnap her front and climb out of her mac.

'He nearly cycled right into the car. I haven't dared look at the bumper.'

'Perhaps his brakes failed.' The babies seemed lost on Anne's armchair breasts.

'He shouted at me, right up in my face. I couldn't shout back. Not with the children.'

There was silence as the room considered the children and the harm that shouting could do them.

'Was he drunk? He must have been drinking.'

The woman said she hadn't got near enough to know. She'd kept her window firmly closed. What with the children inside, and the rain and so on, she wasn't about to smell his breath.

'It was a nightmare,' she said, and Ruthie said to sit down and relax and tell us all the whole story, and that we needed some strong fresh tea. She filled the kettle capably. She opened the tall fridge and peered in. She took a carton of milk out, shook it hard then dropped it into a bin. She wondered out loud if we should inform the police.

'He's not out there now at any rate.'

Anne was standing on a chair, peering out of a window with stained glass at its curved edges. Ruthie had her head back inside the door of the fridge.

'I think we should get some more whole milk in before we discuss this properly, Anne. There's only skimmed in here, did you know that?'

Anne was making lip-smacking noises to a child in a high chair, to encourage him to eat. I'd seen them doing that before, wanting their babies to want what they offered. They ate it themselves if all else failed, as an example, or a punishment perhaps. My own baby was bored with feeding now and writhing away from me with a vague discontent and fisting the shapes of his face. I took his fingers and watched them wrap around my thumb. He might be going to cry. I hoped he wouldn't. I wasn't always able to make him stop, and whereas I didn't mind the noise, I thought it would complicate things in this kitchen.

'Well, we'd better tell someone,' said Ruthie. 'We can't just have lunatics wandering the village in the middle of the afternoon.'

'He was obviously out of control,' someone else said. 'I mean, anything could have happened, couldn't it, really?'

Isabelle agreed, and the new woman too. I wondered exactly what 'anything' was and asked if there was any more tea yet. It was the first thing I had said out loud, and it was clearly inappropriate because everyone stared. Perhaps tea was a triviality now. I should have been considering the dangers of the outside world, joining in with the story. I tried to make amends by standing up and patting Billy's back absorbedly. Anne went to see if there was any milk in the freezer. The woman who'd been all-but murdered by the bicycle man peeled a sandwich apart to feed one of her children. She was saying now that she'd probably over-reacted to the whole thing. She'd been jumpy all day because that woman had rung again this morning and put the phone down when she'd answered.

'That's the third time this week.'

She ate the sandwich her child didn't want, and said that she wouldn't mind, except she'd like to have a talk with the girl. She thought she could help her understand Bill. There was no point in getting het up over the man.

'I mean, I'm his wife. I know what he's like, I'm afraid.'

The room nodded in concerned understanding. How naïve the other woman was.

'So, anyway. What's the story with you this week, Ruthie? Is Romeo still pining for his Juliet?'

Ruth raised her eyebrows, smiled carefully and explained

that she wasn't going to mention anything. That's what she'd decided this afternoon, she said. She'd had some good advice.

'Good for you. That's the only way to handle it, sweetheart. Keep mum till it's over, then let him have it. That's what I did last time, and I'm playing it that way again.'

She smirked and rubbed one of her baby's cheeks, as if there was something hidden under its surface that she must very carefully disclose.

'I mean, there's really no point in discussing it with him. It just makes them feel important.'

I couldn't see what would be wrong with making your husband feel important if he was thinking of leaving you for someone else. They might decide you were important too. Nick told me I was still important, the last time I saw him in London. He threw a tub of goldfish food across the floor to emphasize his point, and I didn't clear it up for days. I'd just take a bit of it from the scattered mess and feed the fish that way, until Danby arrived and got out the vacuum. My floor seemed important to him.

Anne came back from wherever the freezer was in a different jumper but without any milk. She sat down on the couch and patted the spot next to her, to encourage me to move there. I did, and tried to look as if I agreed with what she was thinking, and eager to hear her express it.

'Look, they're shits and that's all there is to it. It's not even worth talking about. They all come home in the end.'

Anne swept crumbs from herself with firm jerks of her hand, then bent to lift a child to sit on her knee, and brushed the legs of that down too. Then she said there was no milk, so someone must go to the post office and get some.

Everyone studied their children. The post office didn't appeal, clearly.

'Anyway, Ruthie, darling, this is not a reflection on you. You're fine. Don't worry about it.'

Everyone then agreed that everything was always the husband's fault. Someone kissed Ruth's ear. I kissed Billy's, which felt cold as seaweed and I wondered why he hadn't smiled all afternoon. He seemed lonelier than usual, which was odd, because we'd rarely been with so many people before.

I stood up, rubbed my little boy's nose with my own. He smiled.

'And at least we've got each other to talk to. I mean, thank God for women, I say,' someone said. 'Thank heaven for the second sex, *n'est-ce pas*?'

There was laughter and happy sighs were heavily exhaled. Eyebrows were raised in my direction. I said I'd go for the milk if no one else much wanted to.

'I'll go to the post office, shall I? I think Billy needs some air.'

I wanted to be outside myself, to meet the man on the bicycle again maybe and say I understood his rage with these creatures, of whom I was supposed to be one now. But Anne said no, she'd go for milk herself, and no, I mustn't be out in this wetness. What madness, they said. Billy and I must stay here, indoors. Babies should be warm and dry.

'Well, I could go by myself then. Perhaps someone could watch him for five minutes?'

I had to get out of there and breathe. I felt sick, I told them, and it wasn't entirely a lie, although the fact that I was taking iron tablets was, but they didn't know that. Isabelle said she had had those wretched things too, of course, and Anne too, now that she remembered. She'd felt nauseous for months, but it was better than feeling too exhausted to breathe. Why hadn't I told them I was anaemic? Anne had dried apricots in the cupboard. No wonder I looked so pale.

Concern for me flooded. They all knew just how I felt. Ruthie took Billy into her capable arms and said I must have fresh air. Anne then took Billy from Ruthie, giving her own child to Isabelle, and said how dreadful that I felt sick.

'I know just how you feel, you poor thing,' she said. 'And of course Wolfie was no help at all.'

And so I became their baby then, and was cosseted into my coat and told to take my time and not to worry myself. Have some time off, but bring back a carton, Anne said.

'A carton, not glass,' she whispered urgently to me. 'I don't have glass bottles in the house any more.'

I said yes, a carton, though I couldn't see why, and I walked out into the wet, which was black by now with white bulbs strung along it, like small-town seafronts, and a sweet smell of beer and damp wood.

The post office was along to the right, beyond the telephone box. I waded through water and past a field of still sheep, and I stopped to watch as they ate their way into night time, and I decided not to cry, which I felt like briefly, leaving Billy alone in a strange place. I wouldn't cry, but I wouldn't be long. Although I would have liked to be for ever in some ways. But I must go to the post office and buy the women their milk. Then Billy and I could go home to Lily and Gabriel, and soon we could go back to London, to our new gas fires and our old friends there. I could tell Danby all about this world, down the road from where his daughter lived. I might write and tell him. Two letters in a week might be too much, but I could buy another stamp in case.

In the post office the shopkeeper was polishing glass. He was in front of a shelving unit with one of everything on it, like a children's shop set. The place smelled of paraffin and sweets. It was closing time, the man said. Five thirty he shut shop on Thursdays. He had a kind face and was neat with his polish. I explained how I just wanted milk, deciding not to mention stamps. Milk would be in the fridge, he assured me, and pointed towards it, then went back to his cleaning until the door opened again, with a window-box lilt in its bell, and the man with the cap who'd been on the bicycle came through, with his corduroy trousers tucked into his socks and a large flat book wrapped in plastic under his arm.

'Drawings,' he explained when I stared. 'Been drawing the trees all afternoon. All the big ones. Good trees in the rain.'

I was surprised he'd been able to see any trees clearly, or find anywhere dry enough to draw. He looked down at his sketch pad fondly, and I did too, hoping he might open the thing to show me his trees, but he didn't, so I asked could I see, which surprised me. I don't usually talk to strangers. The man didn't answer, although I asked him twice. The shop man stopped working to listen.

'I draw a lot,' I told him. 'I'm a textile designer.' I remembered what I was with surprise. 'But I've been drawing my new baby lately.'

He stayed silent, but smiled, with his eyes slits of crinkles. I smiled back. He shook his head, then nodded, still smiling and said sorry, he was hard of hearing. He couldn't make out a word I said.

'Deaf, that's me.' He patted his sketch pad. 'No point talking to me unless you like shouting a lot.'

Then he laughed with not many teeth in his gums and angled himself on past me to the counter. He asked for firelighters. The man in the shop must have known who he was because he didn't say anything to him. The three of us watched the firelighters being wrapped in newspaper, listening to the rain outside and the noise the folded paper made.

'Goodbye then,' I shouted very loudly, and he must have heard that as he opened the door, because he turned back to me and held up a thumb from one of his wrinkled fists and winked. The barman in my local in London does that.

'Nice to meet you,' I shouted, but he'd gone by then. I

thought it might have been nice to show him my baby. He might have shown me his trees if Billy were there.

'Five thirty now, miss,' the shop man said clearly, as if a train was about to leave that I'd wanted to catch. My grandmother used to call us 'miss' when we were naughty. I opened the fridge door and peered inside.

'I'm sorry. I can't see any cartons.'

I was told they were there at the back on the top shelf, but I could only see sausages there. A few packets of cheese were on the next shelf down, with some chalky milkshakes like Edinburgh Rock, but no milk, except some in glass bottles at the bottom with a lettuce.

'There's no milk in cartons that I can see, I'm afraid.' I said the words as Ruthie or Isabelle or Anne would have said them. As if they were important, because I hadn't a clue why I was saying that really, except that I'd been instructed.

'There is milk in that fridge.'

'But not in cartons, is there?'

'There is milk in that fridge.'

His voice was louder. He came out from behind his counter wearing maroon slippers, like soft little tug-boats. There was a label stuck to the heel of one of them. I wondered if he had a wife. A wife would have noticed a thing like that.

'There is milk in that fridge, do you hear me?'

Shouting loudly by then, and I turned to the door, thinking I'd go back and tell the others this story, but he was suddenly there on the lino shop floor, with his hand on my arm in front of the fridge and bits of his face moving fast.

'Have to have it your way every time, you women, don't you?'

I was flustered by the word 'women', although I was one of them, I could see.

'Bloody picky, that's what I call it.'

He let go of my arm, but I didn't move, although a different sort of woman probably would have. If I'd had a husband called Harry I might have moved away quickly from this person with the wrong sort of milk.

'What's wrong with milk in a bottle, eh? Not good enough for you?'

We looked at each other and not at the bottle that he had in his hand, up in front of his face.

'What's wrong with milk like that?'

Then it wasn't in front of his face any more. It was up high above his head, I suppose, because it made a terrible noise as it smashed. We looked together at its splinters and its liquid white that seeped under the fridge and rolled in drops on his slippers, and I said nothing and neither did he. There was nothing wrong with that one. Except that it was broken.

Back at the old Sunday school I told everyone else that the post office was shut. It had closed early today, I said. I didn't want them to know about the man with his slippers, the smashed glass and the milk, or how he'd been when we'd wiped it up. I didn't want them to know that his wife had left him, that he'd held my coat, that his finger bled onto my hand when we said goodbye.

But Anne knew already all she needed to know about Jim Dones, her post-office man.

'He's not the same since his wife left,' she said brightly, and no wonder, poor him. He was always off early, not surprisingly. He wasn't coping well on his own. They all agreed that the post office was a sorry place now and the man was not coping well.

I watched Ruthie sip tea and Isabelle understanding and a baby full of milky rusk and I told them no, they'd got it all wrong.

'It has nothing to do with his wife,' I said firmly, collecting Billy from Isabelle. 'That is not why he shut his shop early.'

I was packing my son into our pushchair and pushing my head into my borrowed Kagool. I was jamming open the door so I could wheel away from everyone watching. They'd stopped drinking tea, and were just watching me now, because I was leaving and they hadn't told me to go.

'This isn't to do with his wife. He closed early to go to a party. He's gone to a party in London. He doesn't care about his wife any more. He's never speaking to her again. Men do that sometimes, hadn't you heard? They leave and they never come back.'

'Jim Dones?' they all said. 'Jim Dones has left without his wife? But how do you know?'

'A man on a bicycle told me,' I said, bashing my way out of their sphere with the pushchair I suddenly loved very much.

'I met a man on a bicycle outside the post office and he told me Jim Dones has given up on his wife and has gone to a party in London.'

Anne was clutching my arm, but I elbowed her off.

'He's happy without his wife now,' I called as I left. 'He's never been so happy.'

And I kept saying that sentence aloud to myself as I walked quickly away, wiping my eyes and the fine rain from time to time.

Twelve Home

MY MOTHER'S HOUSE IN WINTER IS ALWAYS COLD. I DON'T often go there, since she has a friend in Kensington who she visits every November and my flat sees a lot of her then. But the year Billy was three I rang her one blowy March day to ask if she'd meet us in Leeds and she said what a nice surprise, and of course she would. I didn't pack much. We wouldn't stay long, but I had something I wanted to see her to say.

We drove back from the station into the smell of her garden and I walked Billy into the yellow room, which is where people sit in my mother's house. Visits to the place where Isa and I grew up begin with a cup of tea in that high-ceilinged space, next to the fire, across from the leaky French windows, which gust their curtains about like Victorian nighties through the Yorkshire winter nights. By day, the panes are often washed with rain, which collects beneath their blistered frames to puddle on the floorboards my father sanded when we were small.

It was raining hard and loud when Billy and I arrived that cold day when he was almost three, when I was tired and Nick came to stay as well. I should have guessed my visit was to be a complex one by the length of time my mother spent organizing the first cup of tea. You can tell from the time she takes to make tea what mood my mother is in. The cakes she produces are significant too. Christmas cake is always a bad sign – unless, of course, it's Christmas – so I was prepared for the worst when slabs of the stuff were produced.

'So, how have you been? You're looking well.'

I thought this would be a better beginning than anything personal about myself. I decided not to mention, either, that I was hoping to get some work done during my stay. My agent was going to Italy with his winter collection in a fortnight's time.

'Oh, tired,' she said. 'You know how it is.'

I hazarded a sympathetic smile. I had no idea how it was to be my mother, though it had been made clear to me from an early age that it was not an easy task. She looked into the fire reproachfully. I had thrown an unsmoked cigarette in a few moments before. It may have been that which pained her. She doesn't approve of smoking.

'Shall I be mother?' I said as I lifted the teapot, which sometimes amuses us both, and I started to pour, then stopped, mid-flow, because she sighed deeply and told me that Nicholas was arriving that evening. She always calls Nick Nicholas, as if the person she knows of that name has nothing to do with me.

'He rang when I was having my morning nap. Attempting to nap, that is.'

I carried on pouring tea until there was no room in either cup for milk and the one nearest me overflowed. I stared at the small disaster I had brought about as I heard her ask, 'Is that a nice surprise?'

I looked about for Billy, who was being suspiciously silent. He was riding my mother's ancient dog away and out of the room, which was a slow process. The dog only gets to its feet every few days.

'Come back near the fire, Billy, and keep warm,' I said. He carried on just the same, as though everything hadn't changed. I lifted the lid of the teapot and poured steaming liquid back into its depths. I poured milk into the meagre rations left in both cups and concentrated on spooning sugar into mine, aware that I was being watched. I usually let Billy stir my tea. He arrived at my side as I ground the bottom of my cup, as if I might be trying to dissolve a lump of coal in the thing, and he took the spoon from my hand. He ladled sugar into my mother's drink. She shrieked and grabbed the teaspoon, which meant the milk jug tipped over. We watched semi-skimmed seep into the carpet.

'What do you mean, Nick's coming?'

I felt calmer with the question now that I had pulled Billy onto my chair and had him secure between my knees. I gave him a slice of Christmas cake, which felt as heavy as a wet nappy to lift from the plate. My mother left the room and returned with a cloth. She dabbed at the floor instead of answering my question, so I asked it again, and how come Nick was in Yorkshire anyway? Nick was living in Scotland with Isa.

'I ought to get him to finish papering this room while he's here.' My mother smiled, smoothing autumnal hair away from her forehead, looking like Isa as she did so. 'He's been promising to finish that corner for me for the last fifteen years, after all.'

That was a silly thing to say. It couldn't be true. It was only thirteen years ago that Nick had started papering the yellow room blue and I painted its cornice white. We did the ceiling together when I was almost eighteen. I know that's when it was because we stopped work on my birthday and never really started again. Which is why there's still a section of wall by the door that's still a rich mustard yellow.

'Of course you children never do finish things properly,' my mother said, and I looked across at the first piece of paper I'd watched Nick apply on the first day I'd been in this room with him. It was slightly short at the top. Nick hadn't done any wallpapering before my mother employed him, although he didn't tell her that. He'd told her he was a painter, which was what she had asked for when she put a notice in the local Job Centre to get someone to decorate her house. He arrived on a bicycle the morning after the notice went up. The bike was red and his shirt was green with blue buttons and his hair very black in a warm July rainstorm. I was in my pyjamas in the kitchen when he came through the door, and when he'd gone I knew that I'd like to decorate too. I started the same day as he did, and as the days went by and the room became progressively blue, I became accustomed to the way he'd arrive in the mornings and move the ladder I was standing on to a different part of the room, then offer me doughnuts and roll up his shirt-sleeves and tell me endless things I thought I didn't know.

When the room was about two thirds blue, we started walking to the pub at the end of the road for lunch, then home again alongside the river. I spent a lot of time wishing Nick wasn't there, because he made me nervous, but I hated it too when evening came, when the light left our gluey-strewn room and he put his tobacco away and laced his boots and rolled his sleeves back down. I'd watch the skin of his forearms disappear and want to ask him to stay, but he didn't do that for some time. Not until after we'd started to go for drinks in the evening. Then he seemed to be always there, until I went to London, when he came as well, though I didn't ask him exactly. I don't think I ever asked Nick to do anything really. He just seemed to be wherever I was for a very long time. And then he was living with Isa.

My mother threw a squat log onto the fire. It looked like a dog's head in profile. The dog was underneath Billy again. They were over by the window, moving towards the piano, which no one but Isa can really play. It looked forlorn, with its lid jammed up over old maps and newspapers. My mother had done a class in papier mâché about three years before and the house had never quite looked the same since. The corner of the room which was still yellow looked like my local newsagents in London when they put everything that hasn't sold outside in the evenings.

'More tea? Have some cake, Chrissie. I wish you girls would eat.'

I found I was chewing the soft part of my thumb. I stopped and took a mouthful of luke-warm tea, then bent to collect the remains of Billy's crumbed cake from the floor. My mother frowned into my fingers at her feet.

'Why do children take things when they know they don't want them?'

It was the sort of question I'd been training myself not to respond to since Billy was born. I tilted tea leaves around in my cup. I picked a sultana from boulders of cake on the plate that was too small to contain them.

'So why is Nick coming? What's he coming here for?'

Does he know I'll be here? was the question I did not ask.

'Well, he's not coming to finish the decorating, I imagine, dear.' She still does call me dear sometimes.

'So why is he coming?'

My mother poured herself more tea. She sighed.

'He has to teach something somewhere in Leeds tomorrow morning. He does it twice a month apparently.' She made this sound as unlikely as only she can when disclosing information she disapproves of. 'And the person he usually stays with in Leeds seems to have some sort of problem this week, so he asked if he could stay here.'

The word 'problem' was handled with care, like something found on her bathroom floor, which she ought not to have to dispose of. She left a moment's silence, before smiling across to me.

'I don't think it need affect you and Billy too much, dear. I said I'd collect him, if necessary.' She studied her finely made hands, which neither Isa nor I had inherited. 'Although it's not till eight o'clock.'

'I'll collect him. I'd like to.'

She fingered the milk jug, which was one of her best. One of my father's mother's, I'd been told. The doorbell rang. The dog barked and moved violently across the room. Billy protested loudly. He doesn't like sudden movements unless they're his own.

'Well, dear, we'll see. Now that doorbell's for you.' She lifted hair from her forehead again. 'Well, it's for Billy, at least. The Parker grandchildren are coming to play.'

The Parkers are my mother's neighbours, who have their grandchildren to stay over from time to time, and when Billy and I arrive they come over to play. My mother's house then becomes a bowl of noise, which seems to multiply itself as long-forgotten limbs of the place are cranked into sudden agitation. The garden, too, moves into the house. Bits of creeper are used to tie chairs together. Bicycle tyre-marks lace the floors. Empty wine bottles are filled and placed underneath the piano, where Sally, the four-year-old, presses acrid liquids into the hands of anyone willing to be a customer at the bar that this little-known corner of the room is temporarily meant to be. Notes are put on doors, issuing instructions: get lost, keep out, come in, go away. These are printed in crayon by Jo, who is six. Billy worships him, but spends most of their time together in tears.

Before Nick was due to arrive, the children and I made paper aeroplanes. My mother had asked us to do something peaceful indoors, so we huddled together in front of the fireplace, which is the only warm place to be in winter in my mother's house. I leaned against the mantelpiece, which my father had spent my childhood burning layers of gloss paint from, and I watched the children fail to make aeroplanes that would fly.

I studied the frozen grins of the photographs which cluster on the mahogany mantelpiece and was surprised to see Jamie there. He was pushing a pushchair along a beach I didn't recognize and trying not to smile. Behind the photograph of him was one of Isa and myself in front of an open atlas, at school, with our hair in short fringes, like scars across our foreheads. Then one of my mother as an undergraduate, folded in half in the frame to cut my father out.

'You took mine,' Billy said. 'Mummy, Jo took mine.'

'Did not,' Jo said.

'He did,' Sally said. 'He did, Chrissie. Jo took Billy's one.'

'You have to share,' I told their scrambled heads. That is what adults tell children, of course, although why they think it will help them in future years escapes me.

'I'll make you one each, then you can have a race,' I decided, and started in on my task. I was good at making paper aeroplanes. Jamie taught me how to do it when we were painting Lily's houseboat about a hundred years ago. The children stood in a row and aimed their new sleek darts into the scullery. Sally's disappeared behind the washing machine, so I put my hand into the rubbery feel of its back and touched something soft and wet. It was a dead bird, which I rolled out with a broom handle, to slide onto an old train timetable, which was spreadeagled on top of my mother's tool cupboard. We inspected the bird's matted feathers and translucent eyelids, closed in wrinkles on its bone of a head.

'Well, this won't fly again, that's for sure,' I said.

They stared at me. It wasn't a proper response.

'Its legs are like string,' said Sally.

'Let's bury it,' Jo said.

I said we would have to see what Billy's granny said. My mother sighed when she saw the creature, and took the dead weight of the timetable from me. Then she asked the children to remove the wool they'd wrapped around her bed. She was thinking of having a nap.

'If it's possible to sleep with this chaos around one.'

We stood alone with the bird for a moment as the familiar impossibility of sleep hung between us. My mother has always wanted naps when everyone else in the house is having noisy fun. The children had turned the television on. The sound of adverts came through like a crisis. My mother looked tired, momentarily beaten. She put a hand on my shoulder.

'I must be getting old,' she said.

I touched the top of her head. She was only slightly taller than I was.

'I'll take them outside,' I decided. 'You have a sleep.'

'I know you'd like one too.' She smiled at me vaguely. I could feel my nose getting cold in the damp air of the place, where nothing except washing is done any more. My mother has little to wash these days, of course, but this small room was never silent when I was a child. It was never cold, either, unlike the rest of the place. It was warmed by the smell of drying clothes and the hiss of the steam iron on Sunday nights.

'I'll take them down to the river,' I said.

I expected her to sigh and say why complicate life, but she didn't. She turned away and I heard her walking towards the stairs. She has a very particular way of doing that if she's decided she needs a nap.

The river meant wellingtons for everyone, which meant that the Parker children went back next door briefly while Billy and I found some to wear from a pile my mother has always had. His were red and mine black, which pleased us both.

'I like Granny's,' he said, then the door banged open and Jo came through with an ice lolly for Billy as well as one for himself. He said sorry he didn't have one for me too, then we set off into the smudged late-afternoon light, into the field that leads to the river. We trudged over ground, pooled with dark ovals of water, like the markings of a cow. I told the children to have a race, so I could sit on a wall and suck a mint and examine the possibility of Nick, but they kept wanting to start again as soon as they'd run a few feet, so I told them to look for lost baby birds instead.

'There are lots under that hedge if you look closely,' I told them.

It's the sort of idea that gives small people nightmares, I know, but I didn't much care. I had to keep them out long enough for my mother to wake up in a good enough mood to let me meet a train at eight o'clock.

By the time we'd dragged back home to my mother's fireplace, the light was fading. 'Losing', the people who live up there say. The shapes of the garden were silting into the sky and the birds were making an enormous noise. The lights were on in the kitchen, where my mother was frying sausages and beating a floury paste up for pancakes. She can't make pancakes, but has never accepted that. There was the usual fight then, over who would sit where. Cutlery ringing onto the floor and kicking small feet as I bent to collect it. Eggs were forming burnt blisters in a pan on the stove, so I turned it off. My mother turned it on again.

'Why don't you go next door, dear? The yellow room is in chaos.'

She lifted the eggs and started slopping them out. Billy doesn't like scrambled egg.

'He won't eat that. There's no point giving him any.'

Sausages were now on offer.

'Just give Billy sausages.'

'I'm giving everyone the same, dear. I don't make distinctions for fussy eaters.'

'It's not fussy to dislike something, Mother.'

Billy spiked his sausage. It rolled to the floor. I bent to lift it and started to cut it into edible slices.

'No. Like Jo's,' he told me.

I was crushed between the wall and the back of Sally's chair. I told Billy to eat it as it was.

'Don't be fussy,' I told him. Sally's chair tilted backwards, squashing my hand with a sting.

'For God's sake. Can't you sit still.'

She started to cry.

'I want my mummy. I want to go home.'

She started down from the table, tripped and fell. My mother lifted her, smoothed hair from her flushed face and rubbed her heaving back as the child wept into her shoulder.

'Why don't you leave me to it?' she said. 'You all seem terribly tired.'

I said I thought I could give three children their tea, however tired I was, and why didn't she leave me to it instead. Billy was howling by now. He wanted to go home too, he said.

'I don't like Granny's. I want to go home.'

He stuck his fork into Jo's hand. Jo did it back.

'Right,' said my mother. 'I've had enough. Chrissie, go and tidy the yellow room. Billy, eat up nicely, and Sally and Jo, be good or there'll be no pancakes.'

We stared at each other.

'I'm not a child,' I said. 'Please don't tell me what to do.'

'I'm your mother. I'll tell you what I think you should do for as long as that is the case.'

'Well I hope I go deaf pretty soon then.'

She banged a pan loudly. Billy slipped from his seat as my ears banged with blood, and shame, perhaps. Billy cried. I clamped my teeth, dragged him from the floor, snatched a stray sausage from the ketchup-oozed table and left the kitchen, pushing the door shut with my foot as I went. I deposited my son in a chair by the fireplace, found a cigarette and struck three matches before I could get it to light. It tasted foul. I threw it into the fire. I walked to the corner cupboard my father once lived from and poured a large glass of sherry. I sat on the piano stool and drank it down in one, like soluble aspirin that makes you choke.

'I want pancakes,' Billy said.

'Go and get some then.'

He clambered down from his chair and walked into my mother, who was coming to collect him. I ignored them studiously and hoped he disliked her pancakes as much as I had when I was about his size. I tugged at piles of maps and newspapers jammed into the piano lid and dropped them systematically and loudly onto the floor until I came to a coffee-stained paperback, which made my heart hammer in a different way. It was *73 Poems* by e. e. cummings, and on the title page was written, 'Happy 18th Birthday, Chrissie,' above a line of wax crayon roses. 'With love from Nick. Kiss kiss.'

I read the poem about how you must, above all things, be glad and young, then I went to the glass cupboard and took a slender glass, which I filled to its dusty brim. My mother enjoys dry sherry.

'I'm sorry,' I said to her back. I watched her shoulders relax.

'I'm sorry. I'm tired, Mum, that's all.'

Not too tired to go to the station, though.

'I mean a bit stressed. You know how I am.' She turned round. 'Have some sherry.' She took the glass.

'Cheers,' I said.

'Cheers.' She drank it down in one. There are some things we do have in common.

When my mother took the Parker grandchildren home, Billy wept histrionically.

'You'll see them tomorrow,' I told him, which made his drama more vivid, which I understood. Time not seeing someone you worship is deadly, of course, when you know they could easily be seeing you now.

'I'll make you a lovely bath with bubbles.' He subsided, somewhat. 'A big bath in Granny's own bathroom.'

Since my mother had left, this was a safe enough bribe. She dislikes children in her bathroom, or certainly used to. I carried Billy closely up the stairs, which I'd been hoisted up often myself. We passed the gap in the banisters, where I'd pushed Isa through the day she'd killed my goldfish, and the place where the carpet is black, where she and I dropped a candle one long-ago Hallowe'en. We were on the stair where I used to make her wait, while I jumped the last three, when the telephone rang, then stopped, as I did too. The answer machine clicked into action. The flashing light winked. I carried Billy back down as I heard Isa's voice, which I could feel making my face hot as it filled the red hallway.

'Mum. It's me. Can you get Nick to ring as soon as he gets there. It's kind of important. Speak to you later. OK. Goodbye.' Her voice went up on the word, like it does. I could see her forehead wrinkle, and her fingers holding the phone.

'Who is that voice,' Billy said. 'Who said goodbye?'

'A person Granny knows,' I told him. I pressed 'delete'. 'Now, what about our lovely bath?'

By the time my mother returned from the Parkers' she'd had more sherry, as I'd thought she might. She wouldn't drive now, but I had a fail-safe strategy planned in case.

'Mum,' I said, in my best twelve-year-old's voice, which I'd had to rehearse even at that age. 'I think it would be lovely if you read Billy a story. I mean, I haven't let you have any time together at all.'

She smiled.

'That's sweet of you, darling.'

She only says 'darling' once every few years.

'And I'll collect Nicholas while you two tuck in. It's half seven already.'

She yawned and threw a log on the fire, which made it fleetingly spark, then relapse into silence.

'I think Billy and I will have our story in front of the fire.'

Billy should like that, and I'd promised him chocolate tomorrow if he was good for Granny tonight. I'd promised him two bars, in fact. He could tell I was desperate. I carried his sweet-smelling bulk to my mother, explaining that I wouldn't be long.

'I'm not tired, Mummy. I don't go to bed.'

'We'll see,' said my mother, like I've learnt to now, and she told him that mummies go out sometimes, as if he were not aware of that, as I applied lipstick and found my shoes. I squeezed into a jacket that used to fit, before I'd ever had breastfeeding breasts. I kissed Billy again and found the car keys beside the answering machine, which I slid to silent mode, in case.

'Goodbye. We might go for a drink or something.'

A change in her tone, but I'm out of the door by the time she tells me not to be late, then the leaves crack like kindling in the cold of outside, and the weight of the car door is a gift in my fist as I grip the handle to slam it behind me. The headlights hit tree trunk as the handbrake clicks off. Now the wipers, the heater, the radio's voice with the news, and into second gear, then third on the main road to Leeds, where I'm going to the station, about to meet Nick.

I bought a platform ticket and followed the signs to platform ten, which was deserted. The Edinburgh train had been, a lonely guard explained.

'Where are the people then?' I demanded. 'Where's everyone gone?'

'Home, I suppose, lovey.'

The man winked as I started past him into the gloss of tunnels, back to the echoey entrance.

Sloping spray-paint letters flashed past as I moved. 'If it feels good, do it', the words advised. They'd been there ever since I could remember. Since years ago, when I'd come on the last train on Fridays to see Nick one summer when he was screen printing here. He'd meet me with a bag of chips, which meant we had to eat, talk and touch each other all at once in the moments after my train came in.

Back in the station foyer, across the strip-lit crowd, I saw Nick's old rucksack before I saw him, hunched into a phone booth. The receiver was nestled into the collar of a leather jacket I used to borrow a lot.

'Nicky,' I shouted, as loudly as I dared, then ran a few steps, then stopped to stare as he turned, with the phone still caught on his arm, to wave across at me. When we got close up, we kissed each other's cheeks, and I clutched the sleeves of his jacket, smiling, like people in films, at the end, with their faces filling the screen. He grinned. His stubble was flecked with white.

'Chrissie. What the fuck. What are you doing here?'

'Meeting you, you dimmy.'

'No, but in Leeds, now. Tonight.'

'I might ask you the same question. My mother is very suspicious.'

He gave half a laugh, then a long one, then a smile I'd forgotten, then he said, 'Let's go for a drink. Buzzy plays the Wellington on Friday nights.'

'But Buzzy's in London. I saw him in Camden.'

'Yeah, well maybe he's heard of this train thing too. Now let's move. I need a drink.' He lifted his rucksack as he spoke, and we started together for the swing doors and the wind they made. He said he liked my red shoes, so I watched them walk me across litter and onto the pavement. An old man banged into me and I said sorry.

'Why do you apologize when people push you over?' he asked, nudging me into the wall beside us.

'I don't.'

'You do. Want some gum?'

I did, so we chewed through the black walls and the drizzle, through the short cut we took to the Wellington when we were at my mother's house.

We heaved through stained-glass doors into a wall of herringbone coats and a blast of Tamla Motown. A girl in a beret, with a beer in both hands, sang along. A glass smashed.

Someone said, 'I'd rather be in a car crash,' as I followed Nick's back through angled chair legs and elbows and cigarette smoke to the bar. I had to shout to ask him what he wanted, and he bellowed back that he'd get this round. The barman seemed to know him. He frowned as he pulled a pint, and nodded at something Nick told him. A man in a Sex Pistols T-shirt said his was a pint, and Nick grinned and said, 'Get lost.' I'd forgotten he said that all the time. I remembered it used to annoy me.

We pushed our way through hanging ash and handbags to lean on flocked wallpaper outside the Ladies'.

'Do you come here often?' he said and I asked if he did, so he moved closer to explain that he'd been doing some teaching at the art college since September. He usually stayed with Al, but there was some domestic trouble round there this week, so he didn't feel too welcome.

'And here it comes,' he said, as a woman I recognized struggled towards us, dragging a lime-green coat.

'Nick, baby,' she exhaled with some long cigarette smoke. 'And Chrissie, if I'm not mistaken. I thought you were Isa, for a minute there.' She dropped her cigarette, twisting it out with a patent shoe. 'But you're plumper, aren't you? Still gorgeous, of course. Your taste is impeccable, Nick.' She lit his cigarette for him. She stared at my face, then my feet, then at Nick's jacket collar. They must have had an affair.

'Well, this is quite like old times.' She sort of smiled and narrowed her shadowed eyes. 'Nice that you don't forget all your old friends,' she went on, moving her Dior in closer to us. 'Shame Isa couldn't have made it, too. Or is three a crowd?'

It wasn't clear if she disliked me or Isa most, but for a moment I felt sorry for my sister.

'Drink up,' Nick said. 'We'll be late.'

He drained his glass, lifted his rucksack and took my fingers to pull me away, past the beret girl to the door.

'Sorry about that. I'm starving,' he said to the rain outside. 'Shall we go for something to eat? Your mother's place is icy, I assume?'

'Pretty much. Some things never change.'

A moment's silence, like a warm facecloth after the noise of the pub.

'It's nice to see you anyway, Chrissie,' he said, and I would have replied that it was nice to see him too, but he was saying, 'Let's eat,' with a hand on my elbow that stayed there as we huddled between high walls to the car, which was still warm inside.

He threw his rucksack into the back, then pulled up his knees to his chin to fit on the passenger seat. I rolled the window down to hear the weather. It seemed too quiet, suddenly, side by side in a car.

'Shall we go for a curry?'

'Why not?'

Why not was because we hadn't done anything together for years, and I wasn't Isa and I could see I wasn't going to tell Nick what I'd thought I might. I should be at home, telling my mother. I shouldn't be here at all, but I drove neatly, with the windscreen wipers splashing in front of my face, to the place where we always used to eat curry in Leeds.

The restaurant was empty, except for one hollow waiter and a flowery smell. We ate slowly, not talking much. We drank sweet Indian beer from bottles with elephants on their wrinkled paper skins. Nick was exhausted. He'd been helping Isa out with some backdrops the night before and they hadn't really been to bed. Her assistant had fallen off a ladder, he explained, and she wasn't feeling too good, so she'd forced him to help.

'You know how she gets.'

I watched him wipe his bowl clean with his forefinger, then suck it, then scrub at it with a napkin. His nails were bitten.

'Are you and Isa still in love?' I stared at his hairline to avoid his eyes. I wondered who cut it for him now. 'Does she cut your hair like that?'

He laughed and pushed his plate away.

'You mean she wouldn't if she loved me?'

He stood up and reached to slide out a red leather wallet that used to be hers.

'Let's go back. I've brought some whisky.' He winked. 'For your mum.'

A blast of cold wet wind hit us outside, then the car's heater whirred again.

'You can drive, if you want to.'

He did, so I leaned my head back and watched the street lamps' orange flow. I hoped Billy had been happy. I was anxious to see him again. When we got back I ran upstairs, and saw he was deeply asleep, which disappointed me, perversely. My mother was in bed too, but she'd left a note on the hall table to say that Isa had rung. 'She'd like to speak to Nicholas,' it said. I put it in my pocket. Isa could speak to Nick whenever she wanted.

From the yellow room I heard sounds of wood being

snapped. Nick was building a fire with an orange box Jo had tried to force Billy to hide in earlier in the day. It seemed like weeks since I'd dragged them apart. I watched Nick's fingers wedging flat white wood into a wigwam shape in the grate. He'd made snails of newspaper that he nudged underneath. I took more substantial sticks from beside his legs. We took turns to poke those into the pale new flames.

'It's all a question of balance,' he told me as he straightened up, 'and the wind being in the right direction.'

I stood up. My back ached.

'Where's the whisky?' I'd just have a small one.

It was in his rucksack, with a tin cup too, for emergencies. He watched me unbuckle the bundle and root around until I found *A Sentimental Education*, which had once been mine, but he said was his.

'It was mine,' he said. 'It's got my name in it. Can you find the cup?'

I could, with a pair of socks inside it. He pushed his hands into his pockets and watched me pour Famous Grouse into the familiar object. They used to sell them in the ironmongers on Blythe Road.

'Shall I get you a glass?'

But he took a glass of water from the mantelpiece, drank it down and lifted the bottle from me. He poured himself a large measure, then screwed the lid back on with fingers that were long and tanned.

'Have you been in the sun?'

He told me about a trip to Morocco last autumn. He and Isa had hitchhiked and left their tent in a lorry. He took a gulp of his drink and stooped to peer at a picture of Billy. We agreed that he was the image of his father, and Nick asked what had happened to Jamie.

'Nothing much,' I said. 'He's living in Galway.'

'Must be tough by yourself.'

'Well, if I was by myself, I suppose.'

He raised his eyebrows and narrowed his eyes.

'So anyway. How's your painting?'

He drank and ignored the question. He bent to the fire. He stayed there a while.

'Good fire,' I said, for something to say. His T-shirt was stretched out of his Levi's, so his back showed, with the bone running tenderly through it.

'Pass the bottle,' he said, not standing up, so I did.

'Unscrew it, can you?' He still had one hand balancing wood in the flames.

I twisted the lid off and crouched down by his side. A log was burning solid orange by now and hissing consolingly. It seemed pleased with itself as we stared.

'Well. Welcome home, I guess.'

He smiled, with his narrow nose almost touching my own. His face was glowing, his lips very red, and the line of his ear very fine, with a line of pale yellow behind it.

'Welcome home, yourself.' We stared, very close. I knew I must be going to kiss him, so I touched my lips to his cheek and stood up. I put my glass to rest on the mantelpiece, and as I dropped my hand he took it in his. He stood up and stooped to me, and then we did kiss somehow. We kissed for a long and sudden time, holding each other's heads, feeling the planes of our faces with cold fingers, making tiny noises. I moved to the couch, and he sat beside me, sinking in, and we kissed, like teenagers do when their parents are in bed. Like we used to, a long time ago, in cars, on sleeping bags, at stations, at parties. In woods, on beaches, on landladies' beds. On the ladder, in this room, when I'd just left school. On this couch, a lot.

'We used to do this a lot, I suppose,' I said when we stopped one time and I was temporarily shy.

'Mmm. It's all coming back to me now.'

There seemed to be nothing to do but to carry on, so we

did, through into the ponderous chime of one from my father's grandfather clock, which was followed by another, lighter sound, which was Billy leaving his bedroom.

'Mummy,' he called, in that way he has, as if the world has started to spin terribly fast and he's in danger of falling off. 'Mummy, I want you.'

Nick and I stayed very still for a moment, with his hand still on the back of my neck. I wasn't breathing, I noticed, as my mother's door opened and her footsteps moved lightly along the landing. I knew how cold her hand would feel as she felt his forehead, and how her voice would be as she asked if it hurt anywhere.

'I'll be back in a minute,' I said.

The stairs seemed to last a long time.

'Is he OK? Are you all right, darling? Mummy's here. I'll deal with it, Mother.'

The three of us bundled against the banisters then, my mother's sleepy eyes in mine.

'What time is it? Where's Nicholas?'

'He's on the couch.'

She looked surprisingly small in her white pyjamas, with Billy's sturdy legs around her waist. Would she give him to me or not?

'Poor Billy,' I said, holding my arms out. 'Poor Billy, waking up in a funny bed.'

His arms around my neck then, so much lighter than Nick's were, and his face hot on my own. His sapling back I knew so well. The curve of the whole of him fitting into my front. His legs, like spare arms, pressing into my spine. I felt behind me for one of his feet and held it. My mother smoothed my hair, touched Billy's and walked away as I balanced myself against the wallpaper, which Isa and I used to peel off.

'Poor Billy,' I kept saying as I walked us along the corridor to the room where I slept, with its big double bed.

'Have a big sleep now,' I whispered.

'Leave the door open, Mummy. More open than that.'

I decided I needed to brush my teeth. The toothbrush handle seemed pleasingly sturdy and the activity wholly refreshing. I walked downstairs, feeling different. Nick was stretched out on his back on the couch.

'Poor kid,' he said. 'Wonder what that's about?'

'Pancakes, most likely.'

I sat down on a red chair across from the couch. It was cold, so I stood up again.

'What did you do with him anyway?' Nick lit a cigarette. 'Is he OK now? Is he comfy?'

'Very,' I said.

He poured me a whisky and one for himself. He blew smoke and moved his legs from the couch.

'I'm not as comfy as I was. Are you?'

'Not really. But I'm used to it.'

'You're kidding me. Come here.'

I sipped whisky, standing up. I quite wanted to go to bed.

'Sorry about before,' I said. 'It's the couch, I suppose. A knee-jerk reaction.'

Nick looked nice on the couch.

'Would you mind sleeping down here,' I asked before I found myself sitting beside him again. He made room for my shoulders.

'I'd rather share a bed.'

'I'm afraid my bed's already full.'

I rolled onto my side and something crinkled in my pocket. I took out the note from my mother with its instructions for Nick to ring Isa. It was crushed, illegible almost. I threw it into the fire and watched the white flame it made.

I held his ankle, then dropped it. I heard my mother move to her bathroom.

‘I think I’ll go to bed now.’

‘I want to sleep with you, Chrissie.’

‘I know.’

I smiled and shook my head, but he couldn’t see that because I was walking up the stairs, which were the same as always. I heard my mother’s bathroom door close. I hoped Billy wouldn’t notice I hadn’t taken my clothes off when he woke up beside me the next day.

The morning after was white-skied and windy. In the kitchen, where my mother was doing something to the kettle with a screwdriver, I saw that it was after ten. I thanked her for letting me sleep so long, because she doesn’t often do that. She thinks parents should get up before their children, however old the children may be. I thought I should ask after Billy, but waited for her to say something first.

‘Well, I saw the whisky bottle.’ She made a lopsided face. ‘I thought you’d be glad of some sleep.’

‘What time did Nick go?’ We both watched a screw as it rolled slowly off the table to the floor.

‘Early. He had a class at nine.’

Billy came in, wearing swimming trunks and a pyjama top, with a sheet of cardboard under each of his feet. He wanted to water-ski, like Jo did, yesterday. He spread his arms and made a motorboat noise. I asked him to stop. I needed some tea. I filled a deep saucepan with water, lit the gas and thought of *Gone With the Wind*, where somebody has a baby and needs boiling water and blankets.

‘I see Jo today,’ Billy told me, and I was hoping I wouldn’t have three shrill voices in my immediate orbit again all day as the telephone on the kitchen wall rang. My mother started talking.

‘Why do you children make life so complicated?’ I watched her pull a newspaper from under a cushion and frown into an old headline beyond her conversation.

'Well I'll ask Chrissie.' She sighed. 'It seems so unnecessary. I might need the car myself. All right then, Nicholas. We'll see. Yes, do that. Goodbye now, dear.'

Tea burnt my tongue. My mother washed a cup as she explained that Nick had left his wallet, with his ticket in it, somewhere in the house. A shaking head and sighing. Another cup of tea. He couldn't miss the twelve fifty, she explained. Isa needed him at the theatre.

'I despair of you children sometimes.'

A paper aeroplane landed next to her on the table. I adjusted its folds for Billy, who asked when he was going to Jo's house.

'Soon now,' my mother told him. 'I'm taking Billy to the Parkers', Chrissie. They're going swimming and taking him with them.'

Nick's wallet was on the couch, under my jacket. It had £20 in it, some stamps and a photograph of my sister wearing a Russian hat. I slid the soft weight of it onto the yellow-room window sill, behind the half-pulled curtains, and then I washed my hair and changed my clothes. The phone rang as I lifted the car keys, but I didn't pick it up. I thought I knew who it would be, and I didn't know what I would say to her yet, or what my mother had told her, or if it mattered anyway.

In the station café I sat at some scratched Formica with fanned cigarette breath and fried food at my back and female voices discussing a man. He was a bad lot, they'd decided. He must move out right away. She should never have lent him that five hundred. Her mother didn't like him. She couldn't stand the sight of him herself, but the kids would miss his fried bread.

And then there was Nick coming through the tall swing doors, with his rucksack jammed behind him that someone jerked free, and he was smiling towards me with his collar turned up and a newspaper under his arm. I held his red wallet up with both my hands, like a fish I'd caught, for a photograph. Displayed like a diploma, or the deeds of a house, so he came over and took it and ruffled my clean new hair, then he looked up at a screen with white place names and times on it, and he looked like someone I nearly didn't know. A man on his way somewhere, sharing my table. Asking for directions or where someone else was, who he'd last seen sitting here with me. A man with a newspaper who needed a shave.

'Well done. It wasn't too hard to find, I trust?'

He winked, slipped the wallet down inside his jacket. His shirt was untucked at the back. It seemed odd that I'd so recently been touching his flesh.

'I need something to eat. I feel like shit. I didn't sleep. Did you?' He swerved his eyes over my face again, then turned towards the glass counter of cellophane shapes across the room from us. He moved away, then back and took my hand.

'Do you want anything? Have a coffee. We've got an hour. I'm getting the next train, not this one.'

He was squeezing my index finger, which had a ring on it that had nothing to do with him.

'We need to talk. I'm not going just yet. I don't want to go till we've sorted this out.'

'Nick.' I pulled my hand back. He slipped his rucksack to the floor and slid into the moulded orange chair bolted to the floor across the table from me. He moved his eyes fast all over my face. He lit a cigarette, then stared on at me through smoke. The women with the unwanted boyfriend passed by with huge shoulder bags, staring. I wanted not to be there. I wanted to go home to see my mother, which made me feel foolish. He finished his cigarette.

'Nick, this is silly. Don't do this now.'

'Do what?'

'Just go home, Nick. Please. Go back to Scotland.'

'Say you love me.'

That's what I used to say at this same station café, when he'd always decide to take a later train so we could work out how soon we'd see each other again.

'When can I see you again?'

'Nick, you live with Isa.'

'So?'

'So go home. Get this train. This is the train you said you'd get.'

'So I've changed my mind. What's a few hours to Isa? I don't have to go because I said I would, do I? We're grown-ups. We can do what we want.'

'I want us to do what you told Isa you would do. That's what grown-ups do.'

That wasn't quite what I meant to say.

'I mean, Isa's my sister. You have to go home.'

He moved some tanned fingers around my wrist, where my watch should have been, I remembered. I stood up and put my hands in my pockets, to touch a boiled sweet that was stuck to one of the linings from some long-ago swing-park trip.

'Can I ring you if I'm in London?'

Squeezing my arm. Holding my hand. Leaving me now to see Isa, and I was asking him to go.

'Goodbye, Nick. You'll be late. Don't miss it.'

I bent to kiss him somewhere, but he jerked his head away, so I looked down at pink freckled Formica and felt him stand up, then bend to his bag, then put his cigarettes into his trouser back pocket. I watched his hand move to the top of the chair he'd been on. I wouldn't see him again now. I'd done it all wrong.

'Say goodbye,' I said as he started moving away.

He said nothing. He stared at me, walking backwards slowly.

'Go on then, leave,' I said and pushed past him to leave before he could. I didn't want him to hear me cry.

At my mother's house the fire was out. She was in the hallway, talking into the telephone, but looked up when I walked through.

'Where's Billy?' I asked, because she was staring at my face.

She put her hand over the mouthpiece.

'Put the kettle on, darling. It's mended.' She didn't stop staring. 'Billy's still with the others. Did Nick get his train?'

'When's Billy coming back?' I wanted to hear his voice again.

'When they bring him home, darling.'

She lifted her fingers from the phone and talked into the handset again, keeping her eyes on my face.

'It's Chrissie, darling. Well I don't know. Why don't you ask her yourself?'

She took my arm, my hand, my fingers, and wrapped them around the telephone. I knew who it was then and I backed away, but she nodded at me, backing away herself, raising her eyes as she did so.

'I'll make us a nice cup of tea,' she said as Isa's voice grew louder. My sister was calling my name. I made myself say hello, but she didn't say it back. She said, 'Where's Nick, Chrissie? Is he coming home?'

'Of course he is. He's on the train. We just said goodbye.'

She didn't say anything for a moment then. She was making a noise. She might have been weeping.

'Isa, everything's OK,' I said, but she was talking again as the words came out. She was saying something very fast. It was, 'Chrissie, I'm having a baby.'

'I'm having a baby, Chrissie,' she said.

And I didn't say anything at all for some time. I looked at my face in the mirror in front of the phone. I watched my mother's reflection move back into the hallway.

'What do you think?' Isa said. 'Is that OK?'

'It's amazing. It's great.' I could hardly breathe, so I waited a second before I said, 'Does Nick know yet?'

'No. I just found out yesterday. Do you think he'll be glad?'

'I do,' I said, 'I really do. I mean, he'll be ever so glad.'

Then I looked at my mother and thought I might as well say it now, although she'd never met Danby, of course, but it was, after all, what I'd come home to say, so I said to Isa on the telephone, out loud in the hallway where I'd learned to walk myself, 'I'm having another baby too.'

It seemed an odd thing to say after all this silent time, but it was true, so I said it again. 'I'm having a baby too. Mum better start knitting right now.'

I don't know what my mother thought of all this exactly, but tea arrived very quickly after I'd put down the phone. There were flapjacks with it, rather ill-formed and soft, like the ones Isa and I used to make on Saturday afternoons when we were still just children, still living together at home.

THE END

BRICK LANE
Monica Ali

'WRITTEN WITH A WISDOM AND SKILL THAT FEW AUTHORS ATTAIN IN A LIFETIME'
Sunday Times

Still in her teenage years, Nazneen finds herself in an arranged marriage with a man twenty years her elder. Away from the mud and heat of her Bangladeshi village, home is now a cramped flat in a high-rise block in London's East End. Not knowing a word of English, Nazneen must rely on her husband. But unlike him she is practical and wise, and befriends a fellow Asian girl Razia, who helps her understand the strange ways of her adopted new British home.

Confined to her flat by tradition and family duty, Nazneen fills her days by sewing for a living – until the radical Karim steps unexpectedly into her life. Against a background of racial conflict and tension, they embark on a love affair that finally forces Nazneen to take control of her fate . . .

'*BRICK LANE* HAS EVERYTHING: RICHLY COMPLEX CHARACTERS, A GRIPPING STORY AND IT'S FUNNY TOO . . . THIS HIGHLY EVOLVED, ACCOMPLISHED BOOK IS A REMINDER OF HOW EXHILARATING NOVELS CAN BE: IT OPENED UP A WORLD WHOSE CONTOURS I COULD RECOGNISE, BUT WHICH I NEEDED MONICA ALI TO MAKE ME UNDERSTAND'
Observer

'THE JOY OF THIS BOOK IS ITS MARRIAGE OF A WONDERFUL WRITER WITH A FRESH, RICH AND HIDDEN WORLD. HER ACHIEVEMENT IS HUGE. THIS IS A BOOK WRITTEN WITH LOVE AND COMPASSION FOR EVERY STRUGGLING CHARACTER IN ITS PAGES. NO WONDER I FINISHED IT WITH SUCH A SENSE OF GRATITUDE'
Evening Standard

'THE KIND OF NOVEL THAT SURPRISES ONE WITH ITS DEPTH AND DASH; IT IS A NOVEL THAT WILL LAST'
Guardian

0 552 77115 5

BLACK SWAN

CRADLE SONG
Robert Edric

'A REWARDING EXPERIENCE . . . THIS IS MURDER AT ITS MOST FOUL, CRIME AT THE DEEP END'
Spectator

An imprisoned child murderer unexpectedly appeals his conviction. In return for a reduced sentence, he offers to implicate those involved in the crimes who were never caught; providing evidence of Police corruption and, most importantly, revealing where the corpses of several long-sought, but never found teenage girls are buried.

Distressed at what may come to light, yet desperate to locate the body of his own missing daughter, the father of one of these girls approaches Private Investigator Leo Rivers with a plea for help.

Rivers' enquiries stir cold and bitter memories. Long-dead enmities flare suddenly into violence and a succession of new killings. Everyone involved, then and now, and on both sides of the law, is unprepared for the suddenness and ferocity with which these old embers are fanned back into life. As the investigation progresses, it gathers momentum, and now must speed inexorably to the even greater violence and sadness of its conclusion.

'*CRADLE SONG* IS A SUPERBLY PACED BOOK . . . THIS IS CLASSIC CRIME NOIR . . . EDRIC CAN ALSO PRODUCE BEAUTIFUL PROSE AND ARRESTING IMAGES AS WELL AS INCISIVE SOCIAL SATIRE . . . MAGNIFICENTLY ACHIEVED'
Giles Foden

'HIS NOVEL IS SOMETHING SUBSTANTIAL AND DISTINCTIVE . . . EDRIC HAS A CLEAR, ALMOST RAIN-WASHED STYLE, EMINENTLY SUITABLE FOR HIS HULL SETTING . . . *CRADLE SONG* IS A STRONG AND SERIOUS NOVEL, SOBERLY ENTERTAINING AND WELL WORTH YOUR WHILE'
Literary Review

'HIGHLY ACCOMPLISHED . . . FANS CAN LOOK FORWARD TO HIS USUAL SHARPLY REALISED CHARACTERS OPERATING IN A TENSE, PRESSURED ENVIRONMENT'
Independent

0 552 77142 2

BLACK SWAN

THE FOURTH HAND
John Irving

'A RICH AND DEEPLY MOVING TALE . . . VINTAGE IRVING'
Washington Post

'SHARP AND VERY, VERY FUNNY, THIS IS ANOTHER OF IRVING'S FIERCELY ORIGINAL MEDITATIONS ON LIFE'S INHERENT STRANGENESS'
Uncut

While reporting a story from India, New York journalist Patrick Wallingford inadvertently becomes his own headline when his left hand is eaten by a lion. In Boston, a renowned surgeon eagerly awaits the opportunity to perform the nation's first hand transplant.

But what if the donor's widow demands visitation rights with the hand? In answering this unexpected question, John Irving has written a novel that is, by turns brilliantly comic and emotionally moving, offering a penetrating look at the power of second chances and the will to change.

'IRVING HAS A LITERARY STYLE SIMILAR TO A SNOWBALL EFFECT: WITH EACH NOVEL HE CREATES SYMBOLS AND DEVELOPS THEMES TO ACCOMPANY THOSE HE HAS ALREADY ACCUMULATED. GRIEF, LOSS, ABORTION, AMPUTATION, SEX, CHILDREN, AMERICA'S POLITICAL HISTORY AND THE POWER OF FORESIGHT ARE ALL EXPLORED HERE'
Observer

'A CORUSCATING COMEDY OF SEXUAL MANNERS. IN THE MARGINS OF A HARD-HITTING SATIRE ON THE MODERN MEDIA, IRVING HAS PRODUCED SOME OF THE FUNNIEST BEDROOM SCENES OF RECENT YEARS'
Sunday Telegraph

'RICHLY ENTERTAINING READING: PART SATIRE, PART FARCE . . . THERE'S NO BETTER – OR FUNNIER – REINTRODUCTION TO THE LEAST KNOWN TRULY GREAT AMERICAN AUTHOR'
FHM

0 552 77109 0

BLACK SWAN

NOT THE END OF THE WORLD
Kate Atkinson

'MOVING AND FUNNY, AND CRAMMED WITH INCIDENTAL WISDOM'
Sunday Times

What is the real world? Does it exist, or is it merely a means of keeping another reality at bay?

Not the End of the World is Kate Atkinson's first collection of short stories. Playful and profound, they explore the world we think we know whilst offering a vision of another world which lurks just beneath the surface of our consciousness, a world where the myths we have banished from our lives are startlingly present and where imagination has the power to transform reality.

From Charlene and Trudi, obsessively making lists while bombs explode softly in the streets outside, to gormless Eddie, maniacal cataloguer of fish, and Meredith Zane who may just have discovered the secret to eternal life, each of these stories shows that when the worlds of material existence and imagination collide, anything is possible . . .

'I CAN THINK OF FEW WRITERS WHO CAN MAKE THE ORDINARY COLLIDE WITH THE EXTRAORDINARY TO SUCH BEGUILING EFFECT . . . LEFT ME SO FIZZING WITH ADMIRATION'
Observer

'EXCEPTIONAL . . . SHARP, WITTY AND COMPLETELY COMPELLING'
Daily Mail

'AN EXCEPTIONALLY FUNNY, QUIRKY AND BOLD WRITER'
Independent on Sunday

0 552 77105 8

BLACK SWAN